The Highlander's
Outlaw Bride

Cathy MacRae

THE HIGHLANDER'S OUTLAW BRIDE
Copyright © 2014 Short Dog Press

This book is a work of fiction. The names, characters, places and incidents are the products of the author's imagination or are used fictitiously. Any resemblance to actual events, business establishments, locales or persons, living or dead, is entirely coincidental.

All rights reserved. No part of this book may be copied, reproduced, stored in a retrieval system or shared in any form (electronic, mechanical, photocopying, recording or otherwise) without the prior written permission from the author except for brief quotations for printed reviews.

The scanning, uploading and distribution of this book via the Internet or any other means without the permission of the author is illegal and punishable by law. Please purchase only authorized electronic editions, and do not participate in or encourage electronic piracy of copyrighted materials.

Your support of the author's rights is appreciated.

Published by Short Dog Press
ISBN-13: 978-0-9966485-1-6

Published in the United States of America

*This book is dedicated to my wonderful husband,
who is my own happy-ever-after.*

Acknowledgments

During this past year, I am eternally grateful to my critique partners, Dawn Marie Hamilton, Cate Parke, and Derek Dodson, who have endured the changes in my life. I have the utmost respect for your writing, your encouragement and your friendship.

Prologue

September 1386, Wyndham Hall

Brianna glared at her da, hands fisted on her hips, the belligerent thrust to her chin the mirror image of his. "I willnae marry. Ye can burn that contract as easily as sign it."

"Ye will marry, and ye will wed whomever I choose."

"I did that once, and all I got was a dead husband scarcely a year into the bargain."

Lord Wyndham scowled. "Young Mungo was a fool to challenge the lads to a horse race."

"He was a fool to fall off at the first hedge," Brianna scoffed. "And to linger for weeks afterward. I had my fill of his da's arguments and threats during those days."

"He dinnae want his son to die without an heir."

"I wasnae with child and he wanted to solve the matter himself!" Her cheeks flamed as she recalled the chieftain's rants and crude suggestions when he learned his son would never leave his bed again, his duty to the bloodline unfulfilled. Her fists clenched.

"We need the help, daughter. I have written the papers and ye will fulfill the bargain."

"Ye put all of Wyndham into the contract. Wyndham belongs to Jamie. I want to stay here and take care of ye both. And I dinnae need a man to tell me how to run Wyndham." *Nor will I ever put myself in such a situation again, St. Andrew be my witness.*

Her da's face reddened. "Ye need a man to put a bairn in yer belly."

"Ten months wed and there was no bairn. I dinnae believe ye will get yer heir from me. Ye must look to Jamie for that."

Lord Wyndham dropped his gaze and pivoted on his heel, his heavy cloak billowing about his legs. He pulled the wool close about him. "Yer brother is weak—has been since he was born. He willnae live to provide an heir."

His bitter voice tore at Brianna's heart and she slipped behind him, a sympathetic arm about his waist. "I know how ye have grieved since Ma died, but 'twas five years ago." She eyed the whisky flask on his desk, already half-drained at this early hour. Rare was the afternoon that saw her sire sober.

"Though Jamie was born much too early, he has grown into a good lad. He cannae help being sickly. I know he will grow out of it soon."

"Ye are over-optimistic, daughter. And headstrong and disobedient." Da broke from her embrace and stalked to the chair behind his desk. "We have too much trouble on our borders, and Laird MacLaurey has offered his help if we combine our lands."

Again Brianna's hands propped on her hips, frustration boiling to the surface. "And by that he means I am to marry his son. Weel, I dinnae like it. He is a skirt-chasing rogue by all accounts and lost his heart to Laird Macrory's daughter. He isnae likely to be happy finding himself betrothed to me!"

She knelt beside Da's chair and placed a hand on his. "Besides, he is in France nursing his broken heart and who knows when he will return? Will his da honor his word to help us whilst his son traipses around the continent?"

Lord Wyndham eyed the whisky flask and licked his lips. His hand trembled. "We need the help. Reivers have struck us too many times. Our people willnae eat this winter if we cannae protect our cattle."

Brianna bit her lip. 'Twas her da's inability to stay sober that affected them most. She knew her ma's death at Jamie's birth had hit him hard, and his bouts of drinking had gotten worse, not better, since. When he could be roused to remember his duty as lord of Wyndham, he would bluster and rail, swearing vengeance on those who stole from his people. But in the end, he did nothing. Except drink himself into a deeper stupor.

"There has to be another way. Gavin and I—"

Her da smacked the desktop with a ferocious stroke of his palm and Brianna flinched in surprise. "Ye are a lady and willnae consort with the soldiers!"

"But Da—"

"Dinnae disobey me, daughter! We will obtain help from Morven, and ye will wed the MacLaurey's son." He waved his hands in the air. "Be gone! Attend to yer sewing and leave me in peace!"

Gathering her dignity, Brianna strode out the door and into the hallway. The clink of the flask reached her ears as she closed the door.

Chapter One

July 1387, Glenkirk, Scotland

Brianna trembled in the poorly lit entrance to the main hall, a mixture of fear and anger tightening her stomach. Surrounded by surly guards, her hands clenched tight, bound firmly behind her by a ragged rope biting sharply into her tender skin. Four bristling Douglas soldiers, sworn to protect her, stood a few feet to one side, similarly detained. Her heart pounded as she stared into the brutal faces of the sheriff's men. At twenty-and-one, she was about to be hanged for reiving.

She tilted her head slightly, wanting to see her soldiers, needing to draw strength from them. *What terrible fate have I brought them to?* Their faces were still black with fury at being forced to surrender their arms as one of the sheriff's men had dragged her from her horse, a sword to her throat. Gavin, the Douglas captain, met her sidelong gaze and lifted his chin, nodding solemnly. Whatever happened, they would face it together bravely, as befitting Douglases.

Brianna inclined her head in silent acknowledgement. She was Lord Wyndham's daughter and would not bring disgrace to her clan. The sheriff may have caught them with the wrong group of cattle—who could tell in the dark?—but there was no shame in protecting her people. She flinched. The idea had seemed so right at the time. She squared her shoulders and prayed her legs would not buckle beneath her.

A guard prodded her from behind and she took a quick, startled step forward, her men a scant stride behind her. They halted just inside the main hall, awaiting milord sheriff's pleasure. For several agonizing moments, the sheriff ignored them, intent on speaking with a young woman who giggled prettily at whatever he said to her. Brianna's cheeks flamed as she realized the insult he gave by relegating their presence below that of his simpering leman.

At last the sheriff waved the woman away and beckoned Brianna and her soldiers forward. Lounging in his throne-like chair, he surveyed the ragged group with an insolent air of boredom.

"I am Fergus, Sheriff at Glenkirk."

Brianna stiffened as his gaze slid from the glowering Douglas soldiers to roam her boyishly clad form, lingering on her unbound hair spilling across her shoulders. He was clearly intrigued by the fact she, as leader of the group, was a woman—an unexpected change from the rough male cattle thieves normally brought before him for judgment.

"What say ye about yer actions, milady?" Fergus dragged his gaze from her and addressed the small group. Brianna blinked at his question—she had not expected a chance to defend herself or her actions. The sheriff was not known to question reivers before hanging them. Perhaps she was of more interest to him than she'd thought. The possibility sent a shiver of alarm down her spine.

Unsticking her dry tongue from the roof of her mouth, she took a steadying breath. *I am a Douglas. I am Lord Wyndham's daughter and I willnae be afraid.* With sudden clarity, she saw a glimmer of hope. The blood of kings ran through her veins, and to spill it this day would cost the sheriff dearly.

"Neither I nor my soldiers are guilty of reiving." Her voice rang clear and she lifted her chin a notch higher. The Douglases' heads swiveled to her in unison and she noted the pleased respect lighting their grim faces, warming her, giving her courage. They obviously hadn't expected her to be so bold before the sheriff.

Fergus waved aside her claim with a flick of his wrist. "Och, of course ye are. Or have ye forgotten being caught with cattle not yer own?" He wrinkled his nose distastefully. "The odor of the byre clings to ye yet."

Brianna's eyes narrowed at the insult. "I demand the king's authority."

The sheriff sat upright in his chair, leaning forward to jab a finger angrily at her. "And what makes the daughter of a minor lord, caught reiving against the king's direct edict, so special she thinks she can escape her fate?"

Her limbs quaked, threatening to betray her, but she dared not back down. "This daughter of a minor lord is also the grandniece of Lord John of Islay." Anger flared even as a frisson of fear shot through her as she challenged the man who held her life, and those of her soldiers, in his hands.

Fergus leaned slowly back in his chair, stroking his chin thoughtfully. Brianna's confidence grew. Surely he knew as well as anyone that Lord John of Islay, styled King of the Isles, was married to the daughter of King Robert of Scotland. Brianna hoped it was less well known that her lineage traced to Lord John's first wife, not his second. She held her breath.

The sheriff's face crumpled into a scowl, and Brianna was certain he understood hanging the grandniece of Lord John meant hanging the grandniece—however far removed—of the king. Fresh hope spread through her like a flame, thawing the icy fear around her heart. She had been right to challenge the sheriff. No matter what she had been accused of, she had the right to appeal to the king.

The sheriff stood, his mouth an angry slash across his face. "Lady Brianna of Wyndham, I hereby find ye guilty of reiving and name ye outlaw, and yer men as well. I release ye into the custody of King Robert of Scotland for yer doom. May ye find justice at his hands."

Dazed with the unexpected reprieve, Brianna glanced around the noisome cell as the guards' footsteps faded down the rock passageway. "I am not sure what will happen now," she admitted, her voice a low murmur of wonderment.

"Och, ye have done a fine night's work, lass." Rabbie's voice held a proud note. "'Tis enough we are still alive and not dangling at the end of a gallows rope."

Her heady sense of relief disappeared in a cold rush of reality. "But I could have cost us our lives just as easily."

The men quickly disclaimed the events leading to their capture.

"'Tis not yer fault yer da…"

"Laird MacLaurey…"

"'Twas the alliance that failed."

Brianna's eyes flashed. "Dinnae speak to me of the alliance. Or Laird MacLaurey—"

Gavin raised a hand and they quieted. "We all agreed to the reiving to get our cattle back. 'Twas no one's fault we were caught. But we need rest. William and Rabbie, the two of ye sit watch for the guards' return. We have time before they take us to Troon to stand before the king. Wake me and Duncan when ye cannae keep yer eyes open."

Realizing how tired she was, Brianna drifted to one corner of the tiny room in search of a place to rest, unfastening her plaide from her shoulders to spread over the rotted hay scattered across the cold stone floor. She settled gingerly on the woolen cloth, needing sleep but barely able to stomach the intolerable stench of the refuse beneath her cheek. Sleep was a long time coming. Their necks were not free of the hangman's noose yet.

Brianna startled to wakefulness. Blearily she blinked her eyes, struggling to distinguish the nearby shapes in the gloom.

"Wheesht, lass." A large hand fitted across her mouth and another clasped her shoulder, holding her still as the voice rasped in her ear.

She jerked violently at the man's touch, her stomach clenched tight in terror. She twisted beneath the ironlike stricture, but the grip tightened, and the scream rising in her throat bled away to a muffled whimper.

"'Tis Gavin."

Relief washed over her and she relaxed, though her heart still raced painfully in her chest as she swallowed the bitter taste of fear. Next to her, Duncan roused William with a touch, and to her surprise, Ewan was there to wake Rabbie. She longed to ask him how he came to be in prison with them, but the men rose silently, and she kept her questions to herself.

Gavin helped her to her feet and motioned for the others to follow. They slipped into the darkness, closing the iron gate behind them with care against its slow, protesting squawk.

Geordie awaited them behind the stable, horses saddled. Brianna accepted her mare's reins and walked Maude silently into the night. Cloaked in shadow, the sky lit only by a shrouded, rising moon, they cautiously edged the bailey. A single, man-high gate set in the castle wall, large enough to walk through single file, yawned open before them. Brianna's nerves stretched taut as she anticipated cries from the guards on the wall, but none came. Once through the gate, they hugged the shadows of the battlements until they were within easy reach of the forest and Gavin gave the signal to mount.

They rode at a punishing pace, neither slowing nor stopping until the palest hint of dawn appeared and Brianna's muscles knotted with exhaustion. At last Gavin allowed them to rein their tired mounts to a halt. The horses milled about, stomping their feet as they snorted and blew. Steam rose from their hides and the odor of their sweat hung heavy in the mist-laden air. Brianna dismounted and drew a deep breath, savoring the aroma. It smelled like heaven. It smelled like freedom.

Relief was evident in the way the men moved, softly joking among themselves as they checked their horses and gear. Brianna glanced fondly at each one, her chest tight with gratitude as she considered the lengths they'd gone to in their attempt to keep her safe. She sought Gavin.

"May we talk now?"

He nodded and the men clustered around. Brianna burned with questions.

"How did we get away?"

"Geordie and Ewan took care of that." Gavin nodded to the two men. They beamed with pride.

Brianna acknowledged their efforts with a nod. "How did you know where to find us?"

Geordie chimed in. "Ye dinnae make it home last night, and this morning Auld Willie was afraid ye had been caught by either the reivers or the sheriff. So Ewan and me went to Glenkirk, where we heard a lass and her men were to be taken to the king to be sentenced for stealing cattle."

Ewan took up the tale. "It had to be ye, since we hadnae heard of another lass reiving in this land. We found where they were holding ye and, er, *inconvenienced* the guards."

Geordie flushed and jabbed Ewan in the side with his elbow. "We bribed those we could."

Ewan ground the knuckles of one fist in the palm of his other hand. "Aye. A few."

Brianna glanced from Geordie to Ewan, then back to Gavin. "But why did they have to rescue us? The king would have pardoned us. I know it."

Gavin shook his head. "Lass, they werenae taking ye to Troon."

Brianna canted her head in confusion. "What do ye mean? The sheriff said we were to be taken to the king."

He grasped her gently by the shoulders, forcing her attention. "Ewan and Geordie learned that the guards were to take us as far as the River Clyde and kill us there."

A chill swept over her and her knees wobbled. She opened her mouth once, but no sound came out. She swallowed and tried again. "Why?"

"Someone wants ye dead, lass," Ewan informed her solemnly. "They paid the sheriff to ambush ye and see ye hanged."

Brianna tried to understand what the men were telling her. *Why would anyone seek to have me killed?* Head spinning, she listened bleakly to Gavin's next words.

"When ye told the sheriff of yer kinship to Lord John of Islay, he couldnae hang ye at Glenkirk for fear Lord John and the king would be angry. So he plotted to send ye away, telling everyone he was sending ye to the king for him to decide what to do with ye.

"But he gave his men orders to take ye far enough away to keep his hands clean of the deed, then kill ye. Mayhap his men would have reported ye drowned in the river and we either drowned trying to save ye, or became so enraged they were forced to kill us to protect themselves. I dinnae know. But Ewan and Geordie stopped them before they could put their plan into action."

"I am verra sorry to tell ye this, lass," Ewan added. "If there had been a chance the sheriff would let ye see the king, it might have been better to see this through. But the truth is, the king isnae even at Troon."

Exhausted, her nerves frayed by events piled on her the past hours, Brianna took a stumbling step forward, bracing herself against the trunk of a tree as her knees buckled. Finally, she took a deep, steadying breath and faced the soldiers.

"Where is Jamie?"

It stood to reason if someone at Wyndham wanted her dead, it was because of the land entailed to her through her unfulfilled marriage contract. Though a sickly lad, Jamie was the only other member of her family who stood to inherit the property if she died.

"He is fine," Geordie answered. "Auld Willie knows the lad could be in danger and has taken charge of him. Ye needn't worry about him."

Brianna nodded weakly. "What do we do now?" Her voice gained strength as she determinedly shrugged off her shock and readjusted the mantle of responsibility over her shoulders.

Gavin shrugged as though his plan was of the utmost simplicity.

"We wait for the king to pardon us."

Chapter Two

Several days later, in Ayrshire

Connor MacLaurey reined his stallion to a stop at the foot of the hills just south of Troon. Satisfied with the protection the trees afforded, he turned to his two companions.

"We will stop here for the night."

Sliding tiredly from his saddle, his legs trembled as he led Embarr to the edge of the glen. Water gurgled in a nearby burn, winding through the rocks and trees.

"'Twill be good to have this done and be away home." He grunted as he stripped the saddle from Embarr's back. "I shouldnae have stayed away so long."

"I am sorry we are too late for your father's funeral, *mon ami*."

Conn nodded wearily. "I thank ye, Bray. And my sister's warning of my cousin's plan to take over the clan doesnae help, either." He lowered his saddle to the ground with a groan of effort. "If the ship hadnae been forced to berth at Ballantrae, we wouldnae have had this ride to Troon. But at least it has given the mares a chance to stretch their legs."

"Your king will be pleased with his gift. Perhaps enough to pardon your betrothed."

Connor cut his friend a sharp glance. "I dinnae sign a betrothal contract before I left for France, and I dinnae approve my da arranging this for me. She was a plain, straw-headed lass when I last saw her as a wean, and I would suppose she is even less interesting now. And, if I remember, a widow in the bargain. Let us think on happier things, aye?" He shrugged the memory of a fiery-haired lass from the Firth of Clyde from his mind and returned to his tasks.

The two men watered and fed the horses in silence, but the words from Morven's captain, Seumas, included in the letter from his sister, ticked through his head.

Yer betrothed has been accused of reiving but escaped the hangman's noose. The sheriff has declared her outlaw and his men hunt her. Only the king can pardon her. Ye must find her, protect her.

The Wyndham lass an outlaw? Connor shook his head. *Seumas exaggerates. She dinnae have a bold bone in her body.* He dredged up the memory of the lad she'd married more than two years ago. *Nae, she wouldnae have learned courage from him.* As for now being his betrothed—he would deal with that absurd notion as soon as he ousted his cousin Malcolm from his mischief at Morven. With a final glance at the tethered horses, he turned toward camp.

"I will see if Gillis needs anything."

Bray lifted his head. "I smell smoke. I hope the lad has something pleasing planned for our meal."

Conn ventured a short laugh. "Despite his assurances, I doubt the lad is much of a cook. But we shall see."

Conn's stomach rumbled and he hurried to the campsite, where deadwood piled haphazardly next to a small cook fire. He grabbed an oatcake from the stone at the fire's edge.

"Ow!" He blew on his singed fingers, tossing the freshly cooked bannock back and forth between his hands. Deftly swiping two more of the sizzling oatcakes, he settled against a nearby fallen log to eat.

The Frenchman grimaced as he approached the fire. "Bannocks again?"

Conn shrugged off his friend's complaint. He didn't care if Bray ate or not.

Short-tempered Gillis bristled. "Ye willnae find yer Frenchie *mishmak* food here," he huffed, waving an oatcake in the older man's direction. "This is Scots fare, and good enough for the likes of ye!"

Bray leaned down with a glower for the lad. "From what I have seen, Scots food is merely another word for plain and *inintéressant*."

Conn sighed. Why must Bray insist on needling the hot-headed lad?

"'Tis better than ye got aboard that ship!" Gillis glowered and bit into his bannock.

"Is that why you jumped ship when we docked in Ballantrae?"

"I dinnae jump ship!"

Conn felt moved to intervene. "Dinnae *fash* the lad, Bray. He isnae cut out for life at sea. Leave it at that. Ye will get other food when we arrive at Troon."

Bray's feigned chagrin matched the mocking flash of his grin. "My apologies."

With one smooth movement, he bent to snag an oatcake in one hand, delivering a smack to the back of Gillis's head with the other as he stepped past the boy. Gillis sputtered at the abuse, but had enough sense not to physically challenge the older man. Conn watched with mild amusement as Gillis returned to his supper, muttering against all things not Scottish, and against Frenchmen in particular.

Rising, Conn lifted his arms in a bone-popping stretch.

"I am away to the burn to wash." He glanced sternly from Bray to Gillis. "Stay out of trouble whilst I am gone."

Bray gave him a bland, innocent look, and Gillis hunched his shoulders to indicate he couldn't be responsible for Bray's actions. Conn shook his head. Tossing his plaide over one shoulder, he headed for the inviting little pool of water beneath the waterfall.

He halted on the edge of the burn, the high, full moon's silvery light sparkling like diamonds across the rippled surface of the water. He glanced around the clearing, instinctively alert for danger. Seeing no threats, he stripped away his travel-stained clothes and stepped into the pool.

The icy water burst with fine needle pricks over his tired body, washing away the day's accumulation of grit and grime. Adjusting to the frigid water, he lifted his arms, stroked to the center of the pool and dove beneath the water. He surfaced with a shake of his head, sending silver droplets of water flying in all directions. Refreshed, he glided to the bank. Climbing from the water, he strode back to his clothing. The evening breeze rippled softly through the moonlit grass, and the gurgling water whispered a murmuring counterpoint beneath the velvet sky. Appreciating the peacefulness, Conn decided to linger a bit longer, away from the certain strife at camp.

Seated on one corner of his plaide, he used the other edge to wipe most of the clinging moisture from his body. Declining to pull his dusty clothes back on over his clean, damp skin, he rolled onto his back and draped the woolen fabric across himself to block the slight breeze, his sword close to hand. He stared at the spangled sky as the words from his sister's letters ran through his mind.

Ye must come home. There has been an accident.

I dinnae know how to reach ye—pray God this letter finds ye.

Cousin Malcolm brought men with him to Morven. Da is dead. Ye must come home. Please, Conn. Please come home.

Fists clenched against the tightness in his chest, he forced his breathing to slow. *I am sorry yer letters dinnae reach me in time, Mairead. I am sorry I wasnae there to help him. I will finish my business with the king, and then I will right things at Morven.*

Brianna jolted awake, her body awash with the cold sweat of fear. The nightmare from a week ago had invaded her dreams again. This time the rasp of the hangman's noose about her neck felt all too real.

The days in the wild had grown long and tiresome as they moved from place to place, careful not to linger at a campsite longer than a day or two, aware the sheriff's men still hunted them. Ewan and Duncan had been dispatched to Troon to await the king's arrival. Brianna longed to present her plea for mercy to the king, to have her good name restored and the stain of outlaw removed. And she longed for home, her friends and family—even little Jamie's never-ending chatter.

Too restless to go back to sleep, Brianna rubbed the back of her neck, feeling the grime of travel roll beneath her fingers. The gown Rabbie had filched for her from a wash line at a cottage a few days ago had been too long without a good scrubbing for her personal sensibilities, and her head itched from a lack of proper grooming.

The men's sleeping forms lay scattered around her, lit by the glowing embers of the fire and the silvery light of the full moon. Gavin and Rabbie stood watch while William and Geordie snored gently nearby. Gavin glanced up as she rose to her feet, but she shook her head, conveying a need for privacy. *Dinnae stop me, Gavin. I cannae bear yer close scrutiny again this night.* Stubbornly refusing a guard, she hurried down the moonlit path to the nearby burn. The cold water wasn't quite what she had in mind for bathing, but the thought of washing the dirt from her skin and hair sent her feet flying down the trail.

She reached the end of the path, where the water laughed invitingly as it skipped over the rocks of the waterfall. She splashed the water with one hand, shuddering at the chill. Checking the clearing with a quick glance to be sure she was alone, Brianna stripped away her gown and rinsed it in the clear water before hanging it on a nearby tree limb to dry. With two quick steps, she dove cleanly into the burn, surfacing with a gasp at the water's icy bite.

After a moment, the shock wore off. With strong sure strokes, she swam to the waterfall and pulled herself onto the rocks. Spreading her arms wide for balance, she crossed the stones worn smooth by the polishing spray, and ducked beneath the rushing water. She twisted back and forth, letting it pour over her in a cleansing rush.

Her fingers and toes began to ache, and her teeth chattered. Unable to ignore the cold, she poised on the rock ledge for the swim back.

A movement in the tall grass on the far side of the pool caught her eye, and she stared intently into the shadowed depths. Tense moments passed, and suddenly a large form lurched upward. Panicked, Brianna lost her footing on the slippery rocks. Clawing uselessly at the air for support, she landed hard on the water. Her breath left her in a rush as she slid into bitter darkness and the foaming water closed over her head.

Chapter Three

Conn bolted to his feet in a single movement, reaching the edge of the burn in two long strides. Slicing the water in a shallow dive, a few strong strokes carried him to the spot where the young woman had disappeared. He broke the surface with a shake of his head, scanning the area around him, but saw nothing.

With a strangled gasp, the young woman's head burst above the water a few feet away. Sputtering, she flailed at the water. Con raced to her side and grabbed her arm. She fought him, breaking his hold, and disappeared again into the inky depths.

"*Shite!*" He searched frantically for her, his fingers encountering soft flesh. Pulling her warily to him, he pinned her elbows firmly against her sides.

"Easy, lass," he murmured. "Ye are safe now."

Her breaths wheezed and her head fell against his chest. Pale hair fanned out in the water around them. Moonlight struck the strands, turning them to pure silver, and unbidden, Conn's lips formed the word 'faerie'. He gave himself a mental shake against such foolishness, and focused on pulling her to safety.

Stroke by stroke, he towed her to the shore. Her size and weight convinced him the young woman in his arms wasn't a faerie after all. He rolled her onto her side amid the tall grass and pounded her back.

After a few moments of such rough treatment, she coughed up what seemed to be half the contents of the burn before she at last drew a deep, shuddering breath. Before she could speak, she began to shake violently and her skin blanched, taking on a purple hue in the moonlight. Conn bundled her icy body in his arms and wrapped them both in his plaide, using his body heat to warm her. He ran his hands up and down her back as he tried to chase away the chill.

At last her shaking lessened and she relaxed against him. Inexplicable protectiveness swept over him and he pressed a kiss against her hair, wiping her face with a corner of his plaide.

"*Coorie doon*, my faerie princess. Snuggle close and rest."

With a sigh, his flesh-and-blood faerie princess fainted.

Words drifted through her head, urging her to wake. Brianna groaned, snuggling into the incredible warmth surrounding her. She hadn't felt this deliciously warm or content in days, and was loath to leave her bed to face another day in hiding.

Something warm and firm slid across her shoulder and down one arm. It grasped her hand and squeezed gently. She reluctantly opened one eye and met storm-gray eyes in an unfamiliar face. With a start, she realized the heat she'd found so compelling emanated from the large male body tucked close against her. Naked. She panicked.

"What are ye doing?" Her voice climbed in pitch, her alarm rising. Trapped by the confining fabric wrapped around her—and him—she pulled back, swatting frantically at the cloth.

"Hold!" He manacled her wrists with his strong hands.

"Let me go!" Jerking one hand free, she inadvertently struck his jaw.

"Ow!" A muttered curse slipped beneath his breath. "Be still a moment and I will help ye."

Choking back her fear, she struggled harder.

Though exasperated with the young woman's lack of proper gratitude at being saved from drowning, Conn understood her distress. She fought him despite his attempts to calm her, and suddenly her knee jerked upward, making solid contact between his legs. He doubled over sharply in pain, his forehead striking the girl's cheek. With a cry, she raised a hand to her face.

"*Qu'est-ce qui se passe?*"

Conn heard the sharp edge to Bray's question, but could not reply. His teeth clenched tight as sweat-popping nausea swamped his stomach.

The young woman twisted about, clawing at the plaide.

"Enough!" he rasped. To his surprise, she stopped. He heaved a lungful of air, expelling it with a painful gasp. Unable to speak further, he wrenched an arm free and jerked the edge of the fabric loose. As soon as the cloth sagged, she scrambled to her feet, only to fall back to the ground with a sharp cry.

Bray took a step toward her. "Are you injured, *mademoiselle?*"

She struggled to sit and leaned forward, pulling her long, damp hair over her shoulders in an attempt to cover herself. Biting her lip, she grasped one ankle.

Conn shoved his plaide aside and moved awkwardly to kneel before her, taking her foot in his hands. She flinched, choking back another cry.

He forced his words through clenched teeth. "Hold, lass. I will wrap ye back up."

She eyed him warily but did not speak. Rubbing the sore spot on his jaw, he snatched the plaide from the ground and draped it about her shoulders. Catching her wide-eyed stare, he smothered a grin as her cheeks flamed red. He stepped casually to his clothing and pulled them on.

"This does not look well done, Laird."

The girl looked up sharply and Conn noted Bray's assessing stare as he studied her. She hunched the plaide higher over her shoulders.

"Quit staring at the lass, Bray. Ye make her blush."

Bray inclined his head. "*Je vous demande pardon, mademoiselle.* I have never failed to admire a beautiful woman, and your hair is a most unusual color. I did not mean to embarrass you."

"Ye are French, aye?" Her voice was soft and low, rippling like silk. Conn blinked twice, shaking off her spell.

Bray executed a sweeping bow. "*Oui, cherie.* The laird and I met at my father's home in La Rochelle. I am pleased to see you are as intelligent as you are beautiful."

Conn snorted at Bray's outrageous behavior.

"Never trust a Frenchman, lass. He has left broken hearts from here to the French coast."

"I did not know you could find such a beautiful woman in the wilds of Scotland. I am humbled by your Scottish lass."

Conn frowned at the girl. "Och, 'tis no simple Scottish lass ye see before ye, but a veritable faerie or changeling at the least. She is apparently not at all appreciative of the fact I saved her life."

The girl wrinkled her brow. "Ye saved my life?"

"Aye. Ye slipped on the stones at the waterfall and nearly drowned. Ye dinnae remember bathing there? I imagine ye twisted yer ankle when ye fell."

"Ye watched me?" Her eyes widened, her voice incredulous. She glanced down and Conn remembered with a jolt she was completely naked beneath the plaide. Her face reddened and he knew she remembered it, too.

Bray pursed his lips. "I tell you, 'twas not well done, Laird."

Conn squared on him. "I suppose ye would have closed yer eyes until she left?"

"*Non,*" the Frenchman admitted candidly. "But what are we to do with her now?"

"I am leaving!" The girl's determined voice broke into their discussion. She grasped the plaide firmly and pushed to her feet. But her injured ankle would not support her weight and she would have fallen had Conn not grabbed her arms.

"Where is yer home, lass?"

Her gaze slid away. "I will be fine if ye just let me go."

"Ye willnae go anywhere on that ankle, and ye ask for trouble out here on yer own. There is no cottage or village within miles. Tell us where ye belong, and we will take ye there."

She clenched her teeth as stubbornness lit her eyes and she refused to answer.

"At least tell us yer name." Conn brushed a strand of silver-blonde hair from her cheek. She shifted beneath his touch and drew back with a tiny hiss of breath, pulling the plaide closer around her throat.

"If ye snug that any tighter, ye will hang yerself," he noted dryly.

She slowly released a slight bit of the fabric.

Bray stepped closer. "Are you hiding from someone, *cherie*?"

The girl flinched but did not speak.

"An abusive husband, mayhap?" He pointed to the bruise on her cheek.

Conn grasped the girl's chin between his fingers and examined the darkened area. He frowned. "I believe I did that."

Bray's eyebrows shot upward. "You struck her?"

"Nae. She kneed me and I hit her with my head when I doubled over." He grimaced and shifted his weight, remembering the pain. "She is tougher than she looks."

"She kneed you?" Bray's disbelief changed to admiration and he chuckled.

"She couldnae get much leverage, as close as she was. But 'twas enough."

The girl jerked from his grip, eyes flashing her ire. "Let me go. I will fare much better on my own than in yer *care*."

"Much as I would like to, I cannae turn ye out unprotected." Ignoring her squawk of protest, Conn scooped her into his arms. He faced Bray, easily controlling the girl's struggling attempt to get down.

"We need to get back to camp before young Gillis comes looking for us."

Bray nodded his agreement.

"Put me down!" The girl beat vigorously on Conn's chest and he nearly dropped her in surprise.

"Wheesht, lass, dinnae worry. We will get ye home."

"I have never seen a young woman try so hard to remove herself from your embrace. This must be a first for you, *mon ami*."

"True, but the lass is a bit addled from her swim."

The lass tweaked the hair on his chest with a vengeful twist of her fingers and Conn yelped. She glared at him. "Dinnae make a jest of me! I dinnae need yer help."

"'Tis but a bit of fun, lass." Conn tried to reassure her, but her eyes sparked with mutiny. His temper slipped a notch.

"Fine." He let her slide to the ground, careful to support her as she wobbled on her injured ankle. She put a hand out for balance and lost her grip on the plaide. Conn hid his grin but not his interest as she lunged toward a nearby tree, grabbing at a low limb to keep from falling. She inched to the far side of the tree, putting the trunk between them.

With great forbearance, Conn checked the urge to say *I told ye so*. He stepped around the tree and faced her, holding the plaide out for her. She snatched it from his grasp and yanked it about her shoulders. Conn folded his arms across his chest. "Tell me where ye need to go."

Glimpses of fear, indecision and frustration crossed her face. Finally she released a deep breath of resignation. "I have a camp on the other side of the burn."

"Good. Now, come with us. We will let young Gillis know where we are going, and Bray and I will take ye to yer camp. Agreed?"

A slow nod was all the agreement she would concede.

Chapter Four

Warily, Brianna settled the laird's plaide more securely about her as protection from curious eyes and the bone-chilling mists swirling through the trees. Young Gillis hadn't been exactly pleased to give her his only change of clothing, but he'd been too wide-eyed with surprise to argue forcefully. Holding his plaide open, the laird had used it to shield her as she slipped into the breeches and shirt, tottering awkwardly on her uninjured foot as she dressed.

She fingered the loose-fitting leine. Though Gillis appeared to be a few years younger than she, his clothes were overlarge and hung loosely on her. They were definitely better than wearing nothing beneath the plaide, though she regretted leaving her gown behind on the other side of the pool. She eyed the two other men, swiftly dismantling their camp. At least she didn't have to resort to wearing one of their shirts. It would likely fit her and Gillis both—at the same time.

She closed her eyes and dredged her memory. The laird told her she'd fallen into the pool and nearly drowned, and he had saved her. Though the details were a bit fuzzy, she remembered the feeling of helpless terror as she sucked in her first mouthful of water. She also remembered—quite clearly—the feel of his bare skin against hers, and she took a deep breath as sudden heat slid through her body.

Firmly pushing aside her wayward thoughts, she steeled herself for more important things. Surely, one of the Douglases had noticed she had not returned to camp. By now someone should be looking for her. A nagging suspicion that Bray and the laird could be in league with the sheriff went through her mind, but it was obvious young Gillis was not one of the brutish guards they'd dealt with in Glenkirk. He was nothing more than a *ghillie* seeing to the others' needs. The older two were easy-going and almost kind, when they weren't teasing her; certainly not of the same stamp as the sheriff's men. Were it not for her swollen ankle, she'd have escaped the *paukie* pair by now. *Wee scunners, the both of them. St. Andrew bless the lasses who fall for the rogues.*

The men moved quickly, gathering their belongings and saddling their horses. Brianna worried her lower lip as she weighed her decisions. *Should I lead them to the camp or not? If my belief these men are not in league with the sheriff is wrong, I risk betraying them all.*

She gingerly touched the cloth the laird had wound about her injured ankle and winced at the jolt of pain. Resolute, she realized the decision had been taken from her. She needed help, and prayed her instincts were right.

Gavin knelt beside the coals, stirring the embers back to life. Mist swirled about the camp as moisture from the nearby burn wafted upward in the pre-dawn air. Ewan and Duncan rode into camp, the clop of their horses' hooves deadened on the thick carpet of leaves. Tossing his stick into the rising flames, Gavin met the men, encouraged by the exultant looks on their faces. It was time for some good news.

Ewan slid from his horse and tossed the reins to Duncan, greeting Gavin with a hard clout to his shoulder. It was only a moment before the other Douglases rose from their plaides and surrounded them, eager for news.

"The steward said King Robert should be at Troon within the week." Ewan was unable to contain his broad grin. "And they will allow Lady Brianna leave to stay at the castle unmolested until her plea is heard."

He cast his gaze around the small camp, his look of satisfaction replaced by a puzzled frown. "Where is the lass?"

Gavin, distracted from making plans to break camp, took a

moment to look around. His mouth went dry. "Mayhap she slipped off for a moment."

But he had been on watch. He should have known if she was not in the camp. It was true she'd left earlier in the evening, and though he'd not seen her return, he'd spied her form curled beneath her plaide before he turned over his watch. Had she left again?

He strode quickly to her plaide. It was still there, rumpled and bunched on the ground. At casual glance it appeared she still slept beneath it. But standing directly over the fabric, it was obvious she was gone. Gavin's heart leapt with alarm. Could she have stepped unnoticed into the surrounding trees to tend her personal needs? Clinging desperately to that hope, he hesitated, not wanting to intrude unnecessarily on her privacy.

The moments passed and he abandoned his concern for Brianna's modesty.

"Spread out. Find her."

Instantly the others disappeared noiselessly into the forest, aware the sheriff's men could be nearby. But as the moments passed, their desperation to find Brianna exceeded their need for caution.

"Gavin!"

He turned at Rabbie's shout, following the sound to the burn, where they had filled their water skins the night before. Rabbie met him partway up the trail, his face leached of color, a damp gown dangling from his none-too-steady hands.

"'Tis the gown I stole for the lass." His voice cracked with emotion.

"Where did ye find it?"

Rabbie pointed down the trail. "Near the burn, hanging in a tree. Do ye suppose she washed it and willnae show herself because..."

The burly man's face reddened. Gavin took the gown. "I will deal with it. Find the others. I will have her back anon." With more reassurance than he felt, he watched Rabbie hurry up the trail to join the others. He turned his attention to searching for signs of Brianna, scanning the wooded area. The early morning sun cast its light through the trees, the resulting shadows almost darker than the night itself. He reached the water's edge and held the empty gown at arm's length.

"I am the only one here, lass. The others have gone back to camp. 'Tis safe for ye to come out now."

He waited, straining to hear the least sound to indicate where she was, but the forest remained eerily silent except for the merry sounds of the tumbling water. Cold sweat broke on his forehead, sprang beneath his arms.

"Come, now, lass," he wheedled. "Ye must get dressed. We are ready to break camp and head to Troon."

Dread settled hollowly in the pit of his stomach. Even a completely modest young woman would have called to him, told him where to place the gown so she could retrieve it. Brianna was stubborn and impetuous, and not unnecessarily modest. Even so, she would not keep him waiting like this. He must face the truth. Brianna was gone.

He scanned the ground for footsteps around the burn. Rabbie joined him and they swept the area for tracks leading away from the water. A short distance upstream, the burn narrowed, and they forded the creek, making their way to the opposite side of the pool. Here, scuffed marks showed clearly in the damp earth. Small, bare footprints, occasionally overset by two sets of larger feet, one bare, the other shod, told their story. Only the larger feet led away from the burn.

He lightly touched the soil around the imprints. "These are deeper—as though carrying a weight."

Rabbie nodded. "Aye. I fear the lass encountered someone here at the burn and he or they carried her away."

The two men exchanged glances. Wiping his fingers on his plaide, Gavin rose. They quickly followed the trail over a small ridge to a recently deserted campsite.

Gavin grunted. "We must get the others and come back. It should be light enough by then to follow their trail."

They were rapidly mounted and arrived at the site a short time later. Rabbie dismounted and searched the area for any indication of the direction Brianna and her captors had gone.

He struck the earth with his fist in frustration. "The ground is too hard to show a clear trail. And there have been at least two other groups of riders to cross their trail this day."

"Aye, having to duck into the trees each time the sheriff's men approach is costing us time." Ewan faced Gavin. "Do ye think we should split up?"

"I think 'tis best we separate and cover as much ground as we can. Pair up and meet back here just before dusk."

"Do ye not think we will find her before then?"

Gavin wheeled his horse away, keeping his doubts to himself.

Brianna stared at the empty glen where she had laid her cloak only hours before.

"Is this where yer camp was, lass?" The laird glanced about in some confusion.

The remains of the fire had been damped down and carefully covered, the area around it swept clear. Were it not for the trampled grass where the horses had been picketed, she would have been hard pressed to recognize the site.

Why did they leave without me? Her stomach dropped. Her protectors were gone. Had they met with some misfortune? Had the sheriff's men stumbled across them? *Nae, the site would show the marks.* Dragging her gaze from the deserted campsite, she glanced at the man beside her. At the look of sympathy in his eyes, she squared her shoulders and carefully hid her dismay.

"Aye, but no matter. I can fend for myself."

"Brave words from a brave lass, but I have no spare horse to leave with ye, and yer ankle willnae be better for a couple of days." He touched her shoulder in a compassionate gesture. "Ye will be safe with us. We will see ye safely home."

Brianna dropped her gaze, thinking furiously. *What if we chance upon the sheriff? If the price on my head is enough for him to betray his promise, then what my fate?* She tested the strength of her injured ankle, but it did not bear the strain. She had no choice. Without knowing the extent of their chivalry, she was at their mercy.

Chapter Five

The young woman twisted before him in the saddle. "Do ye live far from here? I know Bray doesnae." She gave a dimpled grin to the Frenchman. "And Gillis is from Glasgow. I wonder if ye would rather be heading home now?"

Conn flinched at the question, but gave no sign he would answer. She had chatted with Bray most of the morning, quite a contrast from the mutinous silence he'd gotten from her the night before. She apparently was quite capable of expounding on a multitude of subjects. He wanted to admit he admired her views, her interest in so many things. But since he'd placed her before him in the saddle, the only view he'd been able to consider was the one revealing itself to him from beneath her ill-fitting shirt as she twisted and turned with each animated gesture. A tempting view of soft, luscious curves and a shadowed valley between drew his eyes and warmed his blood.

He shifted his seat as she slid a bit to the side.

"Be still," he growled, jerking her back against him. The contact of her lush body against his sent shock waves through him, and he swore under his breath. He had only himself to blame for the mess he was in. He'd rescued the lass from drowning and was fairly sure he regretted his actions. Though she refused to give him her name, something drew him to her, mocking his decision and taunting his self-control. Her scent, the feel of her swaying against him with each step Embarr took, even her persistence was driving him to the brink of madness.

He'd tried hard to deny bringing her along with them was for his benefit as much as her own, but the truth was, he simply did not want to let her go, and damned if he knew why.

"We would take you to your home if you would but give us direction, *cherie*," Bray observed. His voice sounded kind, but his attitude bordered on exasperation.

"She has pointed us in nearly every direction on the compass," Conn grumbled, shifting his weight once more as the lass again swiveled in the saddle.

"I think I am quite lost," she informed him. Her pert smile did not quite conceal the dark shadow of uneasiness. What was she hiding?

"May I get down?"

The question jolted him from his thoughts and he pulled Embarr to a stop. Grabbing the girl around her waist, he lowered her slowly to the ground, feeling her stiffen as her injured ankle took her weight. Straightening, she walked with pained hesitation deeper into the woods.

"Why do you not speak with *la mademoiselle*?" Bray asked. "She is charming and delightfully well-informed."

Conn scrunched his face into heavy thought, refusing to let Bray see how much he enjoyed listening to the lass' comments. It was better to keep a distance between them—for her sake, of course. "She doesnae matter to me past her safety. I dinnae need to know more about her than where her home lies."

Bray hooted with laughter. "You are disgruntled that she will not give you her name, and mayhap even resentful she speaks more freely with me."

Flashing Bray a sneer of contempt for his assessment, Conn grunted, "See if ye can drag her name from her if ye wish." He shrugged. "I care not."

"Do you think she will run?" Bray's voice was casual as he turned his attention to the spot where the girl had left the trail.

"She willnae get far on that ankle. I will give her a few moments and see if she comes back on her own. It willnae be hard to catch up to her if she doesnae."

Gillis groused his own opinion. "Why is she with us? She has my best shirt."

Conn ignored the complaint. Personally, he rather liked the way the thin fabric slid across her full breasts. He'd certainly never spared the garment a second glance when Gillis wore it.

"Because our laird is unwilling to turn the girl loose to her own ends," Bray answered, his voice mocking.

Conn shot the man a look of irritation. "She isnae capable of taking care of herself. Since I first laid eyes on her, she has been trouble."

"*In* trouble, or just trouble, *mon ami*?"

Conn winced. "Both." He abandoned the conversation, searching through the trees for a glimpse of silver blond hair. Leaves swayed gently in a breeze, but he saw no sign of his faerie princess.

"*Shite*." Nudging his horse forward with his heels, Conn reined him off the trail into the brush. He swatted slender limbs aside, ducking their whip-like recoil as Embarr made his way through the trees. Ahead, dappled light glinted brightly, the sight gone in an instant. Conn peered at the spot, holding his stallion in place. Several yards away, a limb swayed, dipped. A low gasp reached his ears and he urged Embarr forward.

The lass shot him a murderous look from her undignified sprawl on the ground. A long, narrow scratch raked her cheekbone and a hank of her glistening hair snarled on a branch.

"Going somewhere?" He swung down from his saddle, towering over her. "Given yer ability to get lost crossing a burn, ye would do better to stay close to the trail."

She slapped his hand away and rose, dusting her bottom with one hand as she limped to Embarr's side. Without a word, she endured his assistance as she mounted, keeping a wall of indignant pride between them as he climbed up behind her. He reined Embarr back up the trail to where the others waited. Ignoring Bray's raised eyebrow, he urged them on with a curt nod.

His eyes drifted downward, past the rumpled fabric of the lass's shirt. He wondered why she hadn't fought him, why she had yielded after only a token fit of anger. She swayed with Embarr's movements and her back brushed his chest, setting him ablaze. He burned to slide his hand along her curves, push aside the coarse linen leine. See her undressed and passionate in his arms. But he had no right to her. He had no right to anything but her well-being. There were many more important things to occupy his thoughts. Days, perhaps weeks would pass before he could satisfy his curiosity about the young woman he was about to deliver to the king, and no certainty he would ever see her again. He wasn't sure he liked it. In fact, he was fairly certain he didn't.

Brianna eased back against the laird's broad chest, trying to deny the thrill running through her as their bodies touched. For hours she'd ridden literally in his arms, and though she'd escape in an instant if given the chance, she was no longer ill at ease with the man. Quite the opposite, in fact. She found him fascinating.

She liked his joking comradeship with his friends, so different from her dead husband's blustering attempts to best everyone around him, and was growing used to his teasing way with her as well. She admired the way he sat his horse, the calm authority he portrayed. He had also proven himself honorable, unlike Laird MacLaurey's absent son who assuaged his purportedly broken heart amid foreign skirts and taverns. Thanks to his lack of concern, several months had passed since Laird MacLaurey and her da had signed the betrothal, with no sign of him honoring the contract. Not that she wanted to be the unfortunate woman who married the *loun,* but since the laird died and all help cut off, she understood the need for a strong alliance.

This man was different. Though her goal, should she ever marry again, would be to establish a bond with another clan that could offer Wyndham a measure of protection against reivers, not with a self-assured young ass who would disrupt her life. Perhaps a doddering auld laird in his cups and too far gone to accomplish more than drool in her presence would suffice if the coffers were deep enough. She was finished with irresponsible men and had no patience for prattle about love. And her betrothal to Conn MacLaurey? As far as she was concerned, the *loun* could rot far away from Scotland's shores and she'd not shed a tear.

I can run Wyndham with none the wiser to have a woman in charge. With my help, Jamie and Da will never have to worry. I willnae marry again unless 'tis my choice, and I will only wed to benefit Wyndham.

Confidently affirming her silent vow, she turned her thoughts again to the man she rested against. She couldn't see his eyes, but she knew their hooded, impenetrable stare. Her back was to him, but she remembered his chiseled features and the way he showed his displeasure with a simple quirk of his brow. And he'd been displeased with her from the start. Despite the kindness he'd shown her, she knew he was unhappy with her for some reason she'd yet to discover.

She shivered at the feel of his strong arms curved protectively around her, awakening a throbbing deep within her she'd thought long dead. *'Tis a shame he doesnae hold land near Wyndham. I wonder what it would be like to wake in his arms?*

Her thoughts flew immediately to the way his bare skin had felt against hers. She heated to remember the sight of him as he wrapped her in his plaide. *I havenae seen a naked male other than wee Jamie since Mungo died, and even then I dinnae know what I was missing.* A brief comparison of the two men, and Mungo's ghost was quickly discarded for the lean muscle and bronzed skin, the soft furring of hair on the laird's chest trailing down...*Oh my!* She squirmed to remember where her surprised gaze had lingered, and her insides melted in a manner she'd never experienced before.

Rein it in, lass. This man isnae for ye. He doesnae like ye, and ye must remember Wyndham. Brianna's gloomy reflection cooled her interest. Gillis and Bray's banter buzzed around her like verbal midges—noisy and unwelcome and downright pesky.

The laird turned his stallion down a narrow trail and his arm brushed against her breast. Brianna swallowed her gasp of surprise. St. Andrew help her! This would never do! She didn't even know his name, and unlikely was to learn it as long as she stubbornly clung to her refusal to give him hers. Neither her identity as Lord Wyndham's daughter nor as the outlaw wanted by the sheriff held any appeal to her at this moment. She felt much safer being an unknown.

With forced cheerfulness, Brianna chattered away the afternoon. Partly to deflect the bickering between Bray and Gillis, partly because she enjoyed Bray's wide-ranging opinions. The laird said little, but each time he spoke, his voice slid like warm honey down her spine, and his breath on the back of her neck warmed her from her ears to the tips of her toes.

"We willnae make it to Troon before dark. May as well set camp here and ride in tomorrow."

Startled, Brianna's pulse quickened as he lowered her to the ground. "Can we not ride a wee bit farther? I know I will see a landmark—"

The laird landed beside her. "I willnae leave ye beside a stone or a tree of yer choosing. Ye need family, protection, and since we have ridden all day with nary a sign of yer kin, I have decided to turn ye over to the king."

Her heart skipped a beat. *The king isnae at Troon. Only the sheriff's men.* She took a breath against the sudden fear racing like fire through her veins.

"But the king isnae at Troon."

The laird, pulling loose the saddle girth, paused. "How do ye know this?"

She shrugged nonchalantly. "Och, the king left Dundonald Castle weeks ago, and who knows when he will return?"

He gave the saddle a tug and pulled it from his horse's back. "Dundonald is the king's favored residence and he is seldom gone long. But even if he isnae there, his man will give ye respite until he returns." Giving her a crooked grin, he continued with his chores. "I suspect a sweet lass such as yerself will find no trouble fitting in at court. Once ye get proper clothing, that is."

Brianna sputtered, not knowing which insult to address first. "I am not a courtier, and I had clothing—which we left behind." She took a step toward him, biting her lip as her ankle protested sharply. *He called me a sweet lass? But he doesnae like me.* Befuddled, she hobbled to a fallen log several feet away. *He cannae take me to Troon. If the sheriff's man has spoken with the king's steward, he may turn me over to him.* Her pulse quickened as she glanced about the little clearing as the men set about their chores. *I cannae tell them this. I am no more than a burden to them now. I willnae become a hostage.*

She must escape. But how? Riding with the men had been a sensible thing earlier in the day, but the laird's plan to turn her over to the steward at Troon changed everything. It was apparent she was not yet clear of the hangman's noose. Dangerous though it might well be, she must slip away during the night, though surely they set a watch?

Gillis grumbled as he prepared the cook fire and a glimmer of an idea stirred. As he mixed a bit of water into a portion of dried oats, she sighed.

Bray sank beside her on the log. "What is wrong, *mademoiselle?*"

She shook her head, doing her best to appear long-suffering. "'Tis a shame we have nothing to add a bit of flavor to the bannocks."

At Gillis' glower, she waved her hands in a placating manner. "I am not complaining. And 'tis a wee bit late to be setting traps for trout or salmon."

"Or a *petite* rabbit?" Bray flashed white teeth in a roguish grin.

Brianna delicately twitched her nose. "If ye like. I prefer fish."

"You and I think alike, *mademoiselle*. Gillis's bannocks may fill the stomach, but they do nothing to excite the palate."

Grateful for her ma's lessons in herbal lore and praying she could find what she needed, she carefully curbed her growing excitement. The look she turned on Bray was genial, almost kind. "Mayhap I can help."

"Indeed? Then I am much obliged. What do you have in mind?"

"Och, I am sure there are herbs and lettouces near the burn that could be used to flavor the bannocks. Are ye interested?"

"Laird, stay young Gillis's hand. *Mademoiselle* and I will be back in a trice." He stood and helped her to her feet. "Lead on, *cherie*."

She hobbled to the shallow burn, its banks wide and marshy. Plants crowded there in abundance, and she discarded each one as she sought one specific plant.

"Here. Take yer knife and cut it like this."

A white liquid spurted from the cut stalk. "Careful! 'Twill make the bannocks softer—not so dry." She bit her lip against the lie. Bray gathered a handful of the lettouces and she plucked a few leaves from another nearby plant. "Let us hurry before Gillis decides to make his plain oatcakes again."

Bray turned the leaves over in his hands. "What do we have, *mademoiselle?*"

Brianna waved her fingers airily. "Och, a wee bit of lettouce, and this one will add a bit of nuttiness to the flavor." She noted a flirtatious smile stopped his questions, so she bestowed her brightest on him. He grinned back at her and cupped her elbow in solicitous help as they made their way back to camp.

She offered Gillis the herbs and part of the lettouces, then gently mashed the rest of the leaves amid the white liquid. Taking a fresh bannock, she dipped it in the resulting sauce and presented it to Bray. "The fruit of yer labor, so to speak, *monsieur*."

He took a bite and nodded. "Not bad for a quick trip to the burn. Had we time, mayhap we could create something entirely special."

A rudely male snort from behind caused Brianna to jump, heat infusing her cheeks.

"A bit of leaves in yer food is all it takes to proposition the lass?" The laird stalked to the fire and snatched a handful of bannocks. Brianna gave him a crestfallen look when he ignored the mashed leaves.

"At least try it." Bray's reproving voice had its desired effect. The laird scooped a pile of the green pulp onto his oatcakes and munched them noisily. Brianna glanced from one to the other. She needed all of them to eat the prepared mash. The thick, milky substance from the lettouce stem was known to induce a soporific effect, definitely a help to her if she was to escape this night. The added assurance the men would sleep soundly would come as a boon. She could not allow him to turn her over to the king's man—she could not risk it.

But she didn't understand the laird's hostility toward Bray. The man only helped her. *Mayhap he isnae as indifferent to me as I thought.* Intense gratification warmed her, filled her with delight. The urge to escape warred with the possibility of lingering. Again she wondered what it would be like to wake in the laird's arms, but the thought faded with the memory of the worn rope dangling from the scaffold's jutting arm.

Chapter Six

Brianna watched stealthily, huddled deep in the laird's plaide. Bray and Gillis snored gently by the fire. The laird kept watch, his back to the glowing embers, staring into the dark forest beyond. Again, she wondered who he was, wishing her life less complicated.

If I stay, I will have a few more hours' time with him, mayhap even learn his name—if I asked Bray. I could make up a name for myself and mayhap a plausible story that the king's steward would believe. But how many other young women are lost in the area? If the sheriff's man still hunts me, I will be held for him to identify.

She gave a snort and shook her head, angry with herself. *What draws me to him that I would risk hanging? This makes no sense. I will escape tonight and never see him again.*

Impatient now to execute her plan, she steeled herself to wait for the laird to join the others in sleep. Would her plan work on him? Though tired, she was too full of nervous anticipation to indulge in a nap to pass the time, and somewhat afraid she would oversleep. She tried concentrating on the soughing breeze and the flickering embers of the fire. But she found herself reflecting instead on the way it had felt to spend the day in the laird's arms.

She cut her gaze to him. His shoulders slumped forward and his arms, resting on his knees, cradled his head. She drew a slow, deep breath. At long last, he'd apparently fallen asleep.

Cautious, and a wee bit regretful, she slipped to her feet, one small movement at a time. She stood motionless, scarcely breathing, testing his alertness. Satisfied when he did not move, she edged the shadowy perimeter of the fire and padded noiselessly into the woods. Rounding the trunk of a large tree, she leaned against its shaggy bark, blood pounding in her ears. From this point, were she caught, she could plead a moment of privacy. Once she moved deeper into the woods, the laird would be harder to convince. Why must he insist on turning her over to the king? Explaining to him why that struck terror in her might strengthen his resolve to release her to royal custody, believing the sheriff's reach not long enough to snatch her from beneath the warden's nose. Of course, if she was wrong about the laird's sense of honor, he could just as easily see the benefits of claiming the bounty on her head. She did not want to believe it of him.

St. Andrew preserve me from over-protective men! Especially this one, who treats me as though I am a wean and unable to care for myself. Condescending— She swallowed the last uncharitable word and took a deep, encouraging breath.

She pushed away from the rough bark and glided deeper into the forest. Her ankle protested her slow, deliberate steps, but she gritted her teeth and ignored the brief flashes of pain, impatient with her injury yet pleased with its improvement. Reaching the edge of the stream, she considered the best place to ford the water, avoiding the muddy banks that would betray her footprints. She tested the weed-covered ground with a cautious toe.

Something grabbed her elbow, yanking her back from the water's edge. Her shriek of alarm was cut off as she stumbled, spinning with the force pulling at her. She drew up short, her face against a broad, muscled chest, the musky scent rising from beneath the fine leine covering it one she knew instantly. Bracing her hands against the solid wall, she stared into storm-dark eyes, her heartbeat leaping out of control.

"Wha...what are ye doing?" Her voice squeaked shamefully through her tight, dry throat.

The laird blinked owlishly at her. "Ye left the camp. Ye shouldnae have left the camp." His behavior intrigued her. There was something about his mannerism, his hard stare at her before he'd answered, and the way he repeated himself that was unlike him. He peered at her again, leaning forward as though trying to focus on her face.

He reminds me of Jamie sleep-walking. She hid a satisfied smirk.

St. Andrew be praised, he will be snoring with the others shortly. With a serene air, she shrugged lightly and took a step back. "Och, I dinnae mean to bother ye. I needed to wash after the long day."

A confused look rumpled his face. Pulling easily from his loosened grasp, she moved closer to the stream and knelt beside the burn. She reached forward, cupping the cold water in her hands and splashed some on her face. Swiveling on her heels, she wiped her face on one of her voluminous sleeves and gifted him with a wide smile.

"See? Much better." She offered him her hand and he stared at it for a moment before he took it and hauled her to her feet. "Time for bed!"

Her light-hearted quip earned her a frown, and Brianna gritted her teeth as the silence between them lengthened. Keeping her smile in place by sheer force of will, it was all she could do to keep from screaming aloud at the strain in her muscles as she fought the panicked urge to run. Even if he hesitated, she knew she wouldn't get far, and she silently cursed him roundly for her predicament. Finally, he gave a nod of reluctant consent and she forced herself to stroll calmly across the little glen. The laird followed silently at her back and she felt his gaze pricking like a knife tip between her shoulders.

"Where were ye going?" His voice sounded loud enough to wake the dead. Or at least the somewhat drugged. Startled at the sudden outburst of speech, Brianna whirled, hand up to silence him. But he was closer than she'd judged and her palm landed squarely on his chest. A shock raced through her at the contact and she snatched her hand away. Her gaze flew to his face, wondering if he felt it, too. Judging by the way he stared at her hand, he did.

"Why not rest here? We dinnae want to wake the others, aye?" One drowsy man she should be able to deal with. She did not want to risk waking the other two.

"We could talk a bit," she said. She gambled her most winsome smile and dragged the plaide from her shoulders. His eyes widened and she followed his gaze, finding her shirt gaped open to his stare. Rolling her shoulders to bring the fabric to a semblance of decency, she spread the plaide on the grass, motioning him to sit. When he hesitated, she allowed the leine's neckline to slip, baring one shoulder. She dropped gracefully to the ground and patted the woolen fabric beside her.

"Sit here, aye?" she wheedled. "I am too tired to stand around any longer." She yawned and stretched as though to prove how tired she was, aware his gaze followed her every move. Warmth stole through her. She quickly banished the sensation.

After a moment, the laird eased down beside her. *Men are so easily led. Even Mungo, when he wasnae drunk, could be maneuvered by a simple smile.* She beamed at him as though he'd accomplished something incredible, then curled her feet beneath her.

"It has been a long day, aye?" She pitched her voice intentionally low and soothing. She'd had plenty of practice getting her irascible little brother to sleep at night. How different could this man be? But heat crept up her neck, scorching her cheeks as she remembered the ways the man did not resemble the boy. With a sudden twinge of doubt, Brianna glanced at the scowling face too close to hers.

"I am not tired," he informed her, his words slow and deliberate. Brianna swallowed hard, fighting her dismay. She'd pinned all her hopes on the lettouces, and though obviously drowsy, he should be asleep—not talking to her and fighting her attempt to soothe him into a stupor. With a stubbornness born of burgeoning despair, she tried a different tactic.

"When my little brother, Jamie, says he isnae tired, I tell him a bedtime story. Would you like me to tell you a story? You could stretch out here and close yer eyes." She gently pushed one of his shoulders. "Ye look verra tired." *Sweet Mary forgive me for this duplicity. 'Tis the only weapon I have.*

He stretched his long legs and leaned back onto the plaide. His gaze bore into hers as he rolled up onto one elbow. She tried hard to ignore the way he watched her, the way his eyes focused on her lips as she began a story she'd told Jamie a hundred times before.

"The selkies came out of the sea and shed their seal skins to dance on the land in the moonlight." She kept her voice a soft monotone, deliberately pitched to lull him to sleep. The fact it didn't seem to be working only made her try harder, fighting the unsettling effect of his lazy perusal.

"But the man was fascinated by the selkie, and he quickly hid her discarded seal skin as the others fled his approach. Putting their seal skins on, the others disappeared into the sea, but the beautiful selkie could not find hers and was doomed to be trapped forever on the land."

The laird rolled onto his back. Reaching up, he seized a lock of her hair draped over her shoulder. She swallowed as his fingers closed over the strands, feeling the gentle caress all the way to her scalp. She struggled to continue with the story, using it now as an attempt to keep her attraction for him at bay. Her composure began to crumble.

"He promised to, ah, always protect her and she had no choice but to agree. They lived together as man and wife for many years." Memory of what it meant to live as man and wife swept through her. *But I dinnae like it.* He slid his splayed fingers down the length of the hank of hair, separating the strands, blossoming warmth through her. She closed her eyes. *It was never like this.*

She could not have continued the story if her life depended on it. Her tongue stuck to the roof of her mouth, too dry to speak, all moisture pooled warm between her legs. Opening her eyes, she met his heavy-lidded gaze.

Lifting her hand, she touched his shaggy mane, rubbing her thumb across a small scar beside one eye. She stroked her hand slowly down the side of his face, across the short stubble of his beard. He turned his face into the caress and kissed her sensitive palm. She jumped as though stung, the burn of his lips lingering on her skin.

"Ye are quite a sedeu...a seduct..." He frowned, the word he sought obviously not making it from his fuzzy brain to his lips. "Tempting."

Startled at the direction of her thoughts, Brianna shook her head. "Nae! I am not tempting ye. I am—." She broke off, realizing what she had almost given away.

"Ye are what?" He demanded her answer, his voice low, gravely. Brianna frantically searched for an answer. But he relaxed and continued. "I remember ye dancing in the moonlight, the water sluicing over ye." The words barely whispered past his lips as he changed moods and topics with seductive ease.

"I wasnae dancing." Her gaze locked on his smoldering eyes and she shivered at the thought of him watching her bathe naked in the burn.

"I thought ye were a faerie princess." A faint smile slid across his lips. With a sigh of relief, Brianna now felt certain he was at last in the first stages of delirium.

"I saw ye fall into the water and ye dinnae come back up." He frowned.

"Thank ye for saving me." An unexpected ripple of pleasure slid through her to think it mattered to him. Her skin tingled with a thousand pinpricks of heat as she tried to resist the spell of his caressing voice.

"I believe I will turn in now." She started to rise, but he caught her wrist in one strong hand, pulling her off balance to fall across his chest. She started to protest, but he stole the words with his lips, one hand tangled in her hair, cupping the back of her head, pressing her to him.

He finally released her, his breathing as ragged as hers, and she pulled back, dazed. Hovering over him on straightened arms, her hair spilled in a sparkling curtain around them, her over-large shirt gaped open to his gaze. She followed the direction of his stare, but only placed a palm on his chest, fingering the lacings of his leine, ignoring the extent of her exposure.

A wolfish grin creased his face. "Ye tempt me over-much."

Her heart skipped a beat, knowing the tenuous position she was in. *But I am unlikely to meet him again. He isnae likely to remember this night. And, saints help me, I dinnae want to say 'nae'.*

"Are ye trying to seduce me?" Again he turned his attention to her hair, stroking the fall of it as it rippled through his fingers. His eyes, when they met hers, blazed with mockery. "Or do ye think to escape?"

"Nae. I dinnae wish to escape." She leaned closer, yearning to feel his hands on her. With a deft move, he turned her beneath him, nuzzling her neck as he nipped lightly at the soft skin there. She arched against his aroused body, reveling in his groaned response. His lips bruised hers, crushing them hungrily as his tongue slipped inside her mouth. She twined her arms about his neck and returned his kiss with fervor.

He drew back, stroking the back of his hand across her cheek. "Are ye a faerie princess to so tempt me?"

"Tempt ye? With a wee kiss?" Her laugh rippled low in her throat and his eyes darkened.

"I dinnae know who taught ye about making love, lass, but kissing is just the beginning."

Brianna's heart quickened its beat. *No one taught me this.*

He lowered his head and brushed his mouth against hers, this time gently catching her lower lip in his teeth. A low groan rumbled deep in his chest and she caught her breath at the sensation. He slid his lips down her neck, kissing the frantically beating pulse. He lifted her shirt away from her body, pushing it up to bare her belly, raining kisses on her exposed skin. She writhed beneath him, breathless and shocked as his mouth dipped lower.

With barely a pause, he stripped away her borrowed clothing, his hands warming her bared skin, teasing her to a fever pitch. She squelched the tiny voice in her head, ignoring its warning. Her brief married life had never approached this soul-quenching pleasure, and she ached to follow it to fulfillment. She knew what she wanted, and it was here, now, and so close to her grasp she could scarcely breathe. His mouth covered her breast, teeth teasing a taut nipple, and she was lost.

She whimpered as he pulled away, but her interest flared as he discarded his leine and leggings, baring himself to her gaze. He knelt between her legs, sliding himself along her length as he trailed kisses up her body. She arched against him and he plunged inside her. Her fingernails dug into his shoulders at his short, quick strokes, and pleasure swirled deep in her belly. Suddenly, a shout tore from him. He shuddered for several long moments, then stilled. With a groan, he rolled off of her and dropped to the plaide beside her. One arm pulled her against him, and in two short breaths, he was fast asleep. Brianna gaped at him, astounded.

Chapter Seven

Brianna's chest rose and fell in quick bursts, and she blinked in confusion. *What just happened? Does this deep longing make things worse?* She had no words to adequately explain her sense of loss at just the point the laird spent himself. Something slipped from her grasp, and she could not name it. *At least with Mungo I dinnae care when he finished quickly.* She stared at the man beside her.

He grunted in his sleep and reached for her. She stiffened at his touch, wondering at the flames still streaking along her skin and the tightness low in her belly.

Men. No care for anything but their own pleasure.

With a low snort of frustration, Brianna slipped to her feet. The laird muttered and rolled toward her and she saw his eyes glitter from beneath slitted lids. She gave a start. He was no longer asleep and her chance of escape was near gone.

Moonlight glinted on steel. She lunged to his pile of clothing and grabbed the leather-wrapped hilt of his sword, protruding amid the jumble. Testing the cold weight of it, heavy yet carefully balanced, she rolled it over in her hands, tip poised at the hollow between his throat and chest. His eyes widened. He started to sit up, forearms scrabbling on the ground, but Brianna lifted her elbow in warning. He stilled, understanding it would take only an instant to thrust the sword deep in his chest. With a wry lift to his lips, he surrendered.

"I dinnae suppose ye would give it another go? I usually have more care for a lass than that."

Brianna shook her head, eyes narrowed as she noticed his aroused interest. "I dinnae want anything else from ye. I am leaving ye now."

He shrugged, ignoring her pique, letting his eyes roam casually over every naked inch of her. Scowling, she backed away, stooping to her discarded clothing. She quickly dragged on the shirt and breeches, eyes boring into his, daring him to move. With a last look of warning, she turned and ran to the edge of the burn, tossing his sword to the side where it landed in the dark water.

Conn bounded to his feet the instant she turned, but checked when he heard the splash of his sword hitting the water, and his hesitation cost him the chase.

"*Shite!*" Frustrated, he watched her vanish into the darkness, the shimmer of her long silvery hair flickering one last time before she melted into the moonlight and shadows among the trees.

He spent several anxious moments searching for his sword amid the weeds and mud, careful not to step on the finely honed blade. Irritated with the loss of the lass and possibly his sword as well, he ripped a limb from a nearby sapling and used it to prod the marshy ground until it struck against the submerged weapon. He rinsed the sword clean in the burn, wiping it dry with his plaide. Pulling on his clothes, he stomped up the trail to his camp, wondering if he should exchange his short sword for a claymore that would lend itself less well to the delicate hands of a silver-haired lass.

Bray sat at the edge of the fire, idly pushing at the dark red embers with a long stick. He glanced up as Conn stalked past.

"I see *la mademoiselle* is not with you."

Conn shot him a dour look, but Bray merely shrugged. "It was not well done, *mon ami*."

Conn eyed his friend, silently agreeing with him, but unwilling to admit his fault. He could not believe he had spent himself so quickly. But the exquisite pleasure had taken him by surprise. He was not unskilled in love-making, yet the one woman he craved had fled his arms, thinking him an insensitive dolt. His mood soured.

Bray sighed. "I do not understand, with my superior expertise with women, how they always seem to trip themselves over you."

Conn showed his teeth in a smile more predatory than genial. "I dinnae try so hard as ye."

Bray nodded, thoughtful. "No, you do not have to. *Bon*, I assume she is able to fend for herself now?"

"Leave it alone, Bray," Conn growled. He flung a stick into the fire, muttering under his breath. Fortunately, Bray dropped the subject and said no more about the girl with the silver hair.

Brianna skirted the edge of a small loch, tripped and fell at the water's edge. Within seconds, she was up and running again, not pausing to rest her throbbing ankle. She could not afford to stop, not while there was a chance of capture. Did he chase her? How long would it take to find his sword in the weeds? Unanswerable questions were shoved to the back of her mind as she concentrated on her breathing, running—escape.

And then, she had no more breath. Stumbling on weary legs, she threw her hands forward to break her fall. Her heartbeat pounding in her ears drowned out all other sound as she lay on the leaf-covered ground, too exhausted to rise. Her arms and legs shook with fatigue and she rolled to her side, suddenly overcome with nausea. Pulling up against the trunk of a nearby tree, she retched, shuddering with reaction. Gradually, her heart slowed and her gasping eased. The roaring sound in her head grew fainter and she became aware of the night sounds around her. Her skin felt damp and sticky with sweat in the early morning mist. At last she rose, gingerly testing her ankle. She winced at the dull pain, but decided it would do a bit longer.

Pink and yellow rays of morning lightened the horizon. As light filled the sky, she pushed through brush and bracken, swearing as the branches tore at her hair and clothing. She crested the low hill and faltered, startled to see horses and riders moving at a slow pace through the tall grass a short distance away.

She crouched low, watching as they wound their way across the side of the hill. There were six men, but she counted seven horses. The last horse was riderless and its dappled gray hide shimmered in the early morning sun. It was Maude! Six men meant Duncan and Ewan had returned from Troon! She shot to her feet and lurched headlong down the hill, shouting at them to stop.

Gavin heard her first and wheeled his horse to the sound. His face reflected a mixture of relief and anger for the scare she'd given them as he leapt to the ground and rushed to meet her. Grabbing her shoulders, he looked her over from head to toe and back again.

"Are ye well, lass?" He cocked his head at her. "'Tis a relief to find ye hale and unattached to the sheriff's noose."

Brianna sobered at his scold, but could not contain her relief at being back among her clansmen. "Aye. I am well and happy to see the lot of ye."

The others dismounted their horses and gathered eagerly around her.

"What happened to ye, lass?" Rabbie asked.

"I went to the burn to clean up and slipped on the rocks and fell. I swallowed too much water and would have drowned were it not for a man on the other side who saw me go under." She glanced around the little group, wondering if any would challenge her story. Apart from a few narrowed eyes, they said nothing.

"I hurt my ankle when I fell, and needed help getting back to camp. I dinnae know if the men were in league with the sheriff or not, though they treated me well and did not ask too many questions. We searched for ye, but ye had broken camp. I rode with them all day looking for ye, and finally struck out on my own—and found ye!" She smiled happily, and one by one the Douglases nodded, satisfied she was back and apparently none the worse for her absence.

"We have good news for ye," Geordie said. "The king will be in Troon in a day or two, and the steward has given ye leave to stay in the castle until ye present yer petition."

With a cry of joy, Brianna launched herself at the young Douglas and hugged him fiercely, fairly dancing with glee. Geordie blushed furiously, ducking the good-natured swat Rabbie aimed at his head.

"Come, lass," Gavin urged. "Climb up on Maude. We ride for Troon."

Chapter Eight

Dundonald Castle, Troon

Brianna absently drew the brush through her hair, her thoughts far from a mere act of grooming and even farther from her interview with King Robert in less than an hour's time. With little to do for the past two days at Dundonald Castle, her mind betrayed her with heated memories of the laird's touch.

Mystified with a longing she did not understand, she mused over her unprecedented behavior. What had come over her to make her act so wantonly? Was it because he dared hold her, kiss her? Mungo had done those things, though little else, and never stirred the passion she'd felt with the laird. She groaned in a mixture of embarrassment and desire, still unsettled with the way the act had ended.

Thank goodness there is little chance of ever seeing him again! Once back at Wyndham, I will have other things to occupy my mind and I will forget this folly.

She eyed herself critically in the mirror, schooling her flushed face into a mask of calm serenity. Her priority was her petition to the king, not the coupling that had both awakened her passion and left her wanting.

Brianna jerked the brush through her hair with such force it slipped from her fingers and clattered to the floor. The serving girl straightening the room jumped at the noise and hurriedly bent to retrieve the object. Brianna frowned. "I am sorry. I seem to be out of sorts today."

The maid carefully placed the hairbrush on the table. "Aye, milady. Ye have an appointment with the king this day. But dinnae be nervous. King Robert is a kind man, if ye dinnae mind me saying it. Those of us here at Dundonald know him well."

Though facing the king was only one of the worrisome things on her mind at this moment, Brianna seized on the topic gratefully. "I thank ye. I know I shouldnae worry. My cause is just, and the king is known to my family. I will take yer words to heart."

The maid smiled brightly and helped Brianna finish her preparations. Seeing Brianna in her stained boyish garb when she'd arrived two days earlier had sent the maid scurrying to the clothing chests determined to find her something more suitable for life in the castle and an audience with the king. She had done an admirable job with needle and thread adjusting the lovely gowns to fit Brianna's figure.

"This velvet looks fine on ye, milady." The maid fingered the lush dark blue-green cloth, a perfect foil for Brianna's pale hair. "I have never seen hair the color of yers afore, neither. May I add some ribbon to it?"

Brianna considered her hair in the mirror. "Aye. I would like that. My ma's people came from the far north. My coloring is from her." She shrugged. "'Tis a bit different."

The maid excitedly dug through a small chest. With a triumphant grin, she held up a length of ribbon the same color as Brianna's gown and a length of silver ribbon as well.

"I will twine these together. 'Twill will give yer hair a wonderful sparkle."

Taking the mass of Brianna's hair in her hands, she worked quickly to pull the sides up and back, fastening it at the crown of her head and allowing it to fall past her shoulders. Weaving the ribbon through the resulting curls, the maid stepped back to admire her handiwork.

"There!" She handed Brianna a small hand mirror and bade her turn her back to the larger mirror at the table.

Brianna twisted her head this way and that, catching glimpses of silvery blonde hair woven with aquamarine ribbon and beset with silver strands sparkling in her hair like diamonds. She turned to the maid with frank appreciation for her efforts.

"'Tis wonderful! Ye have worked a miracle."

"Ye should always wear such finery," the girl avowed, a pert grin dimpling her cheeks.

Brianna's face heated at the unaccustomed praise and she set the mirror on the table. "I thank ye. Ye are very kind."

The young maid flushed and dropped a curtsy. Hurrying from the room, she left Brianna alone with her thoughts.

Flames from a hundred flickering candles lit the long room. Murmuring voices droned nearby. King Robert studied the young man before him. Connor MacLaurey, newly Laird of Morven, stood patiently before the throne. The king shook his head and sighed.

"I knew yer father, though not well. I am saddened to learn of yer troubles. I can promise ye, if what ye say is true and yer betrothed is innocent of the charges and comes before me, I will grant her pardon and restore her to ye fully."

Conn bowed deeply. "'Tis all I ask, Sire. I had hoped she had reached ye by now, but I will tell yer man of her and leave the matter in yer hands. We arenae truly betrothed, as my father died before the arrangements were finalized, and I was unaware of them until only recently. Yet I feel an obligation to the poor thing."

King Robert rubbed his chin. It was too much of a coincidence. The new laird of Morven petitioned him to pardon his betrothed, whom he could not find, and somewhere in Dundonald Castle a young woman awaited an audience with her king to clear her name as outlaw. They had to be the same person. He quelled the upward tilt of his lips as the absurdity of it struck.

"I am afraid I only arrived yesterday. 'Tis possible she will come to me soon."

"Aye, 'tis my hope as well. She cannae be involved in reiving as the sheriff proclaims. Though I met her only once several years ago, she was a mousy thing, quiet and unassuming. Her short marriage was to a braggart of a fool and unlikely to have done anything to encourage boldness. I wish I could tell ye more about her, but if she resembles the maid she was then, she is scarcely more than a pale, thin woman today."

The king eyed him. "She is plain?"

"Honestly, Sire, she was a skinny, knob-kneed girl of six with nearly colorless hair when I last saw her. I doubt her looks have much improved."

King Robert hid a smile. He had watched his own daughters change from skinny, plain little girls into young women of stunning beauty. The young laird was in for quite a surprise if what the king's advisor told him was true.

"Ye may leave it in my hands. But I ask ye to linger in the hall a bit. Ye will join me for dinner after I have spoken with a few others."

Laird MacLaurey bowed deeply. "As ye wish, Sire." He backed a couple of steps then turned and strode to the back of the room where his companions waited.

Conn motioned Bray and Gillis close, ushering them away from a group of gossiping courtiers. "The king is willing to do what he can about Lord Wyndham's daughter. Though I hoped to be on the way to Morven now, he has invited us to stay and dine with him tonight. We are to await him here."

Gillis gaped. "Eat with the king?"

"I am to assume even the King of Scotland eats oatcakes?" Bray needled Gillis with a lazy drawl and a toothy smile that did not reach his narrowed eyes.

Conn shot them both a crushing look. "See if ye can stay out of trouble for a while at least. I need to remain on good terms with the king if he is to pardon Brianna. The mares are a gift, not a bribe to get the two of ye out of the dungeon."

The doors to the Great Hall opened and a young woman with shining silver hair flowing in loose curls past her shoulders strode through the doorway, radiant and confident in her royal finery. A herald's voice rang out.

"Lady Brianna of Wyndham!"

Conn watched in stunned disbelief as the faerie princess who had haunted his dreams for the past two nights lifted her chin and approached the king.

Chapter Nine

Brianna stopped at the appointed spot before the king and dropped into a deep curtsy. King Robert eyed her thoughtfully, stroking his chin, looking very much like a stern father debating how best to chastise an errant daughter. Brianna chafed beneath his silent admonition, the words she would have spoken to her father in a similar situation best left unsaid.

Remembering her need for clemency, she waited, bowing her head in deference. The moment drew longer, and she became uneasy. Had the sheriff already approached him? Would he believe the sheriff's testimony?

"Come closer, Lady Brianna." The king beckoned with a wave of his hand.

She lifted her skirts and stepped forward until she stood directly before her king. Once again he regarded her in silence, though a faint smile touched his lips.

"I knew yer great-uncle well. Lord John of Islay is a frequent visitor here."

"He was married to my mother's aunt many years ago."

King Robert nodded. "Ye realize he divorced her in order to marry my Margaret?"

"Aye. Ma was fourteen and already in love with my father. She was less concerned with the affairs of those around her, though she always spoke kindly of Lord John. Her own parents never wed, and she was grateful Lady Amy took her in after her father died."

"I understand yer mother passed away some years ago."

A twinge of pain caught in Brianna's chest and she blinked back sudden tears. "Aye."

The king gave her a kind smile and an approving nod. "It seems she did well by her daughter. Ye are forthright and well-spoken. Most people are tongue-tied to address their king."

A smile curved Brianna's lips. "She did her best, Sire. She taught me what she could in the years before her death, though I was quite young. I was an indifferent pupil, I fear."

"I dinnae know yer mother, but Lord John once mentioned her to me. He said she was a beautiful, clever lass who fell deeply in love with yer father, and pined for him every day until permission was given for them to marry."

Brianna ducked her head, dismayed his kind words again threatened to make her cry. She took a deep breath. "I thank ye, Sire. I remember it so. She has been dead these past five years, and I miss her still."

King Robert's eyes twinkled. "Ye seem to have inherited her spirit."

"Mayhap, though I remember her as elegant and composed even under the most provoking circumstances."

"What provoking circumstances was she subject to?" The king's frown was puzzled.

Brianna laughed. "'Twas most likely me, Sire. I would imagine I was the most provoking thing in her life."

King Robert roared with appreciation. "Ye realize Lord John's divorce was a political move, not a personal choice, though I believe he and Margaret suit each other well. And such a move has very likely saved yer life."

"'Twas my thought as well as I stood before the sheriff, Sire."

"Then tell me, Lady Brianna. What is yer petition of yer king?"

Brianna sobered immediately. She bowed her head for a moment to collect her thoughts. In her banter with the king, she had all but forgotten why she was here.

She lifted her gaze. "Sire, my people are clan Douglas of Wyndham. We are small in number, but have always been fortunate in the raising of cattle and crops. Several months ago, my father and Laird MacLaurey entered into a protection agreement against reivers on our southern border, and until two months ago, this benefited us greatly." Brianna paused, her gaze sliding away from the king as she delicately avoided mention of the betrothal that had sealed the agreement.

"But Laird MacLaurey died, and his son has been gone from Morven for some time. His cousin laid claim to the title and dinnae see fit to continue the agreement, and the reivers have now decimated our herds."

Agitated to remember the cause of her problems, she began to pace the floor in front of the king. "Five years ago, Ma died, and since then, in his sorrow at her passing, Da's mind has slowly left him. He is currently incapable of protecting our clan."

She whirled abruptly and faced the king. "Sire, I couldnae bear it. Last year the adults went hungry. This year, since the agreement has failed, the bairns will also suffer." Drawing herself up proudly, she gave the king a frank stare. "I gathered six trusted Douglas soldiers, and together we have been taking back cattle stolen from us. We cannae fend the reivers off—there are too few of us. We know the land well and have been fortunate to locate most of our cattle before they were sold. So far we have returned nearly all to their rightful owners."

King Robert leaned forward on his throne, rapt fascination on his face. Brianna continued her story.

"Two weeks ago, cattle were stolen from Wyndham land. We went to retrieve them, but were captured by the sheriff at Glenkirk and his men. My soldiers and I were to be hanged, but I pleaded with the sheriff to allow us to fall upon yer mercy."

Brianna's voice softened and she spread her hands in supplication. "Sire, we are not reivers. We were caught with cattle not our own, but we dinnae steal from other crofters. We truly believed the cattle to be ours. I have since learned it was a trap set by someone as yet unknown to me. I beg ye to remove the title of 'outlaw' from me and the brave Douglas soldiers who but did as their hearts and circumstances dictated, and let us return to our families at Wyndham."

King Robert nodded, looking thoughtful. After a moment, he smiled. Raising his hands, he stood before his court as Brianna sank to her knees, head bowed as she prepared to hear her doom.

"Lady Brianna, We find ye and yer soldiers not guilty of reiving, but caught trying to keep yer clansmen and their possessions safe. We hereby rescind the charge of outlaw and restore ye fully to clan Douglas. Step forth, lady."

She stood and took a step closer. "Sire?"

King Robert cleared his throat and returned to his chair, spreading his robes across his lap. "I am impressed with yer courage and desire to see yer clan succeed. I release ye from the custody of the crown and send ye on yer way." He lifted a hand in check as she started to speak.

"However, I will send ye back with an escort."

Brianna looked around in puzzlement. She had several perfectly competent soldiers who would be more than adequate escort for her. Perhaps the king meant for her to travel under his banner, though his papers of amnesty would surely guarantee their safety. The king beckoned to someone at the back of the room.

"Inasmuch as I would have this settled, I will see to the union of yer clan with MacLaurey and fulfill the betrothal set forth. Connor MacLaurey, stand forward."

What? Brianna tore her dumbfounded gaze from the king and whirled to see the man once bound to her. She stared at the man as he strode the length of the room. He was tall and well-built, confident, with a swagger to his walk. His face was clean-shaven beneath thick, blond hair, and his eyes—good Lord, those eyes belonged to the man who had tormented her dreams these past nights!

"Nae, Sire, please—" She bit back her words, realizing she contradicted the king. Beneath the regal question in his eyes, she took a steadying breath, clasping her hands before her, gripping them tight to focus her thoughts.

"Sire, please understand, the first priority in my life is to my clan. I care for both my young brother and my ailing father. To protect the clan, he sought an agreement with this..." She cut her eyes to the man standing calmly beside her, quelling the urge to pinch him solely to garner some response from him.

Giving him an uneasy look, she continued. "We received help from MacLaurey for several months, but after the laird died, the arrangement also died and his son, nursing a broken heart, continued to find solace in skirts and wine from here to France, unconcerned with our fate."

A gasp and clang sounded as a jeweled goblet tumbled from the king's cup bearer's hands, reminding Brianna that others were close enough to hear her derisive assassination of Laird MacLaurey's character. Her cheeks burned as a ripple of whispered speculation swept the room. From the corner of her eye she saw Bray's arms fold cross his chest, a scowl on his face. Gillis dropped his oatcake, mouth agape. Beside her, Conn stiffened as though he'd been lashed.

In trembling silence, she waited for the king to consider her plight, praying Conn would not mention their intimate encounter only a few days prior. That would settle the matter entirely, and the king would not be able to see her married fast enough.

I am no maid to be bartered like so much oats or cattle. I want to live my life on my terms, not theirs. She brutally pushed aside memory of the passion ignited in her, the fire that lingered still within. Her heartbeat fluttered and she felt faint. She clenched her fists until her nails bit into her palms. *I willnae swoon before the king!*

The king frowned. "Are ye asking me to deny yer betrothal to MacLaurey?"

She bit her lip and considered his question. Surely Conn could see how unsuited they were and agree to release her from the contract.

"The betrothal died with his father. He has no care for Wyndham."

King Robert turned to MacLaurey. "Would ye still marry her, though she doesnae appear to be pleased with ye?"

"Aye. I would."

Brianna's wide-eyed gaze flew back to the king. "Sire, I am no maid, but a widow with no bairns to bring to the marriage. He should be free to find a woman of his choosing who would give him an heir."

The king looked again to Conn, his eyebrows raised in question.

"I will suffer the risk."

"I willnae see ye seeking another if she doesnae produce an heir," the king warned.

"Her previous husband was young. I believe I can do better."

The Macrory lass dinnae hesitate to abandon yer charms. The sudden tic in Conn's cheek told her she had voiced the words aloud, though a furtive glance assured only he had heard her.

The king stared from Brianna to Conn and back for several nerve-wracking moments. "Lady Brianna, ye need a husband and MacLaurey needs a wife. I am certain it will all work out." This time there was no mistaking the note of finality in King Robert's voice.

"Sire, I have no desire to wed!" Brianna blurted out, partly lifting her hands in desperation.

"Ye wish to retire to a nunnery?" the king asked in surprise. Conn turned a wry, challenging look on her, silently forcing her to remember the passion she was capable of and daring her to deny it. Her cheeks burned with furious anger at both men.

"Nae, Sire," she muttered.

"Then have ye another husband in mind?"

"Nae."

King Robert threw his hands into the air. "Then, instead of seeing ye wed before ye leave, I give ye opportunity to enjoy each other's company for the duration of yer visit and yer travel home. Ye will come to an understanding by then. I give ye, Brianna, a further two weeks to see yer clan's needs are met. At that time, ye will wed without further hesitation."

He stood to his feet, towering over them from his position on the dais. "Connor MacLaurey, I hereby charge ye with fulfilling yer sworn duty to Lady Brianna of Wyndham. Lady Brianna, ye are charged with yer sworn duty to Connor MacLaurey of Morven. Ye find yerself in favor with the crown. Long may ye both live."

Smiling broadly, the king stepped down and took Brianna's face in his hands, placing a kiss on each cheek. He stepped closer to Conn and clapped a hand to his shoulder. "'Twas not by chance she was arrested for reiving. Someone wants her out of the way. Guard her well."

Conn acknowledged the warning with a nod and the king favored the pair with a paternal smile. "Stay with us for a few days. We will host a banquet in honor of yer betrothal two days hence." He waved to his advisor, who nodded at an aide, who scurried away to carry out the king's wishes. Brianna was too stunned to move.

Chapter Ten

Numb, Brianna gathered her skirts. She had no desire to speak to this man the king had bound her to, nor did she wish to stay in his presence a moment longer. Once again she had been manipulated into marriage, and her blood boiled with resentment.

A shudder. Could this marriage be different? She snorted in disgust at the idea. No matter how attracted she may have been to the man, 'twas all for naught in the end.

Her step quickened and she fled the room to the stairway leading to her chamber. An iron grip on her arm yanked her to a stop and she whirled to face Conn, his expression black with fury.

"Let go of me!" she hissed angrily.

Conn released her arm, but did not move away. "What do ye think ye are about? Are ye dead set on being hanged?"

"The king pardoned me."

"Aye, for reiving. Disobedience to the king is treason and will also get ye hanged."

Brianna eyed him narrowly, unable to quell her toe as it tapped the stone floor impatiently. "I dinnae want to marry."

"Well, there will be none to wed ye from the gallows."

He loomed over her, his expression darker still. "And I could have refused ye for yer lack of respect."

She stared at him in disbelief. "Lack of respect? I said naught that is not on any other's tongue, m'laird."

"Ye know naught of me or my past year in France."

"Enough to know I dinnae want to be shackled to a skirt-chaser like yerself. I dinnae want such disrespect in *my* marriage, either!"

Conn exhaled a long breath. "Why are ye so against this marriage?"

"Are ye daft? What is there to recommend it?"

"The reivers—"

"Have stripped my clan of their wealth."

"Yer dowry is of no importance to me. However, I do find myself in need of an heir."

Furious, Brianna tossed her head. "Ye would do better to find a woman ye know will give ye one. I have no desire to be that woman."

"Is that so?" The soft tone of his voice did not match the fire she saw in his eyes. She shook off the frisson of longing before it woke the passion his voice ignited in her, and did not flinch as she spoke the lie.

"Aye."

She braced herself for his scornful rebuttal, certain he would deride her actions of three nights previous. She needed away from this nightmare, a chance to find some palatable option. Before she could move, his hand grasped the back of her head, drawing her against him. She gasped, and his mouth took her cry in a fierce kiss that tore the lie from her. Startled, she returned his kiss, the taste of him a vibrant memory. His hand flared across her bottom, pulling her against his arousal. He was too close, trapping her, giving her no quarter. With a muffled shriek, Brianna jerked away, her hands shoving against his chest. He murmured against her ear.

"That's right. Fight me. Use up yer anger."

With renewed vigor, she kicked at his shins, her slippered feet doing him no damage. Her fingers curved as she clawed at him, leaving a red welt the length of his cheek before he caught her wrists. She writhed against him until her energy was spent, and she sagged against the wall at her back.

Conn shifted both her wrists into one hand and stroked fingers across her cheek, the heat of her skin reflecting her wrath. Taking advantage of what he was sure was only a temporary surrender, his hands took on a life of their own as they released her to stroke her sides, remembering her curves. As his palms moved to cup her breasts, Brianna stiffened with a hiss, and he cursed her willful anger against him. Though a widow, he did not believe she openly sought lovers, for the last time he caressed her, he'd gotten his own sword in his chest for his efforts.

He moved his lips soothingly against her temple as he calmed his raging passion. But instead of settling, she wrenched away, though the wall at her back stopped her retreat. She flattened against the rough stone, her breathing ragged, eyes sparking her fury. He placed his hands on the wall above her head and leaned his forehead against his arms. Admiring the way her breasts heaved against the constraints of her gown, he forced his gaze away from her ample charms and to her eyes.

He read mutiny in their cool blue depths. Mutiny and hatred. Puzzled, he wondered if he had gone too far, but he remembered how she had returned his kiss, for a moment at least. For one sweet moment she had felt like heaven in his arms. Now she fought to get away from him like a rabbit caught in the hunting path of a falcon.

"Explain why ye hate me so." His voice sounded soft and low, both gentling and demanding at the same time.

She glanced past him, her gaze darting from side to side, judging the possibility of escape. There was none, and after a moment she lifted her chin a notch, refusing to answer him. He hid a grin at her courage and pride. And stubbornness.

"Have ye always disliked the idea of marriage, then?"

A disdainful breath escaped her. "I have been married once before. It dinnae interest me much then, either."

"Yer previous husband was only a lad. Heir to a sizeable bit of land, but still just a lad."

"And ye can do better," she tossed at him, repeating his earlier boast to the king.

"Ye know I can." He touched the backs of his fingers to her cheek and she gasped, her skin darkening beneath his touch. "I cannae get our love-making out of my mind."

Brianna shrugged. "Och, there was nothing to recommend it to me. I have already put it from my mind."

"I apologize for that, dearling. Ye willnae feel so bereft the next time, I promise ye."

"Dinnae bother. All I want from ye is Morven's protection for Wyndham."

He met her steely stare. "Ye dinnae want me?"

"Nae," she ground between clenched teeth, her nostrils flaring.

"Ye werenae married long enough to appreciate a man in yer bed.

I bet ye still have yer dowry chest." He teased her lightly, wanting to see a smile on her lips.

"I burned the wood to warm my cold bedroom," she snarled in reply.

"Yer wedding dress?"

"Rags for the stable!"

He leaned closer, his voice a raw whisper in her ear. "I would settle for marrying ye the way I found ye." Brianna eyed him in puzzlement, and he knew the instant she remembered he had pulled her from the burn as naked as the day she was born.

With a snarl of either rage or despair, she flung herself away from the wall. Before he could stop her, she darted beneath his arm and fled down the darkened hallway, her billowing silver hair the last thing to fade into the darkness.

Shite! Does the lass have no sense at all? He rubbed his chin thoughtfully, wincing as he encountered the tender stripe she'd laid down the side of his face. *Why do I pursue her? She openly hates me and has scorned me before the king and his court.* He shrugged, remembering how they'd come together when neither knew the other's name. *I could do a lot worse.* His rueful smile creased the welt and he scowled at the sting.

Pivoting on his heel, he headed for the great hall where the feasting was taking place. Firelight burst across the walls, reflecting the flames dancing in the huge fireplace. Voices raised in cheer reached him and he slowed. *They will wonder if I come to the table alone. Unable to control my bride.* His footsteps halted. *I dinnae want to marry, either. And I escaped to France. But now 'tis my duty to wed and provide my clan an heir. No matter some think I shirked my duty by running away, I willnae turn from it now.*

Surely she hasnae gone far. Biting back another curse, he pushed himself from his indecision and headed down the hallway after her.

Chapter Eleven

Seated on a pile of hay in a corner of Maude's stall, Brianna huddled in anger, arms wrapped around her waist against the night air. The mare showed mild interest, butting her with her soft nose as she begged a treat, but soon returned to her snooze, one hoof cocked lazily on its toe as she flicked her tail from time to time at a persistent horsefly.

Drained from the evening's events, Brianna felt quite content to sit and feel sorry for herself. She was caught firmly by the king's command, for no matter if she obeyed or not, she would soon find herself unable to call Wyndham home. Was there anything about this calamity she could derive happiness from?

Reluctantly, she admitted Conn not bad-looking. Undoubtedly many other young lasses had fallen victim to his imagined charm, but his looks were at least passable. Dare she trust his boast his lovemaking would be different in the future? Dare she hope to have anything approaching the respectful relationship she desired? *From what I know of the man, 'tis doubtful.*

She leaned her head against the wall of the stable. *I dinnae want to marry a man proud of what is beneath his kilt. I dinnae want the distraction from running Wyndham. I especially dinnae want a man who was once in love with another. He is too well known for his dalliances before and since. Marry him? Ha! Murder him is more likely.*

The door to Maude's stall creaked open and Brianna glared at the intruder. To her surprise, Gavin stepped inside the stall, a worried look on his face.

"Are ye well, lass?"

She muttered under her breath, but nodded and motioned for him to join her. He stepped through the deep, sweet-smelling hay, pushing Maude gently on her rump to move her out of his way. The mare stomped a foot in irritation, flicking an ear as he passed.

Gavin settled on the mound of hay beside Brianna and plucked a long stem of dried grass from her tangled hair. With a smiling salute, he stuck the fragrant stem between his teeth. Leaning against the wooden planks behind him, he drew his legs up, hands dangling over his knees. Brianna eyed him curiously.

"How did ye find me?"

"Och, ye always seek the stable and Maude's good company whenever ye are out of sorts."

"I am out of sorts," she admitted. "I begged the king's mercy and received a life sentence."

"The king did what he thought best. 'Twas yer da's plan after all."

"I am a woman grown and not subject to such interference in my life. I dinnae want to marry and leave Wyndham."

"Things will work out. Ye must believe that."

"Why could I not marry someone from Wyndham? So I wouldnae be required to move away, so I could help raise Jamie, keep Wyndham for him until he is grown?" She gave Gavin a frank stare. "Someone like ye?"

"Me? I am years older than ye. I wouldnae make ye a fit husband."

Brianna waved aside his protest. "Ye are honorable, trustworthy, have some kinship and the desire to help our clans-people. And ye are always nice to me."

Gavin shook his head and laughed. "'Tis true, though I care not for the lord's position. And ye are an easy lass to love."

"Ye love me?"

He returned her startled look with seriousness. "Aye. Since the day ye followed me out to the barn and demanded to be allowed to ride yer da's stallion."

"Ye dinnae let me ride him."

"Nae. I couldnae see ye hurt. Ye have always had my heart, lass."

"But ye have said nothing. It could have made a difference. We have so many of the same desires, hopes."

He sighed. "No difference. Ye are betrothed to MacLaurey, and there isnae a man alive who would risk his wrath by touching ye."

Brianna slid a thoughtful look from the corner of her eyes. "What if he agreed to break the contract?"

Gavin's wan smile was tinged with sadness. "There is not a chance in hell he would give ye up, lass."

"No chance at all." Conn's deep, forbidding voice rumbled from the doorway. His face was white with barely-leashed fury, and Brianna drew back in alarm. How much of their conversation had he heard? Apparently too much, she realized as she met his angry gaze. After fleeing his embrace, he now found her in a most compromising position with one of her soldiers—who had just declared his love for her. Did Conn think she planned to run away with Gavin? Likely.

"Ye willnae blame the lass for this." Gavin spoke over her musings, drawing Conn's ire.

Conn snatched the stall door open, motioning for Gavin to leave with a jerk of his head. "The *lass*," he bit out, stressing the word, "is about to become *my wife*. She is now under the protection of the MacLaureys."

Gavin stood his ground. "Until she is married, her clansmen will protect her."

"And let her get caught reiving again?" Conn taunted.

Gavin advanced a step, scowling. Conn relaxed his stance, flexing his hands in eager anticipation of a fight.

Brianna leapt to her feet, planting her fists on her hips in outrage. "Stop it, the both of ye!"

The two men ignored her, their challenging stares locked together, each waiting for the other to make the first move. She turned to Gavin, admonishment on her lips, and Conn's black gaze snapped to her. She froze, realizing that to openly side with Gavin, a man who had declared his love for her in front of her betrothed, albeit unknowingly, would indeed be the spark to set the fire ablaze.

Amadans. Men. Schooling her face to a more tolerant mien, she addressed them both. "There is no reason for the two of ye to act like *paukie* lads. I willnae have it."

Conn sent her a chilling look. "Ye willnae? Then, lady, have a care who ye tumble in the hay with. After our discussion a short time ago, I would be inclined to think him the reason ye told me nae."

"I have told ye my reasons."

"Ye will have to find better ones. The king has already conceded ye much."

"Leave her be." Gavin's voice lost its hostility, his gaze no longer challenging.

Tension arced between the two men, then drained away. But the look that passed between them assured Brianna the matter was far from settled. Conn stepped away from the door, allowing Gavin passage. As the man drew abreast, Conn spoke. "I wouldnae harm her."

Gavin nodded as he strode through the doorway. "That is a good thing."

Brianna watched Gavin's receding back, then met Conn's mocking gaze.

"Ye started collecting admirers somewhat quickly for a lass with no prospects less than an hour ago."

"Still none who would dare challenge ye," she retorted bitterly, musing over Gavin's words and actions.

"Nae, a smart man willnae. I may revise my opinion of the Douglases yet."

"Dinnae insult these men. They have risked much to do what I asked of them."

"Their goal was the same as yers."

"Mayhap, but they swore their lives to me."

"All of Morven will be yers."

Brianna's eyes lit with anger. "Nae."

Conn ran his fingers through his hair in frustration. "Why do ye not accept this marriage?"

"I have told ye. I dinnae wish to marry. My place is at Wyndham."

"I want ye back in my arms where ye were three nights ago."

Brianna lifted her chin, her eyes glittering with warning. "That night was a mistake. If ye persist in this, I will make yer life a living hell."

Chapter Twelve

Dundonald Castle, a sennight later

Brianna tugged the girth strap on Maude's saddle, fitting it tight around the mare's belly. A low whine caught her attention. In the doorway to the stall, a young collie sat, his tail sweeping the straw. Brianna crossed to the pup and squatted before him. She patted his shiny black head and got a lick from his broad pink tongue in return.

"Ye are a right pest, aye, lad?" She ruffled his ears affectionately. "I dinnae bring ye a treat today. My mind was elsewhere."

His tail beat faster and he whimpered as he wiggled against Brianna.

"I wish I could take ye with me. I am in need of a fine herding dog such as ye."

"He likes ye, m'lady."

Brianna looked up, recognizing the kennel master's voice. "He has followed me around the stable the past few days. He seems to be a good lad."

The man rubbed his whiskery chin. "I wondered where he'd been. Of all his littermates, he is the trouble-maker. Not destructive, mind ye, just smart as a whip and always off doing things on his own."

Brianna rose, giving the pup a last pat. He leapt to his feet and slid around her, peering at his master from behind her skirts.

"He is a collie, aye?"

The kennel master grinned, warming to his subject. "Aye, m'lady.

From a very noble and hard-working line. His dam can gather up a flock of sheep quicker than a virgin—er, before I can give the signals. And his sire is tireless herding cattle. Doesnae back down from even the toughest auld besom, yet nearly lost his life keeping a newborn warm out in a winter storm two years ago."

"I could use a dog like that. Mine died suddenly several weeks ago. Do ye know if the pup is for sale?"

"Tam, here? Och, ye dinnae want him. He is too independent and willnae listen. Ask the king's man about one of his littermates. At nearly eight months old, they are already well ahead on their training. They will make excellent herders."

Brianna considered the man's words carefully. "I thank ye. I will speak to the king's man about this."

Ducking his head in a respectful gesture, the man took a step toward her, opening the noose on the end of a narrow rope. He pulled up short, puzzled. "Now, where has the beast run off to this time?"

Leaving him scratching his head in bewilderment, Brianna mounted her horse and set about their daily routine. Careful to keep close to the castle wall, she put Maude through her paces, bleeding off some of the energy the mare collected each day with nothing to do but stand in her stall and munch the king's hay.

Two days later, she tied her bags behind her saddle, distracted as she listened for the soft footfalls of the pup who had become her companion around the stable. He had been absent the day before, and the king's man had nothing new to tell her about selling the dog, though he assured her he'd brought it to the king's attention. Today, however, she was leaving Dundonald, and she regretted not asking the king herself.

She patted the bags, taking a mental inventory of their contents. She'd arrived with almost nothing, and was leaving with more than she'd imagined. The traveling dress she wore was a gift, her maid told her, as was the heavy woolen plaide she would sleep on each night. She also carried a water skin and oatcakes should she grow hungry along the way. In the second bag was an ewer of beaten gold, inlaid with silver chasing and precious stones, given to her by the king as a wedding gift at the banquet two nights earlier.

She'd received a second gift as well. Wrapped in gauze and placed in a soft leather pouch was a sapphire pendant, the stone bound in silver filigree, a gift from her husband-to-be. The pendant, as beautiful as it was, had been pushed to the bottom of the bag. She'd no desire to wear jewelry marking her as the man's possession. Its worth was in the coin it would bring when she sold it. The money, which would buy her people a goodly supply of grain this winter, was of far greater value to her. Conn might or might not agree, but she would worry about that later.

There was nothing left to delay her. It was time to leave Dundonald and the king's protection. Time to look to her new future and make something good of it. She stepped into the saddle and rode from the stable, ducking her head as she passed beneath the portal. Outside, the others were already mounted, waiting for her. The kennel master stood to the side, a black and white puppy at his side.

She nudged Maude over to him. "What is the word on the pup?"

A half-grin pulled the man's mouth to one side. "The steward bade me gift ye with the pup of yer choice. Do ye still want young Tam, or would another suit ye better?"

"This is the lad I want."

"Then St. Francis smile upon ye. He will make a fine dog—once he outgrows his mischievous ways."

He handed the leather lead to Brianna with a small salute. She thanked him and looped the soft leather about the pommel of her saddle. The young dog rose to his feet, tail pluming gently.

"Are ye ready, milady?" Conn asked.

She met his gaze. "Aye."

Brianna stiffened as Conn dropped beside her on the log she used as a seat, his trencher full of oatcakes and roasted rabbit. Her own plate still held most of her own meager meal. Since facing the prospect of marriage to Laird MacLaurey, her appetite had declined noticeably. She set her supper on the ground beside her and nudged it back. Tam, lying behind her, made short work of it.

Tonight they were miles away from Troon and she no longer had the people of Dundonald Castle as a buffer between herself and Conn. And right now he sat entirely too close for her comfort, their truce before the king far from resolved. She scooted once away from his bulk and eyed him warily as he casually licked his fingers. "What are ye doing?" she asked.

Conn glanced at her, his eyes overly wide in feigned surprise. "Why, enjoying yer company, of course."

"Why?" Her tone was blunt, challenging. *Why are ye so persistent? Do ye not understand I dinnae like what ye have done to my life?*

Conn sighed. "Because the king distinctly told us to do so."

Brianna's eyes widened in alarm and she shook her head. "He said no such thing." She racked her memory in an effort to recall King Robert's words. It had been more than a week since he had surprised her with his response to her petition and subsequent reinstatement of her betrothal. She came up empty.

Conn rubbed a hand down the fabric of his kilt and gave her a sideways look. "Yer skill in avoiding me even when the king commanded us to spend time together bordered on insult. Rude behavior is unbecoming and disrespectful."

Brianna bristled under his high-handed, unwelcome tutelage. "Ye follow me around, leaving me little breathing space, disregarding my wishes on matters, and still ye harp on *my* insolence."

"A man needs his wife's respect."

Brianna shot daggers at him. "Few men deserve it. Most men I know demand their respect through loud, angry voices and brutish actions. I willnae be commanded to respect any man. He must earn it."

Cocking his head to the side, Conn stared at her. "Would ye care to tell me how to earn such regard?"

She gave a mirthless laugh. "I willnae give ye some formula for it. It should flow freely between two people, not as a list to be checked off as a meaningless job well met."

"Aye, it should be a mutual thing. Could I, then, tempt ye into a walk so we can discuss this further?" He set his now-empty plate aside and stood, stretching his hand to her. She stared at the proffered limb as though it might bite, and slowly raised her dubious gaze to his. His unwavering stare was perilously close to a command. She lifted her chin in defiance. Conn sighed.

"Dinnae be obstinate, Brianna. Things could go much better between us if ye just admitted ye liked me. Even a bit."

"What on earth makes ye think I like ye?"

Conn's arrogance showed no limits as he prodded her memory. "Ye were soft in my arms as we rode the roads, seeking yer men. Ye were pliant beneath me before we said our goodbyes beside the burn." His smile turned teasing. "And, if memory serves, the king's words were for us to enjoy each other's company of the duration of our travel home. I believe he *wants* us to like each other."

Her lips twitched, but she did not give in to the urge to smile. "Like each other? I distinctly remember saying I hated ye. Liking ye would be a bit of a stretch."

"Come with me, Brianna." He made a small motion with his hand, his voice deceptively soft. Brianna eyed him suspiciously, not trusting his intentions. Finally, seeing no way to avoid it without being accused of being disrespectful yet again, she rose from her seat, though she pointedly refused Conn's proffered hand. Tam nosed the empty trencher once more, then curled up for a nap with a contented sigh. Brianna glanced at the tired pup before turning back to Conn.

"Well?" she demanded testily as he made a leisurely perusal of her person.

He grinned at her unrepentantly, not bothering to apologize for ogling her. Instead, he swept his arm forward, indicating she precede him down the narrow trail leading to a small glade where water bubbled cheerfully over smooth stones.

"'Tis a bit more private here. I would like to talk to ye without being interrupted or overheard."

"If ye think I will succumb to yer charms here by the burn simply because I lost my head once before, ye are sadly mistaken."

"Nae. Ye have adequately informed me of yer intentions. I would not take ye without ye full willing."

"That confident, are ye, that ye will get an heir from me? Conn, even if things were better between us, I was married nearly a year and dinnae conceive a bairn. All yer bold boasts to the contrary, I think ye are daft to believe I could bear ye, or anyone else, children."

Conn scowled. "Nae. No one else. Yer children will be mine, and no other's."

Brianna flung her hands into the air. "What do ye not understand? I dinnae want to wed. I dinnae believe I can bear children. Ye want to wed. Ye want children. Can ye not spare us the misery and ask to be released from this?"

"I dinnae wish to be released from the betrothal. The king has signed it himself. Ye know what ye stand to lose if ye disobey."

Brianna fought to keep from pulling out her hair at his stubbornness. "Ye prattle of honor and duty, and what I stand to lose if I dinnae obey. But what will benefit me if I agree? Will I be allowed to stay at Wyndham, help govern it until Jamie is old enough to do so, keep my da from destroying everything? My clan and my brother mean more to me than anything, and no matter my choice, I will lose it all."

"Ye will marry me, Brianna Douglas. An arrangement can be made for Wyndham's government. But like it or not, we will marry at the king's pleasure in two weeks's time, and ye will be my wife."

"I dinnae want a marriage to someone I dinnae trust. Our short time together is built on lies and little else."

Conn shrugged. "I did ask yer name."

"I was hunted by the sheriff for reiving. As a lord's daughter, I am also a target for ransom. I had no reason to trust ye with my name."

"Would ye trust me now?"

Brianna clenched her teeth and dropped her gaze. "I cannae." Clutching her plaide about her against the cold, she retraced her steps to their camp.

Gavin's frown warned the Douglas soldiers' attention from Brianna as she marched through the campsite, head high, dark stains upon her cheeks. His gaze did not waver as Conn stepped through the group moments later, running a hand through his hair in a frustrated manner.

"She is likely bedded down with Maude." Gavin rose and stepped toward Conn, his movement turning them away from the other men's hearing. He jerked his head toward the horses' picket line, ignoring Conn's hostile glare. "She has always been partial to her horse's company. Especially when something has upset her."

Conn started to push past him, but Gavin stopped him with a raised hand. "'Tis how I knew where to find her the other night. 'Twas no liaison between us. I have known her since she was a wee lass. She had no one to turn to these past years since her ma died and her da became a drunkard in his sorrow. She willnae thank me for saying this, but her previous husband and her da's behavior has left her with little need for men, and little respect for them, either."

"She seems to respect ye well enough." Conn's look was sardonic, his lips pulled mockingly to the side.

"I never rode rough-shod over her wishes. I have gainsaid her when her safety was in question, but the lass has a good head on her shoulders and a soft heart if ye know how to treat her."

Gavin glanced away, giving the moment a chance to resolve Conn's accusation. "Go easy on her. She has been ordered about long enough. She has defended her clan by defying direct orders and tradition. After her first husband broke her heart with his brutish disregard, and his da threatened her with disgrace for not bearing an heir, she came back to Wyndham determined to raise wee Jamie and never marry again."

Conn's eyes glinted dangerously. "Not even ye?"

Gavin stared him down with a hard look. "Mayhap. If I asked her nicely. Ye must turn her mind and her heart. Prove to her ye are different. Let her know she isnae wanted solely as a broodmare, but as a respected wife."

Conn scowled. "I have no desire to break her heart or her spirit. She speaks of honoring her clan. Why should she not accept this betrothal if it brings help to her people?"

"Her desire is to help Wyndham. But aligning forces with Morven meant she had to marry again. And ye have a hard reputation to overcome."

"I spent time in France to distance myself from my best friend and the woman I thought to marry. Rumor wants to believe I drowned my sorrow beneath skirts and tavern tables. 'Tis true I spent a small portion of my time in those pursuits, but the reason I dinnae know my da died was because I spent most of my days—and nights—at horse breeding farms, choosing the right horses to bring home, and as gifts for the king."

Gavin eyed him curiously. "Have ye told her this?"

"Would it matter? I have no proof. She already believes the rumors."

"Good luck to ye, then, and may St. Andrew show mercy. Ye will need it."

Chapter Thirteen

Brianna gazed beyond the velvet night sky, over-sewn with a thousand twinkling diamonds, absently stroking Tam's belly as he sprawled on his back beside her, his body boneless in sleep. She wished she could enjoy such peace.

Maude nudged her, demanding equal attention. Brianna rubbed her hand over her soft muzzle, wondering at the changes in her life. *'Tis been scarcely more than a month since I sat at home, smug in my conviction I helped the people of Wyndham. Scarcely a month ago I believed I was in charge of my own destiny.*

Now, the earth itself had opened at her feet and it remained to be seen if she would find her footing or fall into endless darkness. With her ma gone and her da's actions and thoughts questionable and unpredictable at best, she had no one to trust and counsel her which way to turn.

Nae, that isnae true. Auld Willie is on my side, though he is at Wyndham with Jamie. And Gavin—what a surprise. Always he has been there, whether to tell me I couldnae ride Da's temperamental stallion or comforting me when Ma died. I thought him a friend— what if he had been more?

She felt someone behind her, unnerved to feel Conn's presence so distinctly. "Go away!" she whispered roughly, her voice thick with regret. Regret for the decision she knew she had to make, regret for a life that left her subject to the whim of others.

"May I sit with ye a while?"

Brianna closed her eyes. She could withstand him better if he were cloddish, arrogant, crude or a brute. Aye, these things she knew and could deal with. 'Twas true he was arrogant, but he tempered it with a gentleness slowly slipping past her defenses.

She faced him. He tilted his head in silent invitation and she shifted the puppy down a bit, allowing him to sit next to her.

"This will work, Brianna. Ye know it will."

"How can it when ye dinnae know me?"

"I know ye well enough."

She gave him a look of profound disgust. "Ye are basing yer whole assumption on a few misguided moments we spent together. Ye are squandering my whole life on a foolish moment of passion. When will ye decide ye need to know me?"

Conn took a deep breath and Brianna was aware he clung to a thin tissue of restraint. "Ye dinnae know me, either."

"I know enough," she tossed back at him.

"Ye know rumors. Not me."

"Ye lost yer lady love to another and left yer responsibilities at Morven to drown yer sorrows."

His eyes flashed, but his voice remained even. "The young woman's husband had been missing over a year, assumed dead. He and I had been as brothers. I grew to love the lass, but to be truthful, I later realized I was more in love with her bairn, in love with the idea I could do something worthy for my dead friend by raising his son." His gaze dropped and Brianna saw his hands clench, his knuckles turn white. "To atone for being alive."

Sympathy prickled in her throat. "I am truly sorry for yer loss. And I will believe ye if ye say ye dinnae spend the past year astride any willing lass. But I am not sure how to make our marriage work when we each want different things."

"Had I never met ye, were ye only a name scratched on the betrothal, mayhap I could let ye go. But I have seen ye, heard ye plead for yer people, and felt ye in my arms. I couldnae ask for a better woman to bring to Morven as my wife." He gently cupped her face in his hands. "Will ye marry me, Brianna?"

She touched the side of his face with the backs of her fingers, tracing a line from his temple past his cheek, lingering on the rough stubble of a day's growth. He turned his face into her hand, and kissed the palm. Her fingers closed over where his lips touched, holding the heat of it.

"Ask me again in two weeks."

Conn stared deeply into her eyes, seeing her waver when her words spoke denial. He could point out she really had no choice in the matter—she already belonged to him, decreed by the king. But Gavin's advice kept his practical words unsaid.

She reminded him of a frightened horse, proud in its hard-won freedom, unable to see dignity in submission to another. Unable to trust the hand being held out to her.

"So be it. I will ask ye again in two weeks. And ye will say *aye*."

Brianna glanced quickly away and he was unable to read her expression, but he knew she was not convinced. He had won the skirmish, but had a long battle ahead of him.

"Let us return to camp." He stood, and Brianna brushed off her skirts as she rose. Tam yawned and stretched, then padded after her. Falling into step, Conn walked slowly, hoping to extend their time alone, away from the curious gazes of the men. Out of habit, he glanced at the horses standing quietly at the picket lines, reassuring himself they had been cared for. He caressed his stallion's velvety nose. Embarr snorted and shook his head, then shoved his muzzle into his hand, encouraging the contact.

"He likes ye." Brianna sounded pleased as Conn stroked the horse's long forelock.

Surprised at her statement, Conn considered her words. "Aye, I suppose he does. I only purchased him a few months ago, and I am still learning his ways."

"He is beautiful. Is he from France?"

"Nae. I bought him in Spain. He is an Iberian horse with mixed Barb blood. Bray has several mares from a breeder there, and helped me purchase him."

Brianna stepped past Conn and reached her hand to stroke the horse's face. For a heart-stopping moment he hesitated, unsure of the stallion's reaction to a new person. But the horse leaned over the picket line, his ears pricked forward in interest as he snuffled the palm of her hand.

She laughed, obviously delighted with the friendly overture, and glanced over her shoulder. "What is his name?"

He was taken aback by the vision of Brianna laughing. He'd thought her beautiful before—naked, playing in the water, or wearing a fortune in velvet, bantering with the king. He found himself utterly captivated with her now, in a plain woolen gown, smiling with delight at Embarr's attention. Though mildly disgusted his horse garnered her pleasure while he did not, he managed to answer without sounding surly.

"His name is Embarr, after Niamh's magical horse who could run above the ground and water."

"'Embarr' is also the Irish word for 'imagination'." She ran her fingers down the long bone of his face and the horse gently tossed his head in response. Again, Brianna laughed, and Conn resisted the urge to twine his fingers in her hair and pull her against him. Being patient proved difficult.

They returned to camp, but Brianna was too tired to sit around the fire and listen to the men's stories and songs. Normally she enjoyed the camaraderie, the outrageous tales and the ghost stories she'd heard all her life. But tonight she simply nodded to Gavin and the rest of the men and moved to the far side of the fire where she could have a bit of privacy. Arranging her plaide on the ground, she settled down, the low murmur of voices not enough to keep her awake. Tam curled beside her, tucked against her tummy, his furry warmth welcome.

Her plaide slipped from her shoulders, inviting cool air inside the edge of her gown. As she reached to pull the fabric back into place, another hand settled it snug about her neck, and she felt something warm slide against her back. She blinked, trying to make sense of the new heat running from her neck to her knees. An arm slipped over her and a hand cupped her breast. She stiffened with a strangled sound. Tam gave a low growl.

"Wheesht, lass, dinnae wake everyone," Conn whispered in her ear as he snuggled against her.

"What are ye doing?" she hissed in outrage, now fully awake.

"Keeping ye warm. 'Tis one of my husbandly duties, aye?" He settled more firmly against her, spoon-fashioned.

Brianna shoved him and the confining plaide away and met cold night air. She shivered. "What do ye mean?"

"Warmth, lass. Nothing more."

Cold mist crept into the glen, surrounding the dark embers of the banked fire. Chilled, Brianna settled back against him, and Conn pulled her plaide over her shoulders. Immediately cocooned in warmth, she closed her eyes with a sigh. Her breath turned to a gasp of surprise as she felt Conn's hands begin to wander.

"Now what are ye doing?" she demanded, batting at his hands.

He chuckled, his breath against her neck as he wrapped his arms around her. "Keeping *me* warm. Or at least distracted."

"Och, nae," she shot back. "Ye willnae *distract* me. I am not yer wife yet, and there are men close by!"

He gently kissed the back of her neck, stirring the soft hairs there, creating a completely different type of chill down her spine. "They wouldnae hear ye if ye werenae so noisy."

Brianna squeaked in outrage even as her body shuddered. Panic rose at the thought he would not be gainsaid. "Nae," she insisted, her voice low, close to anger. Beside her, Tam stirred and lunged at Conn, teeth bared. Conn cursed under his breath, snatching his hand away. Tam laid his head across Brianna's hip, eyes glittering.

"*Pax*, Brianna. I only tease ye. The next time I make love to ye will be in private with a soft bed beneath us. Sleep now, and call down yer wee beast. 'Twill be morning soon."

She stilled, stroking Tam's shoulder as he shifted back to sleep. As Conn's breathing evened, she finally relaxed, wondering at the nature of the man who held her.

Chapter Fourteen

Brianna woke alone. Glancing around the campsite, she rose to her feet, glad not to meet any speculative looks from the men this morning regarding the night's sleeping arrangements. All remained busy saddling their horses and preparing for the day's ride. Geordie's laughter rose as he played with Tam. Climbing from her bedroll, Brianna attended her own needs, then grabbed an oatcake as she hurried to saddle Maude. Wary, she eyed Conn as he approached, leading Embarr.

He offered her a pleasant smile. "Are ye ready?"

She nodded and accepted Tam's leash from Geordie as she climbed aboard her horse.

Conn eyed the black and white pup bouncing at the end of the lead, the light of mischief in his eyes. "Do ye think ye can train yer dog not to take bites out of me?"

Watching his face, she decided he was teasing as much as he was serious. "I was told the pup had a mind of his own, so I cannae promise, but I will keep it in mind. Besides, ye woke him."

"Ye dinnae plan on him sleeping with ye once we are wed?"

"I plan to train him to deal with recalcitrant cattle and other such things as vex me." She raised an eyebrow. "Surely that willnae include ye?" She nudged Maude forward, Tam trotting in her wake. "He is the warmest, least demanding thing in my bed right now." Brianna glanced over her shoulder. Conn stared after her, one hand on his hip. "Will ye be walking, then?" she asked him.

The other men rode past with scarcely a nod. Conn flashed her a grin.

"I dinnae plan to be ousted by a pup!" He swung easily onto his stallion's back. Embarr tossed his head, eager to follow the mare as she swished her tail and stomped a rear foot at a pesky fly.

Brianna was surprised when he settled in to ride beside her. The soldiers formed their lines ahead and behind them, leaving space for them to travel in relative privacy. They rode in silence and Brianna soon changed her attention to Tam, who gamboled happily beside Maude. Lean and young, he was full of boundless energy.

They halted for a midday meal on the crest of a low mountain. Brianna sat on a large rock overlooking the valley as she munched a piece of dried meat. Dangling her feet in the air, she turned her face into the rush of wind, relishing the updraft as it lifted the hair on either side of her face. The scent of new green growth rose from the valley below. Tam begged a bite of her food. Conn moved to stand behind her.

"Are ye anxious to get home?"

Curbing her resentment at being disturbed, she surrendered the last bite of her meal to the pup and leaned back, hands splayed behind her. "Aye. Though I know Auld Willie is taking care of Wyndham and Jamie, I worry about them."

"Ye dinnae like this roaming existence, then? Ye are ready to put yer traveling days behind ye?"

She tilted her head back and looked up at him. "Aye. I want a hot bath, a soft bed, and a meal without oatcakes."

Conn roared with laughter. "Then we shall get ye home. One more night in the wilds and ye will be at Wyndham."

Brianna bit her lip. "For two weeks. I have only two weeks to get Wyndham in order."

"Dinnae *fash*. I promise I will help ye see things settled. I know how much it means to ye and it serves no purpose to have my wife anxious and brooding."

She could think of no pleasant response other than 'thank ye', and she was not yet ready to thank him for anything. He had a marital obligation to align himself with Wyndham. He did not have to offer assistance in governing the clan, and no one would show surprise if he took Wyndham land as his own if the leadership fell in contention. She would no longer be there to fill in during her da's lapses, and a sickly five-year-old lad would not be anyone's choice for the lordship should anything happen to her da. She'd fought to save Wyndham for

Jamie and still resented the fact that the right to do so was being taken from her.

He offered her a hand and hauled her to her feet. Brianna took a step away. "Thank ye for not pushing us hard this trip. It is good to hear the men laughing and singing and relaxed in the saddle. 'Twas a wild ride from Glenkirk those weeks ago when we fled the sheriff. I dinnae like to remember those days."

Conn's face lit with a teasing grin. "I wanted to give us time together. I am glad ye approve."

"I dinnae say I approved our time together, but I suppose I should get to know ye better."

"Ye speak aright, however grudgingly. Hoist yerself onto yer mare and we will be on our way."

They checked their horses' girths and mounted, again riding side by side. As they talked, they rode slower, allowing their horses to amble along the trail as the rest of the group traveled ahead to set camp for the night.

"Ye seem to have enjoyed yer time in France," Brianna ventured.

Conn nodded. "Aye. After I saw the mare my friend brought back with him, I decided our stable needed Iberian blood. And I wanted time to rethink my life."

"This is the farthest I have been from Wyndham," she admitted.

"I wouldnae lightly turn over the responsibility of being laird in order to take such a trip again. Learning all that has happened in my absence doesnae set well with me."

Brianna nodded her understanding. "Why did ye not return home when yer father died?"

Conn rode in silence a moment, then reined Embarr to a stop. Brianna pulled Maude in beside him.

"Word dinnae reach me until several weeks had passed. My sister's missive finally found me, but the journey back took too long. Malcolm used the time to his advantage."

"I dinnae mean to pry, but after yer father died, all the help from Morven was taken away from us."

"I am sorry, Brianna. I had no idea of any of this. My da had always been strong and fully in charge. There was no reason to think he would die so suddenly. As for our betrothal, I dinnae know about it, either. I wanted to choose my own wife."

Brianna frowned at the challenging look on his face and refused to rise to his bait. Talking about their lives seemed harmless enough.

She did not wish to return to the issue of their marriage. She offered no comment.

Conn kicked Embarr back to a walk, and Maude snatched another mouthful of grass before lurching forward to join him.

"Tell me about Jamie," he said, startling her with the change in topic.

"Jamie? He is everything a five-year-old boy should be. At least most of the time. His birth was early and he sickens easily." She smiled fondly. "He snuck out one night and followed us when we were after cattle." Chuckling, she shook her head at the memory. "He got more than he bargained for when he had to sit on his fat pony for an hour or so while Gavin waited with him for us to return. He was cold, exhausted, and heartily tired of being shushed by the time we got back.

"He loves bedtime stories and is full of mischief. And he calls me *Anna*. I cannae believe I miss the wee *limmer*!"

They reined their horses to the sheltered area the men had chosen for their camp, and dismounted at the picket line. Maude acted frisky after the long but boring day, and nipped at Brianna's skirts as she moved about, brushing the dust from her dappled coat and setting out the last of the grain for her supper.

"Yer mare is more of a menace than my stallion," Conn commented as Brianna stepped nimbly out of Maude's reach.

Brianna gave a grim laugh. "Aye. She is usually like this when…" She bit her lip, embarrassment heating her cheeks. Her mare played the wanton, openly inviting Conn's stallion to approach her. Brianna was not sure she wished to continue a discussion of her mare's mating habits.

"She is built a lot like my stallion. Sturdy, yet light-boned. When ye are ready, I think a foal sired on her by Embarr would be a good choice."

Conn grabbed his saddle and set it with the others, out of the path of the horse's hooves, and motioned for Brianna to walk with him to the camp. Before they reached the sight of the others, he caught her hand and turned her to him. At arm's length she stopped, watching him warily, but without the open hostility of before.

"Walk with me after dinner?" He drew her closer, inch by inch, until they stood a mere hand's breadth apart.

"Ye ask a lot of me, m'laird." Her voice conveyed her uneasiness.

"Say my name."

"Connor."

"That dinnae foul yer tongue, aye?"

"Be serious."

"I seriously want to walk with ye after dinner. I promise ye will be safe with me."

Brianna lifted an eyebrow skeptically. As much as she distrusted him, as much as she resented being treated like chattel and married at a man's whim, she could not deny the warmth flowing through her from their clasped hands. Talking with him had done unlooked-for things to her this day. The thought of being alone with him had changed from an ideal opportunity to murder him without a witness, to the possibility of experiencing a kiss and possibly something more in his arms.

"Are ye certain about that?" she teased.

Conn lifted her hand and touched his lips to her fingers. His tongue traced the ridges of her knuckles. Brianna gasped and tried to snatch her hand away, burning with the desire to slap him with her other one.

He gave her a devilish grin as he placed her captive hand over his heart. "I willnae do anything ye dinnae wish me to."

The look on his face told her he would see to it she wanted. And desired. And wanted more. She chewed her bottom lip.

"Mayhap—"

Her words were cut off as Conn snatched her bodily to him and flung them both to the ground. Her breath left her in a sharp *whoosh* as she landed hard, gasping as she struggled against the large male body pressing down on her. The air rang with the cries of startled men, the shrill whinnies of frightened horses, and the whistling sounds of arrows.

"We are under attack!" Conn rolled to the side, still using his body to shield her. A bolt thudded shaft-deep in the tree trunk next to them.

"Are ye hurt?"

Brianna shook her head. "Nae. I was winded, not hurt."

"Better than taking an arrow."

With a nod of agreement, she scrambled to her feet.

The fading sunlight glinted off flashing steel blades, and more arrows sang through the trees, seeking targets. A Douglas soldier collapsed beneath a determined assault, and Conn decided he'd seen enough. He dragged Brianna to her feet. "Do ye need yer saddle?"

"Nae." Her head snapped back as he towed her behind him to the picket line, interrupting a black-clad man slicing through the horses' lead ropes as fast as he could. From their left, Gavin crashed between them, Gillis hard on his heels. With a mighty swing, Gavin's sword dealt the strange man a killing blow, and Brianna pulled up with a gasp.

"Get the horses!" Gavin shoved Gillis, who snatched the dangling leads.

"Get her out of here!" Conn shouted above the clamor.

"Nae!" Brianna cried.

Both men looked at her as though she'd grown an extra head.

"I can fight." She jerked from Conn's grasp.

With a snarl, he grabbed her and tossed her onto Maude's back. He whirled to Gavin. "Take her home!"

With a nod of understanding, Gavin grabbed his horse's leading rein from Gillis and flung himself astride his mount.

"Nae!" Brianna leaned across Maude's withers and prepared to dismount. Conn put a restraining hand on her arm.

"I will come for ye. See to Jamie and Wyndham." He caught and held her furious gaze, but at last she nodded and gathered her reins.

He turned to Gavin. "Keep her safe. If these are Malcolm's men, I will find out soon enough. If this is about her, ye may have trouble when ye reach Wyndham. Take as many Douglases with ye as ye can, but leave now!"

A chilling war cry ripped from his lips as Gavin summoned the Douglases to his side, and within moments, he and two others sped away into the darkness, riding so close to Brianna's gray mare that she instantly vanished from Conn's sight.

He turned back to the camp where the fight continued in earnest. Bray parried with his short sword against a claymore, and Conn leaped immediately into the fray. A moment later, the man lay dead at their feet. Bray wiped his forehead.

"*Sacre Dieu*! I may need one of those long swords for myself. What do you call them?"

"Claymores!" Conn cried, the heat of battle overtaking him as he turned to avoid the thrust of another sword. Bray brought the hilt of his sword down hard on the head of a man who overstepped his attack. The man crumpled into a heap of pleated wool and chain mail.

Conn grunted, dispatching another black-clad man, pausing to yank his blade from the dying body. He took a deep breath and looked around the glen, rubbing the sweat and hair from his eyes. To his surprise, the attacking forces faded into the forest, the remaining Douglases close on their heels.

"Hold!"

Uncertain, the Douglases let the enemy go. Conn took stock of the situation, and though most of the men sported an injury of some sort, only one of the Douglas men lay dead, and the injuries of the rest did not appear life-threatening. He bent over one body and rifled through the loose edges of his clothing, searching for a clue to his identity. He found nothing.

He picked up the discarded sword, wiping the blade on its owner's leine, and eyed it carefully in the failing light. The pitted metal was of poor quality, and he saw no identifying marks on the blade. With a snort of disgust, he cast the sword aside.

Gillis stood silently, holding the reins of six horses pawing nervously at the ground, responding to the cries and smell of blood with tossing heads and shrill whinnies. Gillis's eyes fixed, not on his charges, but on the lifeless body lying to one side of the smoldering fire.

Ewan and William sheathed their swords and approached Geordie, who would never ride with them again. They solemnly unwound his plaide and spread it on the ground. Placing his body upon the cloth, they wrapped him securely. With grim faces, Bray and Conn added their hands to the task.

Gillis saddled Geordie's horse and led it to the somber group. Ewan and William lifted the lad's body and placed it gently across the horse's back. Bray and Conn lashed the bundle securely to the saddle.

"Bray, Gillis and I must ride hard to Morven," Conn told William. "Can ye and Ewan take Geordie home?"

"Aye," William replied. "We will take care of the lad."

"Good. Send word if things are amiss at Wyndham. Morven is less than a day's ride away." He clasped William's shoulder, forcing the sorrowing man to look at him, taking his attention away from his dead friend. "Protect Lady Brianna, even with yer life."

William lifted his chin. "'Tis always been our way."

Conn nodded. "I meant no insult. I dinnae need to remind ye of yer sworn duty. I mean to return for her, and she is in danger until we find who set ye up for reiving."

"Aye." William jerked his head at Ewan and they grabbed their saddles from the ground. It took them only a moment to saddle their horses and begin their journey home.

Hands flew as they hurriedly saddled the remaining horses, tying the broodmares with their leads. Bray's horse tossed his head and pawed the ground, eager to be about his business. Embarr pranced about as well, unused to the sounds and smells of battle. Gillis's horse was a good, solid sort, his only difficulty keeping up with the furious pace Bray and Conn set as they headed at a hard gallop toward Morven.

Chapter Fifteen

Brianna and her soldiers raced at breakneck speed to Wyndham, darkness scarcely slowing their headlong pace. The events of the past hours blunted her senses. She didn't want to think about the battle she'd just witnessed, didn't want to wonder how many soldiers would come home bound to the backs of their horses. For all the months in light skirmishes with reivers, this had been her first involvement in a true battle. It left her humbled. And hollow.

She gritted her teeth, so tired she could barely hold herself on Maude's sweated back. Tears, whipped from her eyes by the wind, streaked cold across her cheeks. Still they pressed on.

At last the massive stone hulk of Wyndham Hall loomed through the early morning mist, and Brianna thought she'd never seen anything so beautiful. Home lay at last within reach—her family, everything she loved. Her memory jolted to remember what short time remained to be with them, but she pushed it aside. There would be time later to think about Conn and the life the king had decreed for her.

Shouts rang out from the guards and men scrambled to attention, peering at the ragged group as Brianna and her men rode to the stout double doors of the manor. Maude stumbled to a halt, sides heaving, head low. Brianna slid from the mare's back and dropped her reins, ground-tying the exhausted mare where she stood. Sore in every inch of her body, her legs numb from the hard ride, Brianna limped to the thick wooden doors and beat on them with a trembling fist. It was too early in the morning for the heavy bar to have been removed, and she waited impatiently for the steward to respond to the guards' alert and admit her into the hall.

Gavin followed her inside, leaving the others to see to the horses, the mud and sweat cleaned from their coats, their bellies fed. Though it was early, Jamie was already up and nagging his nurse, Una. Brianna heard his shrill voice trailing down the hall, her heart swelling at the sound. Jamie tripped into the main hall and stopped short, surprised to see visitors. His face lit when he recognized Brianna, and he darted across the hall, shouting as he ran.

"Anna! Anna! Ye are home!" He flung himself into her arms, nearly knocking her on her arse with the force of his welcome. She grabbed him to her, hugging him so tight he began to complain.

"Ow! Ye are hurting me!" He struggled against her grasp.

"Jamie! I have missed ye so much!" Tears blurred her eyes as she held him close, breathing in his familiar scent, his small body fitting her arms so differently than it had little more than a month ago.

Jamie wiggled from her arms and held himself up, stretching as tall as he possibly could. "I have grown, Anna. See?" He craned his neck, showing her how much taller he was. Before Brianna could remark on his height, he planted his fists on his hips and glared at her.

"Ye left me!"

Nonplussed, Brianna stared at the child and blinked in bewilderment, too tired to think properly, amused at the fierce scowl on Jamie's face.

Jamie stomped his foot. "Auld Willie said ye left me."

Brianna drew back in disbelief. Surely her uncle wouldn't have said such a thing to the child. Just then, the old man stepped forward and laid a hand on Jamie's shoulder.

"Wheesht, lad. Dinnae *fash* yer sister so. She has had a hard night of it, so it seems."

Brianna wanted to ask him what he had actually told Jamie, why Jamie thought she'd left him on purpose. But she was too happy to be home and amid her family to question him now. She gave her uncle a weary smile. "I am glad to be home. I must speak with ye, then I would like a short nap so I can think straight again."

Auld Willie nodded. "Jamie, lad, run ask Cook to prepare something for yer sister and the men. They look to be famished and in need of her good food. And help set up the tables, like a good lad."

"I am big now!" Jamie shouted as he ran from the room. "Anna's home and I am almost as big as her!"

His voice faded from the room and Brianna shook her head fondly at his exaggeration. He'd grown taller, obviously much more of a handful than he'd been when she'd left. He would bear watching, and she frowned as she realized she wouldn't be around much longer to keep an eye on him. She turned to Auld Willie.

"Could we sit in private?"

He nodded and led her to a corner of the room where a few wooden chairs grouped around a small table to one side of the huge fireplace. They both sat and Gavin joined them.

"Uncle, I have a story to tell ye, but it must wait." She twisted her fingers and gathered her thoughts. "I was on my way home last night when we were attacked as we made camp a few hours' ride from here."

Auld Willie raised an eyebrow. "Do ye know who it was, lass?"

"Nae. It could have been brigands." Her voice dropped to a pained whisper. "Or someone from Wyndham."

The old man's chin jerked, startled. "Wyndham, ye say? Och, lass. What would make ye say such a thing?"

Brianna swallowed and glanced around the room, looking for something, anything at all that would give credence to what she'd been told. Nothing appeared out of place. Rabbie and Duncan entered the hall, Tam on their heels. The pup gamboled over to her and she ruffled his ears.

"I will tell ye later, but I need to know Wyndham is safe."

"Aye. Wyndham is protected as always."

"And Jamie? We must keep a close watch on Jamie."

Auld Willie rose, patting her shoulder comfortingly. "Wheesht, lass. Dinnae *haiver* so. Ye cannae believe Jamie is in danger."

"Not only Jamie, but myself as well." She placed a hand on her uncle's arm and stared at him, willing him to believe her. "Auld Willie, someone at Wyndham set a trap for us the night we left to gather the cattle. Somehow the sheriff knew we would be out there that night and would have hanged us had I not asked for the king's mercy."

"And the sheriff let ye go, just like that?" Clearly agitated, Auld Willie began to pace the floor. Tam cocked his head at the man's actions. An anxious whine slid from his throat and Brianna glanced at him, surprised. Her next words were for her uncle, though her gaze lingered on the pup.

"Aye, though he had a black heart, for he gave his guards orders to kill us the first night, as soon as we were far enough away to keep his hands clean of the deed. We would surely be dead now had it not been for Ewan and Geordie, who found us and told us of the sheriff's plans. They got us away, and we stayed in hiding for days before the king returned to Troon and I was able to gain audience with him."

She stood, her hand outstretched to halt her uncle's heavy pacing. "We are here and safe now. Dinnae *fash* yerself. I will help take care of Jamie."

Auld Willie came to a reluctant stop and faced Brianna with a wry grin. "Och, lass. Ye have been through a hard time. I will double the guards and be sure no harm comes to ye or our wee Jamie."

Brianna hugged the old man. "I know I am safe here. Thank ye for all ye have done whilst I have been gone. And thank goodness ye were too sick to go with us that night. I know Jamie has been in good hands." Tam rose to his feet and pushed between them. Brianna laughed.

"This lad was a present from the king. I offered to buy him since Dubh died a few weeks ago. He will make a good drover."

Auld Willie eyed the dog and patted Brianna's shoulder awkwardly. "Get some rest. Ye are fair worn out. There will be something for ye to eat when ye wake."

Brianna kissed his dry cheek gratefully and climbed the stairs to her room and comfort, Tam trotting happily at her heels.

Chapter Sixteen

A low keening sound woke her. Bolting upright, she bounced once on the soft mattress as she struggled from the bed. Her feet hit the floor before she was completely awake, and with bleary eyes, she noted the sun was only a wee bit lower in the sky than when she'd fallen into bed. She stumbled past Tam, curled on the rug next to the hearth, to her window overlooking the front of Wyndham Hall. Two mounted men, leading a horse with a cloaked form tied across its back, paced in a slow procession up the long road. A somber group clustered around them, more people streaming from the Hall to meet them, a few in clusters of what could only be acute grief.

Shaking the wrinkles from her gown, Brianna stopped long enough to pull her slippers on before running from her room and down the winding staircase to the great hall below, Tam slinking about her ankles. She darted out the front door and slid to a stop on the wide front steps, overcome by a sense of dread. Her hands shook, and she clasped them firmly to still them. There was nothing she could do but lift her chin and swallow hard against the awful taste of trepidation rising in the back of her throat. As the riders approached, she recognized Ewan and William. Her eyes slid to the bundle between them.

Oh, God! 'Tis Geordie. She dug her fingernails deep into the palms of her hands, using the pain to keep herself from thinking about the young man who had died defending her.

The procession halted in the open space before the hall. She drew a deep breath and walked the necessary paces to them, one firm step at a time, wishing her da or Auld Willie would appear to take this duty from her. Knowing this fell to her alone.

On silent paws, Tam padded hesitantly forward and sniffed the bundle laid across the horse. With an anxious whine, he disappeared into the crowd.

As if in a dream, she floated with excruciating slowness through time and distance. Sounds from the gathered crowd faded from her hearing, the sight of the people growing dimmer, until her entire reality shrank to no more than herself and the dead soldier before her.

She stood beside Geordie's horse and laid her hand gently on the plaide-wrapped body. Stiff and cold, the form in no way recalled to her the vibrancy of the youth, and she closed her eyes against the harsh reality of death. In the recesses of her mind she heard his voice, saw his playful antics with Tam, the way he had sought to entertain them in their exile only days before. He had been the youngest of the soldiers gathered for the raids, but he had lacked in neither courage nor ability.

She opened her eyes, startled to find herself surrounded by silent, expectant villagers. She had no idea how long she had stood lost in her thoughts, but she caught sight of Gavin standing just to one side of William. He gave her a reassuring nod. She turned to her clansmen and saw their reliance on her, their grief tempered with the expectations she would always have their best interests at heart, and the knowledge that dying for Wyndham and clan Douglas brought honor. She lifted her head and addressed the gathering as the breeze gently blew her skirts about her legs, and the sky darkened with threatening rain.

"'Tis a mark of the esteem we hold for Geordie Douglas that he is here today. He was chosen for his courage and his honor to be a part of those who have labored to keep our clan and village safe." Brianna swallowed hard and glanced at the familiar faces around her. "He was a young man who believed in his clan, and who never failed to follow his duty through to the end."

She stopped, remembering just what his duty had cost him, and it was a long moment before she recovered enough to say the final words.

"*Codladh samh*, Geordie Douglas. Sleep ye well." Her throat tightened as grief overcame her. William and Duncan dismounted and led Geordie's horse away to the cottage he had shared with his grandmother who had raised him. A keening rose in the air again, like ghosts welcoming their brother home.

Physically exhausted, she made all the right moves throughout the rest of the day, but her mind raced on without respite. Geordie's death had brought reality home like nothing else could. He had died defending her. Who wanted her dead? Why? Was there a reiver angry enough with the harassment she and the men had caused? Did someone covet Wyndham? If so, Jamie was also a target.

She could not bear to think of Jamie in danger. When it came time for bed, she insisted she couldn't be parted from the little brother she had missed so much. Jamie bounded happily up the stairs and slipped into his night shirt with little fuss before climbing into Brianna's bed, insisting Tam accompany him.

"Tell me a story, Anna!" He bounced on the bed, shrieking with laughter as the young dog batted the furs, growling in mock ferocity.

"Tam, be still! Jamie, dinnae encourage him, or I will make the both of ye sleep in yer proper beds."

Suitably chastened, Jamie wiggled beneath a blanket and Tam curled beside him.

As tired as she was, she couldn't help but smile at the pair before her. She settled on the bed beside Jamie.

"Once there were two brothers named—"

"McGillivray!" Jamie shouted, giving the name a rousing roll from his tongue. Tam's head jerked up, ears perked at the sound. Brianna smoothed Jamie's hair as she began the story.

"Donald's brother, Rory, was fond of music and dancing. One night, the brothers were out looking for some sheep that had strayed, when suddenly they saw rays of brilliant light coming from holes in a very large rock—a rock everyone knew was a place where faeries lived."

She paused, waiting to see if Jamie had drifted off to sleep, but he squirmed under his blanket, far from slumber, his fingers twisting in Tam's thick fur.

"As they approached the rock, the most wonderful sounds of music and merriment reached their ears, and even though they knew the rock was a place where faeries lived, they crept closer and closer. Finally, Rory suggested they pay the faeries a visit—"

"But Donald said, *Nae!*" Jamie crowed, twisting emphatically beneath the covers.

Brianna nodded. "Donald said nae. But Rory was unable to resist, and he jumped inside the rock where the faeries lived, leaving Donald all alone."

"And Donald had to go home and tell his ma and da Rory was gone, aye?" Jamie craned his neck around to look up at his sister. Tam gave his face a vigorous swipe with his tongue and Jamie giggled.

"Aye, and his parents were verra sad. Then one day, a wise man happened by and learned what had happened to Rory McGillivray, and he thought up a plan to get the young man back. *Return a year and a day to the place where ye lost yer brother*, he said, *and, carrying a Rowan cross, enter the rock, boldly and in the name of the Highest, and claim yer brother.*"

"And if he doesnae want to come with ye, grab him!" Jamie's arm shot out, hand fisted as he grabbed the air. Brianna peered at the overexcited lad and wondered if she had chosen the best faerie tale this night. She softened her voice and ran her fingers lovingly through his red-gold curls, causing her mind to dart unbidden to the thick golden hair of the man who would return in two weeks to marry her. She pushed the memory aside and finished the story.

"And so Donald returned a year and a day to the place where the faeries lived. He saw his brother dancing and he ran to Rory and grabbed him by his shirt, insisting he come home immediately."

Brianna dropped her voice to a hypnotic cadence. "And nothing Donald could say would convince Rory he had been dancing for a year and a day until he saw the calves were now grown, the lambs were now sheep, and the babies were walking around the house."

"Did he truly dance for a year and a day?" Jamie asked sleepily. Tam flopped on his side and sighed mightily, closing his eyes.

Brianna pulled Jamie's now-pliant body against her, wrapping him in her arms. "Aye. He truly danced for a year and a day," she replied as she kissed the top of his head. "And all because he wouldnae listen to his brother's warnings. I would imagine his feet were sore."

Jamie snuggled against her and she swallowed against the lump in her throat. She would miss the wee loun once she was married.

Chapter Seventeen

September 1387, Wyndham

"Lass, ye shouldnae be away from the house alone," Gavin chided as he walked through the doorway into Maude's stall. Dropping her grooming rag, her mouth an 'O' of surprise, Brianna stepped into Maude's range.

"Oh!" she cried, whirling as Maude nipped her arm. She reeled backward, straight at Gavin. Reflexively, he caught her in his arms. Brianna stiffened, and Gavin released her and took a step backward. Brianna shifted away as well, rubbing the red and blue mark on her arm.

"Hateful beast," she muttered. But Gavin knew better. Maude was all the comfort Brianna had had when her ma died, all the understanding she sought when her father turned on her in his drunkenness. Brianna loved the mare's willfulness, and delighted in thwarting her attempts to nip and kick. It was a distinct mark of the state of Brianna's nerves to see she had fallen to Maude's mischievous ways and then cursed the mare for it.

"'Twill heal soon and leave a reminder for ye not to turn yer back on the beast."

Brianna flung him a look capable of splitting stones, and he shrugged his answer. "Ye should have someone with ye if ye leave the hall. Ye dinnae even have young Tam with ye. That mare is a menace, but unlikely to protect ye."

"I dislike being followed. Tam plays with Jamie." She glowered at him.

"Nonetheless, as captain I insist on it. Jamie will be watching ye and if ye break the rules, he will, too."

Brianna flushed, obviously restless and out of sorts. She gave a grunt of reluctant agreement. "Will ye stay until I finish grooming Maude?"

He flopped onto a pile of straw in one corner of the stall, well out of range of both ends of the mare.

Brianna rubbed the mare's legs with a rag, bringing a shine to the black stockings where mud had earlier marred her coat. "Do ye know what is happening?"

Gavin gazed into the distance, not sure if he was ready to share his thoughts on the situation at Wyndham. He hated to be the one to broach a subject that would only dismay and disillusion her. "Well, I havenae heard from MacLaurey. Though 'tis been but four days since we parted, and I would guess the laird has his hands full dealing with Malcolm."

Brianna snorted inelegantly at the reminder. "Four days gone leaves only ten until I am to wed. Ten days until I must leave Jamie and Da. Ten left to find who betrayed me to the sheriff. My concern lies with Wyndham."

"Aye. But I have no facts to give ye."

Brianna fisted a hand on one hip. "Then give me yer thoughts."

"I dinnae think ye will like them."

With exaggerated care, Brianna spread her rag on the top edge of the wall, then turned to give Gavin her full attention. He regarded her in silence. She waited, her tapping foot betraying her fading patience. Finally Gavin gave a single nod.

"'Tis only something I have noticed. Nothing more, and I have shared this with no one." He paused, carefully forming his words. "Do ye know if Auld Willie ever married?"

The question left Brianna silent for a moment, a confused look on her face. "Nae. In all my years, I have never known him to have more than a passing relationship with any woman. He has always been devoted to me and Jamie, especially since Ma died. We are his family."

"Ye dinnae know Geordie was Auld Willie's son?"

Brianna stared at him, aghast. "What? Why would I not know this?"

"He is a peculiar man, yer uncle. He never acknowledged Geordie as his son, though Geordie's grandmother was only too willing to tell me the story yesterday. Seems her daughter widowed young, and yer uncle took an interest in her. He was her off-and-on lover for several years before she conceived a child, but by then he had tired of her and when she confronted him with the news, he accused her of trying to push another man's child on him.

"From that time on, he refused to see her, turning his back on her and the child. He told her to find someone else to support her, for he had nothing to offer her or the bairn."

Brianna stared at Gavin, speechless, struggling to come to grips with the fact Auld Willie had sired a child and she had never known. "How could he do that? We should have grown up together, yet he was denied his place in the family because—why?"

Her heart pounded, distressed for the young man now dead and beyond her care. "Nae father would willingly deny his child. Only a madman—" She broke off. "A curse of the family, then?" she whispered. "My da—"

"Nae, Brianna. Lord Brendan was a good da before yer ma died. He loved ye more than life itself, but he wasnae strong enough to face losing Lady Elinor. Had she lived, yer and Jamie's lives would have been verra different."

Thoughtful, Brianna nodded. It was true her da had been a very different man when she was young. He taught her to ride, to swim, and to tickle the trout in the streams. He taught her not to cry over a skinned knee and to be brave and strong—so strong she had been able to hold her head up after her husband's death, amid his father's curses, and take over Wyndham's honor when her da fell into a drunken stupor.

She ached for Jamie, who would never know his father as he'd once been, and for Geordie, who'd never known his father at all. Since Ewan and William returned with Geordie's body, the entire hall had plunged into mourning. Brianna had not seen Auld Willie since then, but had assumed he was busy seeing to Wyndham's protection. Now she wondered if he'd been out of his rooms at all.

"Has anyone seen him since—since Geordie—" She broke off worriedly, unable to finish the question.

"Nae. He has been in his rooms. And the lass who takes his meals to him reports she leaves the tray outside his door. When she returns for it later, the food is untouched."

"Untouched?" Brianna frowned. *Just what I need—another auld man sickening.*

"Aye. But I checked on him this morning."

She lifted an eyebrow. "What did he say?"

Gavin grunted. "He told me to *hie myself away*, in words less suited to yer ears."

Brianna rolled her eyes and tamped down her mounting frustration. Her time was running out. In her absence, her da had sunk deeper into his nether-world and she had been unable to initiate a conversation with him about choosing a steward to help him once she left. And Auld Willie, once her staunch supporter, had holed himself in his room, grieving a child he'd never recognized.

"If he doesnae come out of his room soon, something will have to be done."

"Now, lass. Give the man some space. He has acknowledged his son's existence and his death in the same day. I will keep a watch on him." Gavin rose to his feet. Opening the stall door, he held it for Brianna to step through. She gathered her skirts and gave a curt nod.

"I will leave him to ye, then. I must meet with Geordie's grandmither and see to the funeral preparations."

Gavin nodded. "I will send Rabbie with ye."

She wiped her hands on a rag and rolled her sleeves down, smoothing her skirts. 'Twas not a duty she looked forward to, but she would accept the responsibility to see Geordie got the honor he deserved. Rabbie's support would be welcome.

Chapter Eighteen

September, Corfin Castle, Morven

Conn drew his horse to a stop and stared across the sparkling water to the shining white stone walls of Corfin Castle. Perfect timing brought them to the shore as the tide at the foot of the loch ebbed. Now the horses could be ridden across to the stone causeway before the castle gates.

The barred gates.

How could he have forgotten how easy it was to seal off the castle—and how difficult it was to gain entrance once the gates were shut? He rubbed the back of his neck. Weariness tugged the corners of his eyes and strained his shoulders. It was time to deal with Malcolm.

Bray nudged his mount alongside and nodded at the fortress. "Do you think your *cousin* will let us in?"

Conn stared at the banner flying above the castle keep. Generations of MacLaureys had flown the same standard since they first moved into the big glen and built Corfin Castle, and it infuriated him that his cousin had given himself the right to use the crest when he was merely related by marriage and no true MacLaurey.

"Not if he values his life." He nudged his stallion forward, jaw set resolutely. Before Bray and Gillis could prod their own mounts, the MacLaurey battle cry rolled from his lips and he spurred Embarr into the shoals of Loch Mor.

Water spray flashed like diamonds in the early morning light.

Bray and Gillis pulled abreast of Conn, and together they thundered through the low tide and to the stone path as guards opened the wooden gates, leaving the portcullis down. By the time they came to a halt, men poured into the bailey, many still shaking the sleep from their eyes as their bodies responded instinctively to the summons.

Conn sat astride his stallion, who still pranced with the excitement of the race across the loch. Determinedly, Conn held his ground, surveying the men who peered at them through the stout bars with bristling suspicion, angry they answered to Malcolm and did not recognize his authority.

Embarr suddenly reared, and Conn sank deep into his saddle. "Where is Sir Malcolm?" he shouted, the title a sour taste in his mouth. He pivoted in the saddle, pinning each man with his gaze, as Embarr jarred to the ground.

A gray-haired man Conn did not recognize, approached the gate with an arrogant swagger, picking his teeth with a narrow stick in his mouth.

"His Lordship isnae up." He pulled the twig from his mouth and worked his tongue around before spitting something small and dark onto the ground. "Ye will have to wait." He turned his back and sauntered away.

Conn's jaw clenched in fury. He understood this man, likely one of Malcolm's, would not recognize him, but never during his father's lifetime had a guest been treated so rudely. Before he could react, a missile flew through the air and landed with incredible accuracy on the back of the odious man's head. He stumbled forward, then whirled to face his attacker, his face twisted with fury.

"Who threw that..." He glanced around for the weapon that had hit him. "Oatcake?" His voice scaled upward in disbelief as he spotted the hardened lump of oats on the ground.

Conn's gaze flew to Gillis who had dismounted his horse and still stood with his hand on his saddlebags. The lad fairly bristled with anger and was apparently oblivious to the danger he put them in. Bray leaned in tight. "Surrounded by armed men does not make it tactically clever for young Gillis to pick a fight—*ai-je droit*?"

Conn stared straight ahead. "Hopefully we will live long enough for him to learn from his rash actions." Gillis took two steps toward the gate, hands fisted on his hips.

Bray shrugged. "Mayhap not."

Gillis ignored them and leaned forward, his fists clenched

aggressively. "Dinnae glower at me, ye *crabbit* auld fool! Ye willnae treat yer laird with such disrespect!"

The man squared his shoulders, his bulging forearms folded against his chest. With a taunting laugh, he challenged the lad. "Me laird? The auld laird has been dead these past two months, and there is a new laird now. What are ye about, lad?" The man peered from Gillis to the two men still mounted beside him. Conn kicked Embarr forward a few steps, stopping the stallion only inches from the gate, surveying the men in the yard who stood silent with anticipation.

"I am Connor of Morven, son of Ian MacLaurey." His voice rang harsh through the stone-walled barbican.

Eyes widened as men took a hesitant step closer, eyeing their blustering leader with caution. One grizzled warrior with a pronounced limp and an eye patch jutted his chin at Conn in challenge.

"What is yer mother's name, lad?"

"My mother was Lady Elasaid of Morven and Perth," Conn replied. "And shame on ye, Seumas, for not recognizing yer laird's son."

Seumas stepped forward, peering shortsightedly at Conn, and placed a gnarled hand on the bars of the gate. "Me good eye isnae so good anymore. I know ye now." His look sobered. "Why did ye not come home when yer father died?"

"The message was overlong reaching me. And I am here to find out why."

Seumas shouted over his shoulder to the guards. "Raise the portcullis! Let them in!"

Men came forward to greet him, some pounding his shoulders, others calling to him. It had been a little over a year since he'd left, and the change in his father's men was remarkable. It would likely take some doing to oust Malcolm from his position, but his tight-fisted rule would have gained him few friends, judging from the murmur of approval now running through the men. Conn and Bray dismounted and, passing their horses over to a pair of eager lads, strode purposefully across the bailey to the great hall, Gillis following behind.

Conn stood firm as the doors swung slowly inward. Even in the day's new light, the castle hall appeared dark and uninviting. He squared his shoulders and crossed the threshold.

The white stone which gave the castle its name was dingy with smoke ash, and the tapestries that once glowed with vibrant color against the stark walls were dusty and in need of a good cleaning. As were the rushes strewn across the floor, so old they created an almost continuous mat of crushed reeds mixed with what, Conn shuddered to think. He kicked aside a dented goblet lying unheeded on the floor, and the resulting clang echoed loud in the silent room. Near the back of the room a frightened servant scurried away, disappearing into the darkness.

"I have seen more life in a churchyard at midnight," Bray muttered under his breath. But even his softly spoken words sounded harsh in the nearly empty room, and Gillis jumped at the sound, his earlier bravado obviously fading in the murky hall.

Conn lifted his scowling gaze to the filthy stained glass window, whose jeweled colors were now those of the loch at low tide. With a growl of anger, he swung toward the staircase and halted as a portly form appeared at the balcony above. Conn adjusted his glare to the flustered man, who tried repeatedly to pull his robe closed, though his trembling fingers and excessive girth kept him from accomplishing his goal.

Bray reached behind Gillis and lightly slapped the lad's head. "Close your mouth, *garçon*. It is rude to stare."

Gillis's cheeks flushed as he shrugged Bray's hand away.

The man gripped the robe's edges just below his plump waist, and though he regained some of his modesty, his paunch was wont to poke through above. "My lords." His voice squeaked unnaturally high. He cleared his throat and tried again. "My lords. I am Angus, steward of Corfin Castle. There was, ah, a bit of celebration last night, and the servants are slow this morning. I apologize for your welcome."

Conn gave vent to his anger, his voice thundering in the hall, shaking dust motes from the tapestries. "Where is Malcolm?"

"He isnae here, my lord," Angus squeaked.

Conn took an ominous step forward. "The captain of the guards said Malcolm was still abed," he countered.

Angus looked about frantically, but there was none around who would help him. "I am sure he is abed, wherever he is," he offered weakly.

Whirling, Conn stomped to the hall's open doors and faced the soldiers gathered there. "Let it be known, by Malcolm's cowardly retreat, that he has been holding this clan falsely. I am Connor, now

Laird MacLaurey, and I will have either yer allegiance or yer departure!" Furious, unable to challenge Malcolm to his face, he stared at each man in the bailey with a warrior's eyes, searching for any hint of treachery, demanding their loyalty. Each head began to nod, slowly at first, then with increasing assurance as the men welcomed him home.

"Aye!" they shouted, fists pumping the air in agreement.

Conn sought the belligerent captain who had offered such rude hospitality, but did not see his face in the crowd. "Seumas?"

The old man limped forward. "Aye, Laird?"

"Take charge of these men."

"Aye!" He saluted smartly, then pivoted to the men, whose shouts of pleasure filled the yard.

"You have won that lot over," Bray noted agreeably.

"It wasnae hard. Seumas was their captain years ago, and anyone would have been better than the lout Malcolm chose."

Fierce strides echoing against the stone floor, Conn stalked the length of the hall, kicking debris out of his way. His initial search of the castle turned up seven servants cowering in the kitchen, three disheveled young women of questionable reputation tucked away in various bedrooms on the second floor, and a kitchen boy who stared at Conn and Bray in wide-eyed shock. The castle and its many rooms was otherwise abandoned.

As Conn stalked the upstairs gallery, he scanned the hall below. Its dimensions were immense, and the fireplace, large enough to roast an entire beef in its massive cavern, scarcely filled the far wall. The tables pushed haphazardly against the walls would easily seat a hundred men. In the middle of the floor, light from the stained glass window set high in the wall fell in murky, fractured colors. His anger rose to see the lack of care his cousin had for his home. The fact his father had been spared the sight of the severe neglect and the knowledge of Malcolm's spite was poor consolation, for it only reminded him his father had been laid in his grave without his son to see him honored.

He turned to the servants who had crept to the entrance of the room, their curiosity overcoming their initial fear. "I want this castle cleaned from top to bottom. It will reflect the honor of the MacLaureys, or I will find others who will do the job."

They were quick to locate buckets and rags, and Conn didn't pause to instruct them a second time. He did not have time to waste.

He would bring home a bride in a fortnight's time, and he would not bring her to a home filthy and in need of repair. And he must look to her safety. He did not trust Malcolm and would not rest until the man was captured and faced his peers for his actions. Not for the first time, Conn wished he could talk to his da. His thoughts shifted to the stone memorials on the island in the loch, and the weight of his responsibilities came crashing down.

Chapter Nineteen

Conn stared across the loch to the cairns raised on the tiny island where MacLaurey lairds had been laid to rest for generations. What had happened to his da? How had he died? There was nothing but rumors to guide him, and the only one who knew for sure was now nearly three months in the ground. All Seumas had been able to confirm was that the laird had been thrown from his horse during a hunt, and though he lingered for some days, he never regained consciousness.

Utter helplessness swept over him. The things he'd taken for granted in his life had not turned out as he assumed they would. He had never intended to become laird at the young age of a score and three years. Though he had been raised to assume the leadership of the clan, he felt his da's loss keenly.

"The men have done as you instructed. No one has seen Malcolm or his cronies since sometime last night. Mayhap he fled at the report that his men did not kill you last night." Bray stepped through the archway to Conn's side. "It has been a long day, *mon ami*, and dinner is prepared."

Conn roused as Bray's words reached him. With great effort he turned from the sight of his father's grave and trudged up the path through the small garden behind the castle walls.

The hall glowed with a mellow light, the result of many flickering candles reflected off the freshly cleaned white walls. The stained glass sparkled, shooting colored patterns on the scrubbed stone floor.

Tables had been set up and food prepared, and he was startled to see the men seated quietly, leaving the laird's chair empty.

Conn strode to the chair that had couched the rumps of four generations of MacLaurey lairds, himself now the fifth. He touched the carved wood, the grain worn smooth with years of service. His ancestors had sat in this chair, presiding over their many duties as laird, and their blood ran hot in his veins. He surveyed the faces crowding the room.

"These have been difficult days for me, and for ye as well. I realize I havenae been home in over a year, and much has changed in that time. Understand when I tell ye, word was late reaching me of my father's death. I would have never forsworn my duty had I known."

He paused, breathing through the pain in his chest. "I will, with all my power, honor the lairds who have come before me. I will, with yer aid, keep Morven safe and help it flourish. This is my pledge to ye."

A steady beat began, growing louder as the men stomped their feet and thumped the tables with their fists in support of their new laird. Conn knew most did not understand the distance from the glen to France or the difficulties of travel abroad, and likely still harbored resentment over his absence. But they appeared prepared to trust him, and their approval of his words showed.

With a nod of acceptance, Conn settled himself in the laird's seat, motioning for food to be served. The noise in the room abated as the men and women began to eat.

He stirred the rather greasy stew as it soaked into the crusty bread on his wooden trencher. There was still much to be accounted for in the castle. He remembered the silver and gold serving pieces that once graced his father's table. Apparently Malcolm had wasted no time pilfering the MacLaurey riches.

He lifted a piece of gristly meat on the point of his knife and placed it in his mouth. It took an extraordinary amount of chewing to reduce the food to a state to be swallowed, and he glanced around to see how the others fared. Bray chewed resolutely at a piece of bread, his stew uneaten, and Gillis pushed the unappetizing pieces around, obviously finding it difficult to make anything edible from the food on his plate. Conn sighed. He would inquire of a new cook tomorrow. For tonight, he missed Gillis's oatcakes.

Eyes narrowed with hatred peered through the slit in the door. Exchanging his velvets for stained brown wool and running a muddy hand through his hair had been enough to disguise his appearance among the servants, who he never mingled with anyway. The insolent slouch of a once-rich man had been replaced by a servant's scurry conveying a willingness to accomplish as little work as possible. He stayed out of sight whenever he could, and caused as much damage to the night's supper as could be done with little notice.

The news of Conn's imminent arrival at the castle had filled him with astonishment and fear. His years of soft living had come to an abrupt end, and to his surprise as much as anyone else's, he decided to stay and ensure the new laird's life would be as miserable as he could make it. And as short as possible.

A tall man next to Conn rose and strode toward the back of the hall. "I will see if the *chef* can fry some oatcakes for you, Gillis." His voice was mocking as he tossed the words over his shoulder. Malcolm stared at him as he approached, curiosity warring with his need to remain hidden.

"'Twould likely contain weevils," the younger man groused. Conn glanced up sharply, and Gillis shrugged before slouching deeper in his chair. Fascinated, Malcolm watched as tempers worsened.

He rubbed his hands together gleefully. *I havenae had time to put weevils in the oats, my lad, but 'tis a marvelous idea.*

The door to the scullery burst open, flooding the hall with light. Taken aback, Malcolm scrambled away, trying to keep his face in shadows. The tall man's head swiveled in his direction, and Malcolm dropped his gaze, eyes furtively seeking the closest escape.

"You! Find cheese and fruit that is not moldy, and take it to the head table. I do not know how you have survived this long, eating this *nourriture horrible*."

Bobbing his head repeatedly, Malcolm darted to the back of the room, trying to remember where the cellar was located. He tripped, hands flailing as he tried to catch himself. His fingers latched onto voluminous fabric with soft flesh underneath.

"Och!" a loud feminine voice screeched. Startled, Malcolm's glance fell on the sturdy bosom of one of the kitchen servants, her ample assets filling his hands. He sneered at her before he remembered his disguise. *The auld besom would have been glad for my attentions as laird.*

"The cellar is over there, ye amadan," she grunted, shoving him away with a sweep of her arm. Bobbing his head, Malcolm slipped from the room and down the narrow stone stair.

They will pay for this. I willnae let Conn remain long as laird. I was meant to rule Morven. Corfin Castle should belong to me, not that sniveling arse. He would never wield the power as laird. But me, I revel in it!

He stared at his ragged clothing as he reached for a wooden bowl. The raveled cuff of his sleeve fell back, revealing his reddened hands, once soft and white, now blistered and roughened, attesting to the chores he was obliged to complete in his new role.

Cursed mercenaries! Could they not halt a handful of unsuspecting men? Curse my cousin's luck! Malcolm rubbed a grimy finger across the bridge of his nose. *'Twill not be so easy to rid himself of me as he supposes. I will get Corfin Castle back. I will be laird again. And ye, my cousin, will take yer place beneath the burial cairns of Loch Morven.*

Conn didn't trust an enemy he had been unable to roust for himself. With a critical eye, he oversaw the ordering of the castle as he waited for Malcolm to make the next move, hating the patience it took.

He hired women from the village to help with the cleaning, and men to do the rough work of repairing furniture and roofs and other jobs needed after Malcolm's short reign of drunken revelry and neglect. Soldiers rose before dawn to begin the day's training, and, though hungry, none lingered at the table before seeing to the horses and the rest of the work demanded of them by their new laird.

Young men from the village watched with interest, and many stepped in to swell the soldiers' ranks. Conn suspected some had left under Malcolm's harsh rule, while others who joined his brutish ways had fled with him when Conn reclaimed the castle. Whatever the cause, he was satisfied to see the number of soldiers increase daily and he was even more pleased to see how hard they worked at their new duties.

He assigned Bray to help with the soldiers' training. Bray carefully deferred to Seumas, using the old man's wisdom and popularity to his advantage. Gillis trained alongside the others, though it was clear he considered himself part of the laird's personal guard. Gillis's staunch defense of Conn when they first arrived had won him his place, though Bray worked him hard enough to ensure he earned his new station.

With Conn accepted as laird, the castle and its inhabitants showed much promise, and the wealth of the villagers was in full evidence, their wares of butter and cheese, fruits and vegetables a welcome addition to the new cook's fare. The kitchen fairly hummed with industry, and Conn noted the cleanliness of the tables and floors, as well as the appetizing odors wafting through the doors at mealtimes. This would be the home he shared with Brianna, and he marked its progress as he eagerly counted the days before he would ride to Wyndham to claim her as his bride.

He sought pen and parchment in the laird's private chamber and penned a note to Brianna.

I have reclaimed Morven, though Malcolm escaped me. He is now my top priority as I dinnae wish to bring ye into danger.

Scarcely a week remains until I arrive at Wyndham, and I count each day eagerly.

I am,

Yours, Conn

He blotted the page and sanded it, then sealed the missive with a waxed seal. Giving it over to a young soldier's hands, he bade him carry it to Wyndham.

The young soldier touched his forehead respectfully and handed the sealed parchment into the older man's hands.

"I will see she gets this. Dinnae worry."

With outrageous flair, the young man bounded into his horse's saddle, feet not touching the stirrups. Pulling his steed into a flamboyant rear, he kicked him into top speed and raced down the long road to Morven. The older man ambled slowly across the hall, casting a furtive glance around the nearly empty room. He froze as Brianna crossed the floor, realizing he held the missive in plain view.

"Who was at the door?" Her curiosity showed as she tilted her head to his clenched fist.

"A rider. He wouldnae stay."

"A rider? Who is the missive for?"

Should he say it was for the laird? Would she trust him to deliver it, or would she take it and discover her name on the parchment?

He made a pretense of turning the missive over in his hands, his face registering false surprise as he beheld the address.

"'Tis for ye, lass." Reluctantly, he held it out to her, forcing his fingers to release their grip as she took possession. The corners of her lips tilted upward, but he derived no satisfaction from her pleasure.

"I thank ye," she murmured as she turned away, a finger beneath the flap to break the seal.

Without comment, his face twisted by grief and remorse, he dragged himself up the stairs, feeling the edges of his world closing in.

Chapter Twenty

*B*rianna broke the seal on the folded parchment and opened the flaps, her eyes scanning the contents. A peculiar warmth lit beneath her breast and a smile played about her lips.

M'laird pens his words as skillfully as he speaks them. Her smile broadened. *Mayhap he is committed to this union.*

She smoothed the parchment with her fingers, drawing her hand down the page to linger on his signature.

Yours,
Conn.

The right corner of her lips twitched. *I think I like being wooed.*

Placing the letter in the desk in her room, she squared her shoulders and saw to Wyndham's daily business, feeling the days rush past as she sought to discover who plotted against her. Though she watched diligently, no one under her direct care acted out of the ordinary, and she was at a loss for someone to affix her suspicions to. Only Auld Willie acted strangely, but she was certain his grief would soon ease and he would return to his duties in time.

With Geordie's funeral past, the gloom around Wyndham began to lift, though Brianna still felt an oppressive atmosphere and her temper frayed easily. She could only lay the blame for her attitude on her frustration with her da, for attempts to discuss finding a steward fell on deaf ears. His behavior sank lower than ever before, scarcely acknowledging her, and ignoring all duties laid before him. Time was running out, and she had no answers to her problems.

Auld Willie wandered from his rooms more and more, his body gaunt and trembling, appearing as lifeless as the son they'd buried three days earlier. Brianna saw his eyes, dull with internal pain, and pulled his chair from beneath the table.

"I am glad ye are here, Uncle." She patted his shoulder as she would a child and plied him with food from the laden table, but he refused all but a few bites. "We will plant a rowan tree in Geordie's memory," she told him, hoping to garner a response. But his eyes darkened and she moved away from the topic he clearly did not want to discuss. After several moments in the company of the hall, he rose abruptly and wove his way unsteadily outside. Brianna started to follow, but Gavin held out a hand to stop her.

"He needs to come back slowly, in his own time. Let him set his own pace."

Brianna heard the wisdom in Gavin's words and wondered, not for the first time, what could have happened were she not betrothed to Conn. Gavin was unfailingly kind to her, tempering his words so she easily agreed with him. Despite the letter she received from Conn, doubts lingered. How would he deal with a wife used to ordering a clan?

Moved to send him a reply, she retired to her room after the meal. Seated at the tiny desk, she stared out the window, touching the tip of the quill to her lips pensively.

He has reclaimed Morven, but has he claimed his new responsibilities? Does he still long for the lass who broke his heart, or is he past the hurt? She glanced down at the page before her. *Are these things I can ask him? I dinnae know him well enough—but I will soon be his wife.*

Conn, It pleases me to hear you have regained yer birthright. I know there isnae much time before our wedding to settle in yer new responsibilities, but 'tis my desire to be a true help to ye.

She snorted. That sounds somewhere between stilted and self-serving. She started to crumple the parchment, but hesitated with a shrug. *'Tis what I meant, though not as pretty as his. He promised to look to my advice—and I willnae be shy about giving it.* She dipped her quill in the ink and continued.

It seems as though time is flying past, and I will have leadership set up here soon, though Da falters more each day. I admit to being reluctant to leaving Jamie here, as he has become quite a handful. Ye may be glad to hear I plan to leave Tam with him as they have become fast friends.

That should make him smile. Her lips pursed in a moue of discontent. *How to end this letter? Am I to mirror his signature? Nae. I willnae mimic him, nor am I ready to call myself his.*

Fondly,
Brianna

She placed the quill in the inkstand and sanded the parchment. She glanced over the contents but folded the page quickly before she could second-guess herself. Hurrying down the stairs, she caught Duncan in the hall.

"Would ye have time to carry this to Morven—or find someone who can?"

Duncan gazed at the missive she shoved at him and slowly took it from her. "Aye. I will see it gets there."

Breathing a sigh of relief, Brianna turned the matter over to him.

Her wedding day drew near, and she faltered on accepting the actuality though it was nearly a month since she'd heard the king's decree. She hadn't lied when she'd told Conn she'd burned her dowry chest and its contents. The loss of her mother's wedding gown was another regret, though hardly one to lay at Conn's feet. She'd consigned it to the rag bin soon after her return to Wyndham as Mungo's widow—her vow to never marry again. The arrival of another soothing letter from Conn did much to assuage her skittishness, though she could not say with complete truth she looked forward to her new life. This business with the MacLaurey laird was vexing to say the least.

Brianna glanced up at the soft snick of the door. The figures on the parchment on the desk before her defied her for the third time, and her patience stretched thin. The sight of the priest in the doorway did not improve her thoughts. From his corner of the room, Tam lifted his head, a low growl rumbling in his chest. Brianna raised a hand to silence him and he settled his muzzle onto his paws, his dark eyes fixed on the man in the doorway.

"I understand ye are to marry at the end of this week." The priest's gaze moved from the dog and settled on her with mild accusation.

She held her tongue in check, supposing it was too late to allow Tam to rout the man. She did wonder who had given him the information about the wedding, as she had not. With a sigh, she flipped the quill into the ink pot and folded her hands on the desk.

"The king has commanded it," she replied evenly. The priest met her terse statement with a questioning look. But his disapproval no longer had the power to make her cringe. For several years she had dispensed with his invitation to hear her confessions, preferring to voice them directly to God, certain He was more lenient than Father Roderick. The priest was too shrewd to believe her an unusually pious young woman, and if he believed her particularly heathenish, she most assuredly did not care.

"Ye have much to do in preparation," he reminded her. "There is the matter of guests and food and lodging, and I hesitate to remind ye of yer prayerful provisions."

"The kitchen staff can easily handle the food. There will be few guests, and none will stay the night." She rose to her feet. "My prayers are my own, and currently not being answered."

Father Roderick drew back, shock on his face. "Yer ma—"

"My ma is dead! Dinnae bring her into this. She did her best with me, taught me what I need to know about running a household. But she isnae here to tell me how to live with a man who is scarcely more than a stranger to me." Too late, she bit back her words.

"I understand yer reluctance to marry, Brianna. Though I dinnae countenance rumors, I have heard what is said about the laird and yer husband before him. But it is yer duty to marry to protect Wyndham, and it will be yer duty to be a wife to the MacLaurey, see to his household, his needs, his children."

"I dinnae need yer lecture, Father. I know what my duty is."

Tam whined and slipped from his blanket to Brianna's side. He thrust his nose against her closed fist, and she relaxed. Father Roderick eyed the young dog and cleared his throat.

"Ye have the choice of making yer marriage a thing of joy or of bitterness. Choose carefully, Brianna, for 'tis difficult, if not impossible, to change once ye have decided."

She tossed him a mocking glare. "Where was yer sage advice for my first husband? Seems he could have benefited greatly from it." With a wave of her hand, she dismissed him.

Turning to the door, the priest hesitated. "Resentment will poison not only yer marriage, but the lives of those around ye, including yer children."

Brianna's lips thinned. "I dinnae anticipate children, Father. And the MacLaurey is fully aware of it."

Disapproval etched in the stiff line of his shoulders, Father Roderick strode from the room, closing the door behind him.

Brianna stared after the priest long after he left. Slowly, she paced the room. Her fingers flew against the cloth of her skirt as she counted. Over and over again she counted, but the numbers came out the same.

Damn! It couldn't be true! She'd had ample opportunity to conceive a child in her first marriage. The fact she had not, had been laid repeatedly and wrathfully at her feet, both her husband and his father furious to find her barren each month. Never had she been late or missed her woman's cycle. Until now.

Damn, damn, damn!

She whistled for Tam and swept from the room, ignoring the gawking faces of those she passed as her feet flew faster and faster. Once at the stable, she paused only long enough to toss a bridle over Maude's head. She swung herself onto the mare's back and sent her skittering out the double doors, Tam leaping joyfully at her heels. Maude flattened her ears against her skull and took the bit firmly in her teeth, hitting a hard gallop in two bounding strides. Brianna urged her faster, riding to outdistance her new problems, the only sound in her ears the whistling of the wind, the pounding of Maude's hooves, and the nonstop chanting in her head.

Children, children, children.

Nothing silenced the words, for in her heart she knew the answer. For whatever reason, she'd never conceived a child with Mungo, but it had taken only one moment, one illicit incident beside the burn to put Conn's bairn in her womb. It was too early to be completely sure, but she knew her body too well to hope differently.

She reined Maude to a stop and let her blow. Tam collapsed at her feet, tongue lolling, chest heaving, his tail thumping the ground. After a few moments, she urged the mare down the wooded trail. Tam's nose led him in and out of the brush as they wound past the village and back to the hall. Approaching the stable, she spied Gavin sitting

The Highlander's Outlaw Bride

outside, cleaning his saddle. She eyed him narrowly. He had no need to clean his tack. He would never have put it away dirty, and there were plenty of stable boys to attend the task for him. It was clear he waited for her, and she bit her tongue against his coming reprimand.

She slid from Maude's back. The mare dipped her head and gave a mighty shake. Tam drank from the water trough, then leapt into the water, splashing around in youthful high spirits. Without a word to Gavin, Brianna led the mare into her stall, where she fed and groomed her before turning her out to graze in the paddock beyond the stable.

When she returned to the front of the stable, Gavin remained, Tam wriggling in the grass beside him, still dripping water from his swim.

"Good ride?" He quirked an eyebrow, his face calm, though his lips turned down at the corners.

"Aye." Brianna checked her stride, holding one hand out, palm down, to keep Tam from jumping on her skirts. The puppy danced about, then took off with a bark toward one of the stable cats stalking out of the door. "Keeping yer saddle clean?"

"Aye. Busy hands and all. Something wrong, lass?"

"Och, there seems to be something *wrong* every day."

"Do ye still fear for Jamie? Ye are wound tighter than a warm plaide on a chilly day. Come, tell me what is bothering ye."

Brianna fixed him with a blunt stare. "I think I may be with child."

Gavin stared at Brianna, at a complete loss for words. He had imagined a lot of things that would bother her—Jamie, her da, Auld Willie, her wedding, Conn. But this turn of events wasn't even on his list of possibilities.

"I think we both need to be sitting for this one." He motioned for Brianna to seat herself on the bench next to his, and she complied. Waiting patiently, he considered her profile as she stared into the distance.

"Do ye remember the night we camped beside the burn outside Troon—and I disappeared?" she asked.

He nodded, easily bringing the night to mind. "Aye. Ye gave us quite a scare."

"I went swimming in the burn as I told ye. I slipped and fell, injured my ankle, and Conn rescued me. He played the gallant, helping me look for ye. I dinnae want his help, but I had no choice." She gave a small shrug. "I havenae had much use for men since Mungo. I prefer being in control of my options."

Gavin shifted on his bench in the ensuing silence. There was really no need to agree with her. Her tendency to take charge was well known.

"We rode for a full day, then he announced he would be taking me to the king rather than leaving me on my own. I was unsure where the king was, if the sheriff's man had reached him—or not—unsure if I would be imprisoned. It dinnae sound like a good idea to me. So I planned my escape.

"I got them to add lettouces to their meal that night, and Bray and Gillis were soon asleep. Once I thought Conn also slept, I slipped away, but he followed me. We sat beside the burn and talked, for I could tell he was drowsy, and I thought he would soon sleep as well."

"Did he force ye, lass?" Gavin shoved the words past the fury building in his chest.

Brianna sighed. "Nae. I am not sure what my intentions were. I admit his attentions to me were—well, nice. I never planned to remarry, and for a few moments I wanted to know what it was like to be attracted to a man and have him love me. To not cringe at a man's touch. I never thought to see him again."

She stood and stepped a few feet away, hugging her arms about her waist. "I never thought I could conceive a child. I never did in all the long months as Mungo's wife. I dinnae think it possible."

Gavin watched as she relaxed and slowly rubbed her palms against her skirt. "How sure are ye?" he asked.

She shrugged. "Fairly sure."

He thought he understood her answer. Raised with four sisters, his knowledge of women's issues had few holes. He had learned much as a lad, and he knew better than to ask her what the hell she'd been thinking. Censure was not what she needed.

"Ye will be wed next week. No one will notice."

She faced him and he was startled to see uncertainty on her face. "I still feel the distrust from my first marriage. Conn speaks well, but I dinnae know him."

"I dinnae think ye need worry. He seems honorable. I willnae pass judgment on the husband of yer first marriage, but the MacLaurey doesnae act like a man who is a fool."

"He doesnae act like a fool, or would be a fool to miss the wedding?"

Gavin was pleased to see a slight smile on her face. "He would have to be either dead or a fool to miss wedding ye, and a bigger fool to hurt ye."

"Then mayhap I worry for naught. I believe it is time to set things to rights here at Wyndham and prepare for the wedding. Will ye act as steward in my absence?"

Gavin nodded. "Aye. Ye know I will do anything ye ask. And Wyndham is my home. I will protect it for wee Jamie."

She lifted a hand, then dropped it back to her side. "Thank ye, Gavin. Ye are a staunch friend. I couldnae ask for better."

The swing of her skirt kicked up little puffs of dust as she walked the lane to the hall. Gavin sat on the bench a moment longer, tamping down the familiar longing to comfort the lord's daughter with more than sympathetic words.

Brianna rested a hand gently on her da's shoulder. He looked up from the small object he turned over in his hands.

"What is it, Da?" She pointed to his hands. "What do ye have?"

He blinked at her, then down, slowly opening his hands to reveal a small golden pendant glowing in the light of the candles. Brianna sat beside him and touched his fingers.

"Where did ye get this?"

He nodded at the pendant. "'Tis yers."

"May I see it?"

After a moment's hesitation, he handed her the jewel. Light warmed the mellow gold and flashed off the single diamond set in the middle. She ran a fingertip over the smoothly hammered surface.

"'Twas yer ma's before she died."

Brianna nearly dropped the pendant in surprise. For him to speak so calmly of her ma's death had little precedent. He was more likely to bluster and shout and demand more whisky. Her throat tightened and she put an arm about his shoulders, shocked at how thin he felt, how frail he was beneath his robes.

He frowned. "She had many things that are yers, now."

"Mayhap ye will help me go through them one day."

"They are for yer wedding, lass. Ye may get them when ye are ready."

She clasped the pendant to her breast and leaned against him, the pain of Ma's death much less with his shoulder to lean against. She dared not wonder how long his clarity would last.

"Da, I appointed Gavin to help ye when I am gone."

"Aye. A sotted lord and a young lad cannae govern by ourselves."

Brianna nodded. "He is a good man. I dinnae know why I dinnae see it before."

Chapter Twenty-one

Corfin Castle, Morven

Conn nodded his satisfaction. The people of Morven had worked hard to set the castle to rights, and as a sign of appreciation he ordered an informal gathering on the castle grounds, a taste of the festivities he planned for the day he brought his bride home. He glanced at his friends and smiled. In two days, he would ride to Wyndham amid a large party of MacLaurey soldiers and Morven representatives and marry Brianna. Despite his initial dismay at finding himself betrothed, he felt assured by the rightness of it.

Nothing could mar his happiness. Even the somewhat stilted letter he'd received from her several days earlier showed she tried to overcome her reluctance to wed. She hadn't quite mustered the courage to address him with endearing terms, but she had at least admitted she would be his wife soon. Oh, so very soon.

Servants busily supplied the tables with food and drink. With no possible way to seat everyone, all who came were invited to browse the offerings, and the area was thick with well-fed guests. Conn at last stopped his stroll through the crowd and filled a platter. He collapsed into the chair set aside for his use and motioned for a servant to fill his glass.

A haggard man hurried over with a flagon of wine and leaned over the edge of the table to pour. He lurched forward, spilling the wine and knocking Conn's cup to the ground. He caught himself and tried to grasp the cup, but it rolled across the mud-churned ground. Conn rose to his feet and peered over the table.

"A moment, m'laird. I will fetch a clean one." The man hurried away, clutching the dirtied cup to his chest.

"I fear you flustered the man," Bray murmured, lifting his own mug to his lips. He grimaced. "Though the wine is not fit to be served in a dirty goblet, much less a clean one."

"Ye would have me serve the best wine to the untutored crowds?"

The servant scurried back to the table, placing a new goblet brimming with wine carefully before Conn.

"The better wine is still in the castle, Laird," the man murmured as he bowed and slipped away.

With a grin, Conn took a sip. "I certainly hope we aren't pouring *this* down the throats of thirsty villagers." He handed the cup to Bray. "Here. This will appease yer palate."

He looked for the man who'd brought the wine, half-rising from his chair as he spied him several feet away.

"Hey!"

The man flinched and partly turned his head.

"Bring the wine to the table."

The servant nodded and shuffled away, returning several moments later with the flagon. Conn thanked him absently and poured himself another draught.

"A toast to friendship and good wine." The men clinked their goblets together and took a sip.

Bray rolled the wine across his tongue, eyes partly closed as he separated the flavors. "A nice fruity flavor with a hint of smokiness. Not bad at all."

"I shall appoint ye in charge of the wine cellar."

Bray nodded agreement, eyeing the rather dusty young man who approached their table. Stopping directly before Conn, the lad pulled a folded letter from his sporran. Conn bolted upright in his chair.

"Ye are from Wyndham?"

The young man nodded. "Aye. I am to give ye this." He handed Conn the missive.

With eyes only for the letter, he quickly broke the seal and scanned the contents.

Bray laughed. "Walk the tables and refresh yourself, *garçon*. The laird thanks you for your service."

Conn waved a hand vaguely in agreement, his attention on the words before him.

Conn,

Having only ever received letters from a man in the form of bills—and these were addressed to Da, though I dealt with them—I can say yers refresh my heart. They are a gentle encouragement for our life together, and I am ever hopeful it will be thus.

Thank ye for making this time of adjustment a bit easier. I can truly say I at last (I am certain ye would say at long *last) have decided our marriage has much potential and, as ye pointed out, much to recommend it. In all seriousness, ye have warmed my heart.*

Please send word on the number in yer wedding party. I will see to their comfort.

Yours,

Brianna.

"She said 'yours'!" he shouted, waving the parchment in the air. His face heated as heads swiveled in his direction, aware he acted like a heartsick lad. In truth, he had been wary of Brianna's response to his letters—the previous one scarcely more than an acknowledgement of receipt of his. While this one would hardly fall in the category of a love letter, he relished the subtle humor and looked forward to teaching her the ways of love.

Gillis grunted as he flopped into a chair opposite him at the table. Conn took a deep sip of wine, his mood expansive.

"Shall we share?" Conn asked Bray, nodding to the lad.

Quirking one eye in appraisal of the youth, Bray nodded. "Let the lad tutor his palate with the wine. Once he is tipsy, he will not notice when we change it for the common stuff." He poured a measure of wine into Gillis's cup.

"I am hungry, not thirsty," Gillis protested.

Conn laughed. "Let the lad eat. Ye have worked him entirely too hard to deny him sustenance."

Gillis ignored the ribbing and set to his dinner with gusto. Conn and Bray dug in to their own food and emptied the bottle of wine between them. Bray lingered over his last glass as the evening deepened and the villagers began to make their way to their homes. Servants cleared the debris.

"This was a good *célébration*," Bray remarked, slouched deep in his chair.

Conn grunted. "Merely a prelude to the one next week when I bring home my bride."

"A month ago I would not have said you would have been so eager to wed."

"I wasnae," Conn admitted ruefully. "I dinnae know her then. I know her scarcely better now, but I definitely like her spirit."

Bray roared. "You like her form and the way she fits in your arms. *Mon ami*, you are smitten."

Conn's face heated, but he could not deny Bray's words.

The night was dark and still. Too still. Conn lay in his bed, unsure what had roused him. A sudden, sharp pain tore through his abdomen and he rolled onto his side, drawing his knees to his chest against the agony. Scarcely able to breathe, he waited for the pain to pass. Slowly it eased, and he carefully straightened his body.

His stomach revolted and he jerked upright. Flinging the bedclothes aside, he lurched across the room for the chamber pot. He managed but two steps before he collapsed to his knees, vomiting onto the cold, hard floor. His head spun and his stomach heaved. He was cold and hot at the same time. Unable to summon the strength to rise, he slumped unconscious to the floor.

Voices rose and fell in the hall outside his door, but Conn couldn't be bothered to care. Heavy pounding on his door jolted him to partial wakefulness, but he ignored it, resentful at being forced to move. The door burst open and Seumas and Gillis bolted into the room, sliding to a stop at his side.

"Get him up." Seumas knelt and rolled Conn to his back, placing his hands beneath his shoulders. Together, he and Gillis lifted Conn and bore him to the bed. Conn groaned as the movements caused his world to shift dangerously. Seumas quickly brought the chamber pot to the bedside.

"Here ye go, lad." He wiped Conn's face with a damp cloth. Conn lay back on his pillows, exhausted, the room swimming about him.

"Ye have that out of yer system good and proper. Ye need yer rest now. Young Gillis and I will take turns watching over ye."

"Has anyone else been affected?" Conn whispered hoarsely,

glancing anxiously at the pair. Seumas shot Gillis a quelling look, then answered.

"Mayhap one or two, but dinnae *fash* yerself over it. They are being seen to."

Conn tried to sit up, but only made it to his elbows. "Something we ate?"

Seumas pushed him back onto the bed. "Lay yerself back, there's a good lad."

Too weak to protest, Conn collapsed on the pillows, his breaths coming in short, rapid succession. Seumas wrung out a wet cloth and placed it on Conn's brow. With a sigh, Conn closed his eyes and fell into an exhausted sleep.

Wyndham

Wedding preparations at Wyndham soon grew out of hand. Villagers and hall residents alike vied with each other with greenery and flowers for decorations, and their promises of food and pastries to feed hungry guests. Brianna surveyed the festive room with a critical eye. A serving girl approached her.

"Milady, how many rooms do ye wish us to prepare?"

"I dinnae know, but I will find out."

With a brief nod, the lass hurried away. Glancing to the doorway, Brianna called to the man entering the hall. "Rabbie?"

He turned at the sound of his name, his good-natured face beaming at her. He hurried to her side. "What is wrong?"

Brianna pinned a half-smile on her face, determined to keep her frustration from showing. "Could you find how many are coming from Morven and when? The wedding is in two days and I havenae heard word from his lairdship."

Rabbie waved her concern aside and reached for a hunk of bread from the basket on the table. "Och, dinnae *fash*. Put the women in the rooms upstairs and the men on the floor here. Like as not they will just come for the day, one night at the most. Morven is only a few hours' ride from here."

And like as not the men will be fair puggled and not care where they sleep. Brianna gave an exasperated sigh. No one seemed to be concerned the groom hadn't put in an appearance yet or even bothered to inform them of the wedding party arriving with him as she'd asked. Was she the only one who worried about this?

"Rabbie, I havenae heard from him in the past few days. The wedding is the day after tomorrow and I find this verra troublesome."

"He has likely had much to occupy him—rousting Malcolm and getting Corfin Castle ready for his new bride." Rabbie grinned. "He is a lucky man, the laird is, and he wouldnae be so foolish as to muck this up."

With that heartfelt piece of wisdom, Rabbie strode away, popping the bread in his mouth before reaching for a mug of ale. Brianna scrubbed her hands over her face, damping down her inner turmoil. *Damned inconsiderate if ye ask me. Leaves me to do all the work for the wedding and thinks all involved is a 'come hither' look from him on the wedding night.*

Well, he can show up when he likes. If he cares so little, he can sleep on the floor with the guests. She started to call Rabbie back and instruct him to ride to Morven anyway, but hesitated. *Even if I send Rabbie to Morven for information, he will scarcely get back before Conn arrives. I am too worried about such a thing. I willnae think on it again.*

<hr />

"Ye look beautiful, lass," Una said as she brushed Brianna's hair to a lustrous shine. "And ye will look like a faerie princess in yer finery."

Brianna sat before the low table in her robe, unwilling to put on her new wedding dress until just before the ceremony for fear of wrinkling or staining it. Una had stayed up far into the wee hours for several nights putting the finishing touches on the teal velvet gown, edged in silver satin.

She shifted on the hard chair.

"Quit yer fidgeting." Una pulled the brush through Brianna's curls. "He will be here soon enough. Ye are acting like a new bride, not one who knows what to expect from her groom."

Amazingly, Brianna felt heat steal up her neck. The reminder this was her second wedding also brought to mind what she'd worked herself to exhaustion these last few nights to forget. She was also a pregnant bride. Certainly not a rarity, but it pained her personal sense of rightness. She swept from the chair and crossed to the window on the far side of the room to peer outside, seeing the milling crowd at the front of the hall. To her consternation, there still was no word from Morven.

"Anna! Anna!" Jamie bounded into the room, Tam on his heels. "Look at my new shirt!" He leapt onto the bed, bouncing high on the plump mattress, spinning around as he showed off the garment. Tam barked happily, dancing about on his hind legs, mimicking Jamie's moves.

"Jamie!" Both Una and Brianna cried together as the lad's feet nearly trod on Brianna's new gown. She snatched Jamie from the bed as Una swept her hard work into her arms, smoothing the gown over a nearby chair. With a frown, both inspected their charges, finding neither the child nor the gown the worse for the near disaster.

"Ye nearly ruined the dress Una made for me," Brianna scolded as she placed Jamie on the floor. Tam nosed him as though checking him for harm, then sat his furry rump on the floor, his tail swishing softly against the worn wood. Brianna propped her fists on her hips and tried to look stern.

"Now, show me how nice ye look in yer new shirt—with yer feet on the ground!"

Jamie pouted at the scolding, but instantly brightened as he whirled about, arms spread, showing her the shirt she'd finished for him only yesterday. It was her gift to him to make him feel included in the wedding preparations.

Her heart ached to think she'd be leaving him in a little more than a day, and though her da was showing surprising interest in his son, Jamie hardly knew him, and she knew it would be difficult for Jamie to adjust to her being gone—really gone this time. It was time she considered leaving Tam for the lad to play with. Perhaps the dog's ready friendship would help ease the pangs of parting.

"Ye look fine, Young Jamie," she told him proudly.

"I am not Jamie!" he announced with a glare, hands on his hips, mimicking her emphatic stance. "My name is James. Jamie is for bairns!"

Brianna reached and tweaked his nose. "Och, James, ye will always be *Jamie* to yer big sister."

"James! Call me James!" he shouted as he ran from the room. Tam lurched after him. Brianna looked to Una, who shook her head.

"Are ye sure ye can handle him?"

Una smoothed the fabric of Brianna's gown one more time. "Wee Jamie had best learn to behave himself with ye not here. 'Tis unlikely the laird will be letting ye bring him along after the wedding."

Brianna slowly shook her head. "Nae. I dinnae think he will ask Jamie to come with us."

She chewed her lip pensively as she reached for her wedding gown, feeling the weight of responsibility increase instead of lessen as the wedding hour drew near.

The murmuring sounds of the guests faded as one by one they noticed Brianna on the stairs. She clasped her hands tightly, striving to appear composed, chin up, tension singing through her body. Speculation ran rampant as the day passed and the groom failed to show. The hour was now late and she knew her guests were hungry. Delinquent groom or not, they deserved to be fed.

At her sign, Cook nodded to her assistants, who jumped into action, scurrying to and from the kitchen, laden with platters of food and flagons of wine. Brianna picked up her skirt in one hand and turned. Instead of joining her guests, she returned to her room.

The next morning, she greeted the lingering guests as though they'd merely stopped by for a brief stay, her smile strained. She waited until after the noon meal before she warmly thanked her guests for their visit. Meeting Gavin in the hallway, she brushed aside his look of concern.

She held out her fist, palm down, and let the sapphire pendant fall into his outstretched hand. Her eyes bored into his.

"Sell it."

Changing into breeches and a shirt, she fled to the stables and quickly saddled Maude. Releasing Tam from the stall where he'd been kept during the anticipated festivities, she mounted and turned the mare loose to run.

Wind whipped her face and she cursed herself for how much her heart ached, how much Conn's letters now hurt.

I should have known not to trust him. I did know. But I believed his pretty words. His lies.

His lies—his lies—his lies. The words echoed in the tattoo beat of Maude's hooves.

I willnae trust him again. And he will never be welcome at Wyndham—never.

Much later, as she returned, she tugged on the reins, halting just beyond the manicured yard around the hall. The sky blazed with shades of vermillion as the sun set. *Surely the guests are long gone.*

She rubbed a palm over her belly and inhaled deeply. What was she to do now?

Chapter Twenty-two

The sun was riding high the next time Conn woke. He tried to sit up, groaning aloud at the effort. Instantly, the bedroom door opened and Gillis stuck his head inside.

"Are ye better, Laird?"

Conn slowly slid to a sitting position, though the effort left him dizzy. "Aye. Give me a moment." Waiting for the pounding in his head to subside, he motioned Gillis closer. The lad hesitantly crossed the room and stood several feet from the bed.

"Ye expect me to bite?" Conn asked when Gillis stopped short, surprised at how thin his voice sounded. Gillis took another cautious step toward the bed. "Tell me what happened."

Gillis shifted his feet and glanced around the room. The silence lengthened and a tuneless whistle dribbled from the lad's lips. Impatient, Conn swept the covers from his lap and swung his legs over the side of the bed. Gillis rushed to his side as his legs buckled beneath him. Catching Conn with his shoulder as he tumbled forward, he guided him back onto the bed.

"What the hell is going on?" Conn demanded. His head pounded again, and he was angry. Very angry. The door opened, and Seumas entered the chamber.

"Here, now, Laird. Ye arenae strong enough to get out of bed yet."

"Why not?" Conn ground out through clenched teeth.

Seumas gave him a bland look. "Ye have been sick."

"Why have I been sick?" Conn grunted, his effort to speak making his head pound harder.

"I believe 'twas something ye ate."

"Was anyone else taken ill?"

Gillis and Seumas exchanged looks. Conn glared at the pair through narrowed eyes. "Well?"

Finally Seumas laid a gnarled hand on Conn's shoulder. "Bray has been verra ill."

Conn lurched forward. "How ill?"

"He will recover, but it will take time."

"What happened?"

"Rest a wee bit. We will talk again when ye are stronger."

Conn's hand shot out, grasping the other man's wrist. Seumas winced as the grip tightened and finally nodded. "I will tell ye," he said. "But ye must promise to stay abed. Ye cannae do more for him than has already been done, and I willnae watch all my good work here go to waste."

He gave Conn a glower meant to keep him in place. Conn returned it with an even stare of his own, dangerously close to losing his temper.

Seumas grunted. "The night of the dinner, the three of ye were taken ill. Young Gillis was still downstairs when his spell struck. I was there and thought the lad had too much to drink. I had a potion made up to ease his stomach, then sent him to bed. On his way, he heard a ruckus in the stairway and saw Bray fighting a man there.

"He said Bray appeared to be weakened and stumbled on the stair, though he'd drawn his sword and was holding the man at bay. Gillis shouted and the stranger turned. Bray's sword sliced the man's arm. He immediately returned to the attack on Bray, and that is when Gillis jumped into the fight."

Conn glanced at Gillis with a sincere look of gratitude. The lad shuffled his feet, dropping his gaze to the floor.

"The man fought only a moment longer, then ran away. Bray suffered a deep wound to his shoulder and the bleeding took a long time to staunch. He has been ill as ye have been, but he also lost a lot of blood and is unable to do much more than lift his head."

"Who did this?" Conn's voice was silky smooth, dangerous. Seumas blanched.

"After the man ran off, Gillis dragged Bray to his room. He did what he could, then came and got me."

"Who?" Conn demanded.

"I believe 'twas Malcolm. Gillis told me the man was short and stout and left-handed. I dinnae think I am wrong."

Conn closed his eyes, thinking furiously. *No matter how long it takes, I willnae let Malcolm get away again.* He was no longer content to run Malcolm out of Morven. This time it would be death for one of them.

"How long have I been abed?"

"Two days."

Conn swore under his breath. His wedding should have been yesterday. There was no help for it now. He would bring Malcolm to justice and forestall further misdeeds before he brought Brianna to Corfin Castle. He would not subject her to his cousin's treachery.

I will send someone to let her know what has happened. He glanced at Seumas's worried face. *What does he not tell me?* "Bring me some food."

Seumas patted Conn's shoulder. "Aye. Ye need feeding now ye are better. I will have Cook send something up."

Conn swung his legs over the side of the bed, testing his resolve. He found he could bear the dizziness, but the overwhelming weakness caused sweat to pop on his forehead. He gritted his teeth and grabbed Gillis's shoulder as he stumbled.

"Send the tray to Bray's room."

Walking on shaking legs and sheer stubbornness, Conn made it down the hallway. When the food arrived, he forced himself to eat, encouraging Bray to take what sustenance he could. The next morning, Conn felt much better, and he filled the ensuing hours with short bursts of exercise, rebuilding his strength. Bray struggled to join in, and two days later they formulated a plan to capture Malcolm.

By the end of the week, twenty hand-picked MacLaurey soldiers were packed and ready to leave.

"Keep an eye on things here." Conn placed a firm hand on Seumas's shoulder. The older man frowned, his unwillingness to be left behind clear.

"Aye. I will watch over the place for ye." His chin jutted forward, his brows knitted together ferociously. "Ye tell Malcolm a few things for me when ye catch him."

"I will," Conn assured him. He addressed the other men. "We will head north. I received word from scouts yesterday that Malcolm was seen crossing the river just two nights ago. We start our search there."

"There are too many places he could be hiding." Bray stared at the rugged land around them. From atop the mountain they saw little but unbroken wilderness. Conn stood, hands on his hips as he contemplated their options. They had ridden hard to the river and northward into the mountains deep in the Highland ranges. Word had spread of their hunt, and while no one denied their trespass across clan lands, no one could say for sure where Malcolm hid.

"We are ever a sighting or two behind Malcolm and his men," Conn murmured, a bitter tone to his voice

"There were many eager to help us a week ago, but information has dried to a mere trickle the past few days," Bray replied. "The men grow weary and frustrated."

Conn glanced at Bray, noting his pained slouch in his saddle that bespoke his wound not completely healed. His heart lurched with guilt. "If we receive no further word by morning, we will return to Morven. I willnae give up the search, but we cannae continue chasing him blindly through the mountains."

Conn strode from the summit to where his soldiers took their ease after long, hard hours in the saddle, struck at how worn down they appeared.

"We will set camp here for the night. I have decided we will return to Morven on the morrow if there are no further sightings of Malcolm. We have traveled well and tried hard to bring the man to justice, but this may take longer than we expected. When we return home, I will send men to seek out word of him. We will not let it lie."

The men nodded agreement. They seemed loath to return to Morven without capturing Malcolm, but Conn knew they needed time to rest. He also knew they would be willing to continue the hunt in a few days. *And I dinnae send word yet to Brianna.* He sighed, shouldering guilt yet again.

The men quickly set up camp, digging through lean saddlebags for the last of their foodstuffs. There would be opportunity to obtain more food on the trek home, but tonight was a night for smoked salmon and oatcakes.

Three days later they were less than a mile from home. Conn and Bray rode silently, deep in their own thoughts, the men following slowly, exchanging desultory remarks, obviously feeling the effects of the past days on the hunt. Gillis was the first to spot smoke churning just above the trees.

"Look!" He swung his arm urgently, pointing at the black stain across the sky. Conn and Bray both looked up sharply, and the soldiers reined in their horses with combined shouts of anger and dismay. In one accord, they surged ahead, their horses straining to keep pace as they galloped hard for Morven. They reined to a stop at the edge of the village, the sight before them setting their blood to boiling.

"Malcolm!" Conn snarled, the word a curse from his lips. His face hot with anger, he surveyed the desolation that had once been the village of Morven. Ahead of him lay scattered pyres of smoldering cottages, belching black smoke into the air. Dead men and women lay scattered on the ground, indicating the suddenness and viciousness of the attack. Conn heard a child crying nearby, and with a curt gesture of his arm sent Gillis to seek him out.

"We will find your *cousin, mon ami*," Bray vowed to Conn, who was too furious to do more than nod. The soldiers spread out over the village, searching for survivors and dousing what fires they could. Conn and Bray dismounted and joined them, soon covered in soot and teetering between dispiritedness and deadly rage.

Villagers slipped out of hiding, and men joined the efforts at putting out the fires. Women stood aside, clutching crying children to their skirts as they surveyed the smoking ruins with dull, stunned faces. A few rummaged for sound vessels and managed to gather water for the men, who were soon parched with thirst. Gillis returned the foundling to his mother, flushing as she planted a grateful kiss on his cheeks. Eventually all the villagers were accounted for, though the short row of covered bodies lying on the ground made Conn's jaw clench in fury.

A shout rang out. Conn jerked his head. A young boy, his clothes in dirty disarray, burst into the edge of the village glen. He skidded to a stop, his gaze taking in the destruction around him, his eyes wide and bewildered. Bray stepped forward to reassure the boy.

"Easy, *garçon*. You are safe now."

The lad stared at him.

Bray angled his head toward Conn. "That is Laird MacLaurey. Tell him what is wrong."

The lad's harsh breathing subsided and he nodded. "I live at Corfin Castle. I work in the stable." He flung an arm behind him in the direction of the castle. "Malcolm is back!"

"Tell me," Conn demanded, striding forward.

"He burst into the castle—I dinnae know how—and he has taken over again!"

"What of the people there?"

"Ye are either with him or no, 'tis what he said. Them what could, ran away. The rest have been ordered to work, cook—or get thrown into the dungeon!" The boy puffed out his chest. "I worked for him before. I willnae do it again! And I dinnae like the dungeon, neither."

"It looks as though Malcolm has tried to make Morven uninhabitable for you and the villagers," Bray noted quietly. "It was not well done of him," he added. "He will not have the foodstuffs and other things from the village once the supplies run out at the castle."

Conn grunted. "'Tis revenge—nothing less." He placed a hand on the lad's shoulder. "Ye did well coming here. Someone will find ye a place to stay until this is finished."

He turned to Bray. "We will retake the castle."

They sat their horses, looking across the loch at the white walls of Corfin Castle, gleaming in the morning sun.

"Shall we besiege the castle?" Bray asked.

Conn shook his head. "The walls are too thick, the loch at the base of the castle too deep, and the men are untrained in siege tactics. For years it was enough to protect our own. Da was largely satisfied with the lands he possessed, and not ambitious enough to challenge others for their lands."

"What is your plan, then?"

"We will start by seeing how long their foodstuffs hold out. We have a limited supply as well, since Malcolm burned the village, but we can hold out for several days."

"And then what?" Bray asked impatiently. "I have been in positions like this before in France. We could build a battering ram—"

"And have to haul it across the loch."

"Or a catapult."

"Ye cannae get one close enough to the walls."

"A siege tower, then."

"Again, the loch."

Bray made a frustrated gesture. "I have to admit respect for the ancient MacLaurey who built the castle. How are you going to accomplish this if they do not surrender before our food runs out?"

Conn kicked Embarr into a walk and reined him toward the camp. "We will put young Gillis to good use."

Heaving a sigh at Conn's enigmatic statement, Bray turned his horse after him. He pulled to an abrupt halt when he heard Conn instruct the men to begin cutting down trees at the edge of the forest.

"Cut only the tallest, straightest trees," Conn told Seumas, who had been visiting his daughter in the village when Malcolm and his murdering band attacked Morven. "Bring them to the edge of the loch and pile them here, and here, keeping out of range of their archers." He pointed to two areas close to the water, in clear view of the castle.

"When that is done, have some of the men strip the bark from the trees. Keep everyone busy."

"To what purpose is this?" Bray asked as the men moved away as bid. "I agree we need to keep the men occupied, but to what purpose is cutting down these trees? You have already pointed out siege weapons are useless against Corfin Castle."

Conn allowed him a slight smile. "The men need something to do, and Malcolm needs to think we are up to something."

"They cut down trees to confuse Malcolm?"

"Nae. We need the trees to rebuild Morven as well. And I wanted the land near the castle cleared anyway. Cutting down the trees will accomplish much."

He beckoned to a nearby soldier. "Ride to Wyndham. Tell Lady Brianna I will be late."

And with that, Bray had to be satisfied.

"The men on the wall no longer jeer at us, Laird," the young soldier reported.

Conn considered the man's statement. "Good." He nodded, but cared not what insults the men in the castle hurled at his soldiers. After a moment, when Conn said no more, the soldier glanced at Bray, who shrugged and dismissed him with a jerk of his head. When he had gone, Bray leaned forward and clasped his hands together, resting his forearms on his knees.

"What, exactly, are you waiting for? Malcolm's men have quit insulting ours, and that pleases you. But to what purpose? For days you have sent men to the edge of the loch, in full view of Malcolm's men, for what reason you do not share. And still we sit here, accomplishing nothing."

Conn glanced at Bray, noting his frustration. "We have accomplished enough. Come. Let us take a walk."

He strolled through the camp, Bray buckling his sword at his waist as he followed. As they passed young Gillis, Conn motioned for the lad to join them. They left the shelter of the trees to the edge of the loch, which was much shallower than it had been only four days earlier.

"It appears the waters have ebbed," Bray noted.

Conn nodded. "Aye. The waters of the loch cycle each day. It is shallower at this end in the mornings and the approach to the castle is somewhat easier. Each day the guards have diligently watched the approaches at low water, and have been less attentive when the water is too deep to launch an effective attack. The deeper water slows the horses and the noise is enough to alert the guards."

Bray studied the waterline for a moment. "But the shallow water is in daylight. We cannot attack the castle then."

"Nae, we cannae," Conn agreed with infuriating calmness. "But this night the water will stay shallow enough."

"And if we attack tonight, how will we breach the walls?"

"We willnae. Young Gillis will." Conn looked at the lad, who hung on his every word. "Do ye know what I ask of ye? If ye are caught, ye will get no mercy."

Gillis swallowed hard, but nodded. "Aye. But Malcolm cannae be allowed to get away with what he has done."

"There could be other ways."

"But ye said it could take weeks or months, or mayn't even work," Gillis replied.

"True. But I need to know if ye understand the risk."

Gillis drew himself up. "Laird, ye said I could make this work. I am ready."

Conn nodded. The lad was sure of himself and loyal, traits Conn had noted more than once since allowing him to join himself and Bray on their trek to Morven. He grinned suddenly, the heaviness of indecision gone.

"Ye will make it, lad. I know it."

Gillis grinned back, the joy of challenge hot in his eyes.

Conn clouted the lad's shoulder. "Get some rest. I will send for ye closer to dark."

"Tell me, Laird," Bray drawled as Gillis disappeared into a rough shelter. "How will the *garçon* help us breach the castle walls?"

Conn glanced at Bray. "I am sorry, my friend. I could say nothing until I was certain Gillis felt he could do what I asked of him. I dinnae want to coerce the lad into anything he wasnae sure of. Here is my plan."

He motioned for Bray closer. "I dinnae want this overheard." He squatted, feeling jittery, as though he'd forgotten some crucial part of his plan, though he'd gone over it a hundred and more times in his mind. He knew it would only create problems if he over-thought the plan, but it was essential he talk it through with Bray, both to include his friend and in order to satisfy himself he had covered every possibility.

"There is a hidden door in the wall of the castle. The few of us who know of it call it the Laird's Stairway. To reach it from this side, ye must have a low tide, both to cross the loch and to reach the door, which is inset along the wall at the base of the west side of the castle. And, of course, Gillis must approach under the cover of darkness.

"I have had Malcolm's guards watched. They are bored with their work and dinnae even take pleasure in taunting my men any more. They are becoming inattentive in their tasks. Tonight the water will be shallow, the guards are certain we are still preparing our siege weapons, and Gillis will have his best chance to gain his entrance."

He stared at the dirt at his feet and picked up a short stick, using it to draw his plan in the dust. "If Gillis is able to enter through this door, he will follow the tunnel up the stairs to the laird's chambers.

The door to this room is behind a heavy chest set against the wall."

"How will Gillis move the chest away?"

"He willnae have to. On the back of the chest is a small door. Another opens on the front of the chest. It was made so a child could escape alone should the need arise. Gillis is small enough to use that door."

"How do you know Malcolm does not know of the hidden stair?"

Conn looked steadily at Bray. "I dinnae."

"And if Gillis is captured?"

"He is on his own."

Silence stretched taut between them. Finally Bray nodded. "What is your plan once Gillis is inside?"

Conn scuffed away his marks in the dirt with a broad, angry stroke of his hand. "Acting on my orders, Gillis will burn the castle."

Chapter Twenty-three

Shivering with cold and anticipation, Gillis crossed Loch Mor on foot beneath the bare sliver of a waning moon. On cautious feet, he slipped ashore and darted to the base of the castle walls, hugging the uneven rocks, the nearly moonless night cloaking him in deep shadows. He made his way to a ragged niche and crept inside. Running one hand lightly over the rough stones, he stepped deeper into the inky darkness. Suddenly, his hand encountered the upright planking of a wooden door, and he swept his hand across its face until he encountered the iron ring in its center.

His breath rasped and his heart raced painfully. Murmuring a quick prayer against rusted locks, he reached into his pocket for the large iron key made by the smith in the village, guaranteed—so he said—to unlock any door. He ran his fingertips across the door's warped surface, searching for the keyhole. To his relief, the key slipped easily inside. Steadying his shaking hands with a deep breath, he slowly turned the key, every nerve in his body straining to hear the groan of grating iron. A low sound like gravel being ground together broke the silence, as loud to his over-sensitive ears as the fall of a tree. He hesitated, then firmly turned the key its full rotation, ignoring the resulting squeal.

Opening the door, he saw only darkness beyond. Carefully shutting and latching the door behind him, he stared into the impenetrable darkness, squinting his eyes, hoping to gather even the faintest hint of light.

The cloying dampness smothered him like a dense fog, and he wrinkled his nose against the odor of mold and decay. After a few moments his vision adjusted, and he discovered shades of gray amid the blackness. Encouraged, he started forward, quickly stubbing his toes against stone risers. Using one hand against the cold stone wall for guidance as well as balance, he took a deep breath and mounted the stairs.

Conn stood at the edge of the tree line, unable to do anything but stare across the water as Gillis began his task. He could see nothing but the pale glow of the white castle walls, hear nothing but the pounding of his own heart amid the gentle swish-swish of the waves of the loch against the shore. Though he heard no shouts of alarm, there was no way of knowing if Gillis had reached the inside of the castle yet. Time dragged slowly, but there was nothing to do but wait

Bray jostled Conn's arm, pointing to the castle.

"Look!"

Conn glanced to where a dark cloud stained the soft pink-gray sky above the white walls. Moments later, shouts from the guards could be heard. As the sky lightened, another cloud of smoke appeared, then a third.

"Gillis seems quite adept at starting fires." Bray noted the multiple columns of black smoke billowing in the early morning breeze as it drifted into the pale sky.

"Bring the men out."

Held at the ready since Gillis left camp hours earlier, the men quickly formed their lines, moving to the edge of the trees as the smoke clouds grew bigger and blacker. Cries of alarm inside the castle reached a fever pitch, and suddenly the gates opened.

"Now!" Conn kicked his horse into a run. The men charged across the loch, their battle cries mingling with the shouts of fear and panic from the castle. They poured through the gates, past men who stumbled, coughing and choking, on their way out the gate. Some who drew their weapons, saw the futility of fighting both armed men and the raging fires and simply surrendered. Others fought briefly, but fled at the first opportunity. As Malcolm's men quailed before the soldiers of Morven, Conn gave orders for those in the dungeon to be released.

"I want Malcolm!" Conn shouted, reining Embarr to a rearing halt inside the bailey. He surveyed the blackened walls and battlements dispassionately. The castle would require some repair, thanks to Gillis's resourcefulness, but regaining the castle had been worth it.

He glanced at each face as the men were subdued. But there was no sign of Malcolm.

Swiveling in his saddle, he snarled. "Bring him to me!"

A scuffle sounded at the door of the keep, and two soldiers emerged, dragging a man between them. Dressed in robes befitting royalty, the man shook himself as the soldiers released him. He settled his clothing around his plump body with a shrug, twitching the heavy gold chain at his neck into place with one hand. Drawing himself up to his less-than-impressive height with an arrogant bluster, his eyes nonetheless failed to hide his fear. Conn let him stew for a few moments before he dismounted and approached his disloyal cousin with angry, pounding strides.

He loomed over the shorter man, fists clenched at his sides, barely able to control his rage. Malcolm quaked before Conn's fury, held in place by the fierce glares of the men surrounding him.

"Why, Malcolm?" Conn finally asked, the words falling harshly. "Why would ye do this to these people?"

Malcolm sneered. "'Twas never about them. 'Twas the power. Ye wouldnae have used it."

"Ye are wrong. It is always about the people."

Leaning forward, Malcolm pointed a finger accusingly at Conn. "If only ye had died on yer trip to France. I counted on it. How hard could it be? People die abroad all the time. Ships sink every day. Morven would have been mine. 'Tis why I sent ye no word of yer da's accident. If yer sister hadnae interfered, it may have been another year before ye made yer way home. A lot could have happened in that time."

"Ye failed." Conn's voice was flat, emotionless.

Malcolm sniffed. "'Twas nae for lack of trying."

"Then it was yer men who attacked us that night as we approached Morven."

"A lot of good it did me! Fools! The lot of them, useless fools! And now I have nothing!" Malcolm whirled amid the stony-faced soldiers surrounding him. There was no mercy in their eyes.

The Highlander's Outlaw Bride

With a cry of frustrated anger, he snatched a sword from the soldier nearest him. He waved it at Conn, blocking the startled soldier with his arm as the man reached for his weapon.

So this is how it ends? Malcolm challenges me for the title and his life? Grimly, Conn slid his own sword from its scabbard with a low rasp of metal on leather.

"We were boys together, Malcolm."

The man cut an anxious look at Conn's sword. "But never friends. I was always in yer shadow. Ye were the laird's son and I was nothing."

"Ye could have become anything ye wished."

"Never laird. Not with ye or yer father alive."

Conn shook his head. "Tell me ye had nothing to do with his death."

Malcolm smirked. "I dinnae throw him from his horse. But I dinnae grieve when he was laid in the ground. I will say nothing of the time he lay abed, unable to move or speak."

Conn's breathing grew heavy. He had heard enough. He sheathed his sword. "I willnae waste my blade on ye. Ye will stand before judgment of yer peers." He jerked his head at the soldiers standing on either side of his cousin. "Take him away."

Disgusted, afraid to contemplate Malcolm's role in his father's death lest he cut him down here and now in cold blood, Conn turned his back and took a step away.

A man shouted a warning. Conn swung about, his weapon clearing its scabbard before he completed his turn, the blade singing in the sudden silence. The sword continued in its arc, high in the air, as Malcolm rushed inside Conn's guard.

Conn leaped to the side, barely missing Malcolm's thrust. Too close to engage him with his blade, he grabbed the laced leather guard close to the hilt and slammed the weighted metal into the side of Malcolm's head, sending him sprawling in the dust.

Malcolm cried and lifted a hand to the wound. Blood poured from the gash. He rose slowly, the sword still in his grip. He spread his hands wide as he shook his head, swaying off-balance, eyes blinking rapidly. Conn circled him slowly, waiting for his next move. Malcolm turned with him, facing him always, his hands trembling.

He lunged forward, but Conn had been expecting such a move and evaded him easily. He held his sword up and to one side, both hands gripping the hilt. Again Malcolm attacked, and Conn's blade swung to meet it, the clash of steel ringing in the air. Malcolm lurched back, his sword hanging limply at his side as he fought to regain his breath. Conn stared at him dispassionately.

"Throw down the sword, Malcolm. Ye cannae win."

"Nae," his cousin spat, his labored breathing betraying his exhaustion and the depth of his emotion. With a desperate cry of rage, Malcolm threw himself at Conn, swinging his sword in a heavy arc. Conn stepped backward and parried neatly, his sword stopping Malcolm's blade with ease. But the sword Malcolm had stolen was an inferior piece and did not bear the force of the contact. It snapped in two above the guard, and Malcolm stumbled forward, the force of his charge carrying him beyond his intent.

Conn stepped back, startled by the loss of Malcolm's weapon. A snarl on his lips, Malcolm whipped a dagger from his robe, ripping its tip across Conn's side. Flinching back from the slicing pain, Conn drew back his sword and, without further sympathy for his treacherous cousin, slid the honed blade through Malcolm's chest, six inches of the tip protruding from the man's velvet-clad back. Malcolm gasped once in pained surprise, but the life left his eyes before his body touched the ground.

Conn pressed a hand to the shallow wound across his ribs as he watched Malcolm's blood drain into the dirt. *"Tha e ullamh,* Malcolm," he said quietly to the man at his feet. "It is finished."

Chapter Twenty-four

Wyndham

A discolored flower, its petals shriveled and torn, floated from the corner of the pillar where it had lodged two weeks earlier. Without pause, Brianna ground it into the rushes beneath her feet as she strode through the hall. The sight of the dried flower sent a jolt through her, a reminder of the humiliation of being abandoned on her wedding day.

Her hand drifted to her middle and she jerked it away when she realized what she was doing. There was no reason to wonder. She was certain she was with child, and she hardened her heart against the bairn's father. Reportedly, he hunted for his cousin Malcolm who'd apparently instigated some form of poisoning at the castle. He'd not bothered to send word of explanation or apology to her, and as far as she was concerned, the contract between them was broken. She owed allegiance only to Wyndham. And her bairn.

"Anna! Anna!" Jamie's voice resounded as he raced into the hall, leaving the heavy front door open in his haste. Tam bounded behind him, barking as he leapt about, tail waving happily.

"What is it, Jamie?" Brianna broke from her thoughts to Jamie's soaring excitement, motioning for the dog to settle. Jamie skidded across the floor, tilting himself full force into her arms. "We have company, Anna!" he announced, his eyes shining. It was a rarity that strangers rode openly to Wyndham, and he was clearly elated. "I will tell Da!"

Though pleased at the progress between him and their sire, she was uncertain how Da would react to the news of guests. She patted Jamie's arm and shook her head. "Let us see who it is, first, Jamie." She smiled to take the sting from her words. "They may not stay long, and we dinnae wish to disturb him over nothing."

Jamie pouted as she took his hand. "Come with me and help greet our guests." Being given such a grown-up task obviously pleased him, for his face brightened and he skipped beside her, his spirits revived.

They stepped onto the front steps of the manor house. Two men dismounted their horses, a group of Wyndham folk clustered about them. One broke from the crowd and strode toward her. Brianna took one look at him and spun abruptly on her heel.

Conn caught the edge of the door before it slammed shut. He crossed the threshold into the hall and stopped, staring at the woman regarding him with narrowed eyes.

"I am here," he managed in an even tone as he registered her anger. "Admittedly a few days late, but I am here." He was worn out and wanted a bath, a nap, and her, though not necessarily in that order. He knew he sounded gruff and looked even rougher, but he had paused barely long enough to clean and dress his wound and change into clothes that were now as rumpled as he felt.

He was tired of treachery and ruin, and he wanted to bury himself at Morven and set the wrongs to right. But he had one more duty to attend to first—her. He could tell she was surprised to see him, but she lifted her chin and stepped forward. Fury flashed from her eyes and he could feel the scorching heat of her anger.

"A few days?" she scoffed, her voice scathing and low. "Hardly!"

Her scorn scraped at him. *How dare she deride my decisions? Setting the wedding back a few days—Three? Four? —whatever—could hardly make a difference.* "Damn it, Brianna, I dinnae stay away on purpose—and I did send word I would be late." He clenched his teeth. Someday she would tame that temper of hers. But he was too tired to get sucked into her annoyance, and he crossed his arms over his chest, stonewalling her defiance.

"Och, yer man delivered yer message—nearly two weeks after the wedding. So why bother now? Had ye cared to ask, ye wouldnae have wasted yer trip." She leaned forward, her mouth forming her words carefully. "The wedding is off!"

Her statement struck him as unreasonable. Perhaps she did not understand the seriousness of Malcolm's actions. "Ye will be pleased to know I finally caught Malcolm. He is the reason I wasnae here—" Damn, he had lost track of time. Had it been that long?

Brianna coldly supplied the answer. "Two weeks ago."

Conn gave a brief nod acknowledging her words. "He hid himself at Corfin Castle and nearly killed Bray," he continued. Even now he felt the same hollow fear to remember Bray more dead than alive. Brianna shot him a startled look and stepped quickly past him, scanning the thinning crowd. Only Gillis rode with him, and his dusty, rumpled clothing matched Conn's. Brianna turned questioning eyes back to him.

"Is Bray well?"

Conn took a deep breath. "Aye," he said shortly. He had no desire to relive the past days—weeks—now. Out of the nightmare all he wanted was for Brianna to return with him to Morven. Judging by her less-than-cordial reception, she had no intention of going anywhere. He simply was not in the mood to put up with it.

"Get whatever ye need," he told her shortly. "We will return to Morven as soon as we have watered the horses."

He shifted uncomfortably as Brianna's eyes widened, her cheeks flaming with color. She advanced on him slowly, and he wondered at the folly of standing his ground.

"Ye think I will go with ye? Have ye completely addled yer mind? How dare ye ply me with sweet, empty words? The first time something arises, ye forget yer promises and make all decisions on yer own, not bothering with the courtesy to give me word of yer plans. I trusted yer word—I believed the lies ye wrote, but never again, Conn MacLaurey. Never again."

She jabbed a finger at his chest angrily. "I once was the wife of a man who saw to his own pleasures long before my barest comfort, and I willnae endure it again. I told ye I willnae marry a man I dinnae trust, and I wouldnae marry ye if ye were the last man on earth!"

"Ye wouldnae?" Conn returned, hating that he sounded like a five-year-old, and angry she could provoke him so. "Ye are betrothed to me, like it or not, and here is where this argument ends."

"Save it for the poor lass who has the misfortune to marry ye!"

she shouted. "I would rather be turned out to starve than marry the likes of ye."

Conn stopped in his tracks, a blistering reprimand hanging on the tip of his tongue. The line of her body, the bright spots of color on her too-pale face told him she was deadly serious. The fine trembling of her hands, the quick, shallow breaths betrayed the depth of her emotion, and he held his peace for a long moment, hoping to give her time to calm down and come to her senses.

Brianna bristled. Two weeks ago, she would have forgiven him anything, especially to avenge Bray. One week ago, word from him would have made a difference, though he would have been hard pressed to present it, and she would have seen to it he paid dearly for his omission. His callous disregard for her and his rejection of his promise to include her in his decisions still stung, however unintentional it may have been.

She tossed her head, loosening the tight muscles in her neck and back. "Ye can hie yerself back to Corfin Castle. When ye find the betrothal contract that bids us wed *two weeks ago*, burn it!"

Tam's low whine tore her attention from Conn, and she glance down. Jamie stared at her, his eyes huge in his small face as a single tear slid down one cheek. Tam wound his body in front of the lad, providing a physical barrier around him.

Brianna caressed the top of Jamie's head. "Jamie, be a good lad and go find Gavin. Take Tam with ye. Look near the smithy's shed."

With an uncertain glance at her and the men about them, Jamie sidled from the hall, his hand buried in Tam's thick ruff. Brianna turned back to Conn.

"I could petition the king to confiscate yer lands for breaking the contract. I would rather ye simply walk away."

He looked at her askance. "I havenae broken the contract. 'Tis still intact as far as I am concerned."

"Read the wording, Connor. It specified a wedding two weeks ago."

"Gather yer things. We will still have the wedding at Morven."

Brianna drew back, her brows arched, chin tucked close as she pinned him with a regretful stare. "I told ye, I want a marriage based on respect. Ye asked what that meant—since ye havenae learned, I will tell ye. It is trust and consideration, not pretty words that lose their meaning before the ink is dry. Had ye considered me in yer decisions and actions, I would have banded with yer cause, trusted ye to keep yer word."

"I was sick and lost track of the days. Capturing Malcolm took longer than I expected."

"Aye. I sent a man to find out why ye dinnae arrive for the wedding. But ye chose not to send word. I willnae be forever chasing after ye, wondering each day if ye will be home or nae, questioning how I fit into yer life."

She sighed and shook her head. "Ye are still a lad, playing at being a laird. Ye have a lot of growing up to do before ye take on other obligations—such as a wife. If ye cannae keep up with yer daily responsibilities, hire a steward or nursemaid who will."

Conn's face flushed and he scowled. "That is yer final word? Ye willnae honor the contract?"

She turned cold eyes on him. "I have already burned mine."

With a glare to match her own, he strode to the fireplace where a small banked fire lay in readiness for the evening. He pulled a length of paper from his sporran, and, after a brief hesitation, held it to the embers until it caught fire, letting it burn until the flames reached his fingers. He dropped the remnant onto the hearth, where it glowed briefly red as it was reduced to a pile of pale ash and thin smoke.

Jamie threw himself onto the chair at Gavin's side and scowled mightily. "Anna willnae talk to me."

Gavin stared at the lad. Were he older, he would look very formidable, but for now, he just looked cross. Cross and unhappy.

"She doesnae like me anymore," he wailed. Pouring out his woes onto Gavin's lap, he stomped his feet, demanding his world back to its rightful order.

Gavin ruffled the lad's hair. "I will see if I can help. Do ye know where she is?"

"In her room. She willnae speak to me."

With a frown, Gavin rose, heartened at the bright grin that leapt to Jamie's face. He strode up the stairs, confident he would hear nothing more than morning sickness or such she wished to keep from general knowledge. *Though she refused to wed the laird, she has a good head on her shoulders and wouldnae mope about.* His step quickened. What if there was a problem with the bairn? *Surely she willnae put her life at risk. Everyone will know of the babe soon enough.*

He tapped lightly on her door and waited, but heard no answer. Testing the latch, he found it opened without protest. He stepped inside the room, hesitant lest he disturb or embarrass her. Or himself.

Seated on the cushioned bench at the window, she glanced at him over her shoulder. Gavin stopped mid-stride, shock arresting him as he saw the drawn look to her face, the tired lines of her body. *St. Andrew's teeth!* He swore under his breath. *I should have taught that young whelp a lesson when I had a chance. She doesnae deserve this.*

He crossed the room and seated himself on the edge of the seat, an arm's length from the temptation to soothe away her worries. "Och, lass. Is it as bad as all this? Where is the daring lass who stole her own cattle back from the reivers? Ye willnae marry the laird—ye have what ye want. Why the despondency?"

His words had the desired effect. She drew herself up like a wildcat preparing to strike. "Dinnae tell me how to act. I have shouldered the burdens of this clan for nearly two years. I believe I have earned the right to a day or two of quiet—I certainly willnae have peace from the likes of ye."

"Ye are expecting a bairn for certain?"

"Aye. But it doesnae change my decision on the marriage. I willnae marry Laird MacLaurey, nor will I tell him of the bairn."

Gavin's eyebrows rose and he fought to keep his jaw from dropping open. "What do ye think he will do once he discovers he has a child?"

Brianna shifted on the cushion, drawing her knees to her chin as she tucked her skirts about her feet. "He has too much on his mind setting Morven to rights. He isnae likely to consider me or Wyndham's plight."

"Ye have no intention of telling him?"

"Why complicate his life? He will marry a woman who will give him plenty of children. I willnae give up the bairn to him to raise, nor will I have him tugged back and forth between Wyndham and Morven, uncertain where home is."

Gavin was not taken in by her firm yet flippant statement. He had no doubt she would keep the bairn's parentage a secret, but there was a sadness in her eyes that belied her attempt at bold detachment. "There is another side to this ye havenae spoken of. Tell me why, knowing ye carry his child, ye burned the marriage contract and sent him home with a flea in his ear."

He knew she heard him. Her fingers twisted in her lap even as she returned to stare out the window into the darkness. At last she faced him, and for the first time he realized how much the cares of her life weighed on her.

"I saw him once when I was a lass. Golden-haired and charming. He had ridden to Wyndham with his da. There was some issue about buying horses. I was seven or eight at the time, but he was kind to me and dinnae mind when I followed him around as they studied each animal. I think I fell in love with him that day."

She sighed and shrugged. "But I had no choice in who I married, and we never crossed paths again. I heard the gossip, of his easy way with the lasses, yet believed I could be the one who settled him down. However, I was soon married off to Mungo, and I quickly lost interest in dreaming about love—discovered it was a cruel faerie tale at best."

"Then why not give it a chance now?"

"I wanted to. I did—eventually. But I still dinnae believe in love. I want nothing less than respect, and he cannae give me that."

"What of the bairn?"

"I dinnae want tongues to wag. I suppose I could travel to my aunt who lives in Edinburgh. She is widowed and will likely take me in for a time. I could then bring the bairn back as the child of a deceased, distant cousin."

"But ye would leave Wyndham for months. That isnae what ye wanted."

"If I stay, I will need to marry quickly to keep the gossip from reaching his ears."

"How will ye do that?"

"By doing what I should have considered years ago."

"What is that, lass?"

She tilted her face to his, her gaze solemn. "Ask ye to marry me."

Chapter Twenty-five

Late October, 1387, Wyndham

Brianna sank onto the bench outside the stables as her knees gave way. Dizzy and nauseated, she covered her face with her hands to keep her world from spinning out of control. The sensation passed, and she rose slowly to her feet and made her way up the path to the hall. Gavin caught up with her as she entered the door, and his good-morning smile became a frown.

"Are ye feeling unwell?"

Brianna gave him a wan smile. "Nothing to worry about. Just the bairn making his presence known."

"A bout of sickness, then?"

For reply, she cut off his words with an abrupt wave of her hand as she whirled and fled the room. Shivery sweat glistened on her forehead and trickled down her spine. Bracing her hand against the rough wooden wall of the privy, she waited for the nausea to pass.

Why can I not be like other women and have this pass? I am nearly three months gone, and still cannae keep my breakfast down. The sensation passed, and she rose, scrubbing both palms against her skirts. She walked into the sunlight, pausing before she entered the hall. Too many curious eyes awaited her, and she turned back to the stable. Tam wandered to her side and thrust his cold nose against her hand with a whine.

"Dinnae *fash* yerself, lad. Gavin and I have it all worked out." He padded beside her into the building and flopped down on a pile of straw in the corner of the tack room. "We will wed next week and an early bairn willnae be taken amiss. Who would have thought I would have a bairn in the first place?"

Pulling Maude's blanket from a shelf, Brianna gathered needle and thread and a scrap of cloth to patch a worn spot in the fabric. She was sure to make a poor job of the busy work any stable lad could do, but it would take her mind off her stomach, and relieve her of the speculations in the hall.

She eyed the blanket critically. Nowhere near perfect, the job was, however, done and she doubted the stable lads would ever breathe a word of complaint. She bit the heavy thread in half and rose to return the blanket to its shelf. Reaching high, she stood on her toes to give the blanket a final push into place. Tam gave a warning growl as the door opened behind her.

Expecting Gavin or one of the stable lads, possibly even Jamie, she was unprepared for her visitor. The sight of Laird MacLaurey, his form filling the doorway, stole the breath from her lungs. She stood there a long moment, open-mouthed in surprise, until she collected her wits.

"What are ye doing here?" she demanded over her racing heart.

"Is it true? Ye are marrying Gavin?"

Brianna stared at Conn, noting a haggardness about his eyes and mouth. The last time she'd seen him, he had been tired, even exhausted, but he hadn't looked like this. She caught herself before she could feel sorry for him, and measured her words, aware her slightest slip would tell him about the bairn.

"Aye. I am."

"Why?"

Why, indeed? Her best answers were the ones she couldn't give him, so she fell back onto the glib statement she and Gavin passed to anyone who asked. "Because we suit each other. We both have Wyndham's good at heart, and it is time we both were married." She shot him a cold look. "And we respect each other."

"Ye said ye dinnae need a husband."

"I have changed," she lied smoothly.

Conn snorted. "Like hell."

"I want to settle down, watch Jamie grow up, and know I will grow old with someone." She cut her eyes away from his steely gaze. She could have had all of that with him, only she had been too proud and too angry to give it a chance.

He eyed her critically, his gaze covering her from head to toe, and she felt heat creep up her neck. He scowled.

"Have ye been ill? Ye look terrible."

"That sort of talk isnae likely to turn a lass's head," she replied tartly, not answering his question.

"Ye appear to have lost weight. A good bit of weight." He strode toward her and she stiffened as he circled her, inspecting her from every angle.

Within seconds Brianna was seething, her foot tapping an impatient tattoo on the dirt floor. At last Conn came to a stop in front of her, standing much too close. She took a step backward, hoping he wouldn't follow. Tam leaned against her legs and whined.

"Are ye satisfied?" she snapped.

"Nae. Answer my question. And call off yer dog."

She ignored his complaint about Tam. "'Tis none of yer concern, but I have been sick for a few days. I am fine now, but it was a stomach complaint and I did lose a bit of weight."

Conn shook his head. "Being sick a few days doesnae make ye look like this. Tell me the truth. Why are ye marrying Gavin?"

Brianna flinched. *What does he ask? Does he wish to know the truth of my illness or why I will marry Gavin?* She felt the blood drain from her face. *The answer to both questions is the same.*

She realized she still stared at him, and his eyes darkened, a sure indication of either passion or anger, and she was quite willing to bet this time it wasn't passion. "I am marrying Gavin because he asked me to, and...and he loves me." Belatedly, she remembered Conn had heard the words from Gavin himself three months earlier.

"Are ye with child?" His stony look dared her to look away from him again. Anger rose in her, the leaping pulse in her throat betraying her. With a muttered curse, Conn reached for her, encircling her waist with his hands. He stared at his thumbs which refused to meet by a good hand's breadth around her middle, then perused her again, a much closer inspection this time.

"Ye are!" he ground between clenched teeth. "Ye not only look different, ye feel different." His hands drifted upward, his palms against her breasts.

Brianna hissed and Tam snarled as he launched himself at Conn in Brianna's defense. "Keep yer hands to yerself, Connor MacLaurey!" she snarled, hauling Tam bodily back amid the sound of ripping cloth. "The bairn isnae yers!"

"Ye lie!" he thundered as he grabbed his arm, his leine torn but his skin intact.

"'Tis Gavin's," she lied boldly, refusing to drop eye contact. He nodded his head once and took a step backward, then pivoted abruptly to the door. Once his back was turned, she whirled to face the wall, drained of all energy. She braced herself against the wooden boards, one hand twisted in Tam's thick fur, her eyes closed tight as she waited to hear Conn's footsteps in the hall.

A hand clamped onto her shoulder, and her eyes flew open in fright. Tam wriggled in her grasp, but she held him firm as Conn's voice sounded low in her ear.

"If ye have lied to me, ye will wish the sheriff had hanged ye on the gallows," he snarled. "Is the bairn mine?"

Brianna struggled to find her breath as she held Tam tight against her. "Nae."

Without another word, Conn released her. He was gone in an instant, slamming the door behind him. Tam tore away, barking as he flung himself against the closed portal. Hot tears slid down Brianna's cheeks. *St. Andrew's blue bollocks! What a mess!*

She did not fear his retribution. She knew him well enough and he wouldn't take out his wrath on a woman. But she knew now she couldn't live with not telling him. The question was, how to say the words? She'd asked for his trust and respect, but when put to the test, she fell as short as he.

Chapter Twenty-six

Gavin glanced across the practice field toward the stable. Worry lines creased his forehead. *She shouldnae still be in there. Her sickness has her weaker than she will admit, and that mare of hers is a handful.* He wiped his sweaty brow with the back of his forearm and froze, noticing a strange horse standing in the shade of a tree near the stable. Squinting against the glare of the sun, he saw the horse shake its glorious black mane and instantly recognized Conn's bay stallion. Gavin sprinted to the barn, his heart pounding in his chest.

Conn burst through the doorway, slamming the door with angry force behind him. He saw Gavin and whirled toward him, smoothing the torn sleeve of his leine.

"Why is she lying about the bairn?" he demanded.

"I dinnae know her to lie," Gavin replied carefully, assessing the likelihood Conn received the worst of his discussion with Brianna—and Tam.

Conn sneered. "Ye would make an admirable diplomat. Can no one here state the truth?"

Gavin took a deep breath, damping down the tremendous urge to start a brawl neither could win. Though a handful of years older than the laird, they were too well matched in size and brawn, and Conn was frustrated and angry, two traits likely to tip the odds in his favor.

"I will stand by what she has told ye. And remind ye she neither likes nor respects ye."

Conn flinched. "So I have been told."

"She is also certain, should ye decide the bairn is yers, ye will take him from her."

Conn stared at him, his eyes wide with disbelief. "I wouldnae take the bairn away from her. She may grow vexed with the sight of me, and I would expect him to know I am his father. But I wouldnae take him from her. I couldnae do that."

Gavin met Conn's stare evenly, unable to detect a lie in him.

Conn jerked his chin over his shoulder in Brianna's direction. "That bairn isnae yers. It hasnae been a month since I last saw her. And she wouldnae have slept with ye while betrothed to me."

His voice contained a mixture of challenge and accusation, but Gavin did not rise to the bait. "Nae. She dinnae."

"The bairn is mine. His mother, too."

"Nae. The bairn may be yers, but his mother undoubtedly isnae." Gavin's denial was harsh, his hands fisted at his sides.

"Ye know she belongs to me."

"She is no longer a pawn to be used between the clans."

"Pawn? Nae, she will be my wife!" Conn retorted with heat.

"She has agreed to marry *me*."

Conn shook his head, denying Gavin's claim. "What would it take for ye to give her up?"

"What made ye let her go?" Gavin challenged.

"I couldnae bear to see her so unhappy. She wouldnae listen to me, but I would sooner lose an arm than make her feel so miserable again."

"Ye released her out of grief and sadness. I would only release her into happiness. She must choose ye of her own free will—and be glad."

"How much time?"

"We marry in less than a week."

A look of panic swept across Conn's face and Gavin hid a smile. It would take days, if not weeks, just to get Brianna to agree to see, much less speak to him again. *The laird may as well try summoning the spirits in the standing stones on the hill. Getting stones to talk to him would be easier.*

Brianna entered her bedroom and shut the door firmly behind her.

Leaving Tam and Jamie wrestling in the hall, she sought quiet to sort her thoughts.

Conn had been angry. Furious. It had rolled off him in palpable waves, and her breathing had yet to return to normal. Though he had shouted at her, even threatened her, he had been aggrieved. Strained. Until he discovered she was with child, he had only wanted to know why she was marrying Gavin. *Why?* She cringed as she remembered the longing in the single word.

She crossed the room to stand before her mirror. Shrugging out of her gown, she stared at her body through the filmy shift in the silvered reflection. There was a subtle difference—her breasts were a little more full, her tummy a bit rounder. She placed a hand hesitantly on the slight swell of her stomach. There was no movement. But it was real. Soon she would feel the flutter of the life inside her. Her baby. Conn's baby.

Oh, Conn. What am I to do?

Flowers lay beside her platter, their harvest colors warm on the scrubbed wooden table. Brianna stared at them in surprise. Glancing around the room, she sought Gavin to thank him for the thoughtful gift. She knew he was a kind man, but she never thought him to be the sort to give her flowers. He was aware of her encounter with Conn earlier in the day, and she warmed at this silent statement of love, or support, or whatever the bouquet of flowers was meant to be. But he was not in the hall.

She ate, pushing aside the accusations in her head over her decision to not tell Conn about the bairn. She wanted him raised as Gavin's child. So why did her heart twist inside her each time she thought of it? And, why, by St. Andrew, couldn't she stop thinking about it?

At last Gavin walked through the door, and lightly brushed his lips across her forehead. She brightened. *I have made the right decision. Gavin is a good, honorable man.* She smiled warmly at him. "I thank ye for the flowers."

Gavin frowned. "I dinnae give ye flowers."

"Oh. Then whoever—" She searched the room, thinking to catch the eye of the person who had put the flowers at her seat. At last she shrugged. "Well, 'twas well-intentioned, I am sure. Mayhap young Jamie brought them." Jamie's shriek of laughter echoed across the room and Brianna smiled to see him romping amid the other children, Tam keeping pace beside him.

"I think I will go up to bed," she told Gavin, giving his hand a squeeze.

In her chamber, she sat at her dressing table and reached for her hair-brush. Her hand touched not the familiar smooth handle, but a roughened, slender stem. She jerked her hand back, surprised to discover the stem of a rose, its prickly spines removed.

She picked the flower up carefully, studying it from every angle as she twisted it between her fingers. The deep red petals were aglow with health and so fragrant she was surprised she hadn't noticed it when she entered the room.

Her eyes strayed to the tabletop where the rose had lain. There was a small piece of paper tucked against a lotion pot, and she picked it up.

I am sorry. Conn

She dropped the slip of parchment as though it burned her fingers. Her heart raced and she glanced quickly about the room, wondering if he might still be near. But she was quite alone in the room, and after a moment her heart rate slid back to normal.

I am sorry.

She read the note again, staring at it where it lay on the table.

Conn.

She stood, letting the rose slip through her fingers to land next to the note. Slowly, she went through the motions of preparing for bed. Slipping beneath the covers, it was a long time before sleep claimed her.

Brianna woke to sunlight streaming through her window. She blinked, rubbing her eyes, shocked she'd slept so late. Flinging the covers aside, she scrambled out of bed, splashing water on her face before dragging on breeches and a shirt. Skirts were too clumsy for the way she rode, and today she meant to be alone, amid no more worries or cares other than the best spot to sit beside the burn and breathe.

She hurried down the stairs, noticing the tables stacked at the edge of the room. The morning meal was apparently long past, and she detoured through the kitchen to filch an apple and a piece of bread to still the rumblings of her stomach.

Thank the sweet Virgin my belly is back to normal. She grinned as she munched her snack on her way to the stable. In high spirits because her morning sickness was apparently at an end, she let Maude stretch her legs as soon as they were out of sight of the hall. The mare's black mane whipped along Brianna's cheeks as she rode tight against the dappled neck, her face buried amid the silky strands.

Maude at last began to tire, and Brianna reined her to a walk. They meandered next to a narrow burn, its waters flashing in the sun. After a bit, Brianna dismounted and tied the reins to a nearby bush, allowing Maude to graze. Walking to the crest of a low hill, Brianna sat beneath the sheltering branches of a large tree, looking over the wild lands beyond Wyndham.

A light breeze picked up and she watched the clouds as they rolled across the sky, promising an afternoon shower. Brianna stretched lazily, turning abruptly at the soft whinnies behind her. She gasped, startled to see Embarr standing next to Maude, Conn astride his massive beast, an inscrutable look on his face.

Squaring her shoulders, Brianna stood and walked to Embarr. She gave him a pat of recognition as she swept past his rider without a word.

"Still likes the horse better than me," Conn remarked.

Brianna didn't reply, but her step faltered at the sound of his voice. She untied Maude and led her to the burn to drink, hoping Conn would ride away.

She sighed when he didn't take the hint. Not that she actually imagined he would give up so easily. Nothing seemed easy between them, and she longed to call a truce.

"Why are ye still here? Could ye not go home?" She bit her lip at the querulous tone of her voice.

"I did."

Lifting an eyebrow, Brianna glanced pointedly around the glen. "This is Wyndham land."

"I know." He threw a leg over Embarr's withers and slid to the ground. "There is nothing at Corfin Castle for me without ye there." He strode to her side. "Home seems to be wherever ye are."

Stunned by his response, Brianna didn't move when he took the reins from her hand and walked Maude forward a couple of steps.

"She is trying her tricks on ye." With a deft hand, he jerked the saddle's girth, taking up several inches of slack in its length. Maude gave a whoosh of surprise and flicked her ears.

Brianna frowned. She knew Maude's tricks well enough. Within a few steps the saddle would have slipped, an extremely dangerous move if she'd taken off at a gallop as she was wont to do. She mumbled her thanks as she retrieved Maude's reins.

Conn splayed a palm on the mare's shoulder. "Did ye get my note?"

"Aye." Her voice softened as she remembered the words on the paper. *I am sorry. Conn.*

"I meant it. I am truly sorry. Mostly for causing ye more pain after ye'd begun to trust me."

Brianna scowled. "'Tis over and done."

Conn shook his head. "Nae. Not until ye understand why I was late. Ye never allowed me to explain, and I was too tired and wrapped up in my own problems to try to make ye listen."

"I was upset."

"Ye were hysterical," he disagreed.

"I was tired of being taken for granted. Wyndham's very existence has been my only concern for the past two years, and to find myself with an unwanted marriage, an absent groom, and a child— aye, I was a wee bit distraught."

Conn's face registered only slight surprise at her admission she'd known she was with child nearly a month ago when she'd broken their betrothal. There was no need to pretend. Brianna was certain if he thought for a moment the child was Gavin's he would not have sought her out today.

"I am sorry for the way things have turned out between us. Would ye listen and at least try to understand what happened to make me break my promise?"

Brianna nodded, relieved he did not press her to reconsider their betrothal. She looped Maude's reins over a low branch and gave Conn her attention.

"Instead of fleeing the castle the day I arrived, Malcolm changed his appearance and stayed behind. He lived as a servant until two days before ye and I were to wed. That night, he poisoned the wine sent to my table.

"Bray and I both were sick. Gillis had verra little of the wine, and

Seumas was able to give him something to help his nausea. Malcolm accosted Bray on the stairs as he stumbled to his room, and wounded him. Gillis happened upon them and fought Malcolm off."

Conn frowned and clenched his teeth, a bleak look shadowing his eyes. Brianna's hand lifted to smooth the tight line of his jaw, but she stopped before it was more than a mere hint of motion, unsure why it bothered her to see his distress. Conn stepped in a tight circle before he continued his story.

"It took us several days to recover our strength. I thought—briefly—about sending ye word. But I forgot and was consumed with preparations. 'Tis not a good reason, but..." He spread his hands before dropping them to his side.

"We took twenty men to hunt Malcolm and his henchmen down," he continued. "The trail led deep into the Highlands. We chased him for almost a week, always just a few hours behind him. And then we lost his track."

He reached for Brianna's hand, and she allowed him to take it.

"It was already more than a week past the time I had promised ye, but time dinnae mean anything to any of us by then. Right or wrong, there was nothing in our world beyond finding and punishing Malcolm. We decided to go back to Morven and regroup. Three days later, we were close enough to see the smoke from the village."

He gripped her hand, and she squeezed it back, encouraging him. "That is why I was late, Brianna, why I was less than patient with ye when I came to Wyndham. Malcolm left the village in ruins and barricaded himself in the castle."

"We received word about Morven."

"Aye. And the people were glad to receive yer supplies. Ye deserved my thanks that day, not harsh words."

"I have seen Corfin Castle. It is nearly unassailable. How did ye get Malcolm?"

One corner of Conn's mouth quirked upward, but there was no humor in his eyes. "Gillis crept in through the Laird's Stairway one night. It is a hidden escape route for the inhabitants should it ever be needed. Gillis has a knack for blending in—usually to avoid trouble or work—and he managed to enter the castle unchallenged."

"But how did he open the gates?"

Conn's jaw clenched and his face darkened. "He fired the castle."

Brianna's eyes widened, shocked. "He what?"

"He burned the castle from the inside. By the time the men

opened the gates in order to flee the castle, the rest of the small army Malcolm had with him was too involved with putting out the fires to notice him." Conn shrugged. "A tactical error on their part, but one that benefited us quite well."

Brianna's curiosity piqued. "How much did he burn?"

"Enough to require repairs. The clan is currently at work rebuilding the village and restoring the castle."

She stared at him in silence for a moment, letting his words sink in. His dogged determination to bring Malcolm to justice and the stubbornness that led him to burn his home to achieve his goal astounded her. And proved him to be much like herself. Uncomfortably so.

"I must get back." She snatched her hand from his and grabbed Maude's reins. Maude snorted and backed a step, reacting to Brianna's abrupt move.

"Brianna!" Conn raised his voice, claiming her attention. She cut her gaze to him. "This isnae over between us."

"I will marry Gavin on Saturday."

His determined gaze held firm. "That gives me three days to change yer mind."

Chapter Twenty-seven

Brianna flung her riding gloves across the room, slamming the door behind her. *I should marry Gavin today and be done with this madness.* Her eyes strayed to the spot on the table where Conn's note had lain, half-expecting another. *Or should I marry Gavin at all?* She paused to splash cold water on her face, then jerked open the drawer where she'd hidden the note.

I am sorry.
Conn.

She wished she could believe him. What made him pursue her? He'd said he admired her courage. Did that mean he would allow her freedom to act? Would he ask and honor her opinions once marriage vows were spoken?

He'd obviously enjoyed their coupling that night beside the burn—he'd told her that, too. It was true he had awoken something in her she'd not experienced before. Though there was surely something more? Her insides clenched and heated to remember the intensity of the sensations his touch had ignited. And though she felt comforted and loved with Gavin, he did not curl her toes or set her insides afire. Conn's touch challenged her to something she did not fully understand.

And there was the bairn. Would Conn still pursue her if he did not know of the bairn? She gripped the back of the chair, sinking onto the cushion. He hadn't known. Not at first. When he'd walked through the stable door yesterday, he'd come back for her. Only her.

Brianna laughed as Tam darted into the thicket, in hot pursuit of a leggy rabbit. Her basket swung lightly from one hand as she strode the path to Wyndham village to purchase spices from a merchant there.

Beside her, Rabbie whistled happily. As they approached the last bend in the path before the village, Brianna drew to an abrupt halt. Conn, seated on a fallen log, eyed her steadily. To her surprise, Rabbie saluted him smartly and turned on his heel, leaving her in Conn's custody. She planted her fists on her hips, a glare for both men. Rabbie's tune never faltered as he headed back up the trail.

"How on earth did ye convince him I would be safer with ye than him?" she demanded.

Conn shrugged as he rose to his feet. "He is an astute observer of human nature."

Brianna snorted her opinion on his answer.

"And I bribed him."

Tam raced out of the woods and shoved his nose hard into Conn's crotch. With a groan, Conn captured the dog's muzzle between his hands and gently pushed him away. "Ye are a rare beast, Tam. I understand ye dinnae know yer own strength, but have a care, aye?"

"He takes his job of protecting me seriously." Brianna tossed a look over her shoulder. "Unlike others I could name."

Conn quickened his step and drew abreast. "I always have a care for ye, Brianna."

"My care shouldnae be yer concern."

"But it is."

Brianna stopped, whirling to face him. "Why?"

"Why do I care for ye? I have told ye before."

She tossed her head. "Ye told me I would make ye a good wife. I understand that. I was an excellent wife even when married to Mungo, though he was a deplorable husband. Why would marrying ye be any different?"

"Because I know what is in ye." He touched fingers to her hair close to her ear. "In here, ye are shrewd, quick-witted and smarter than many men I know. Unlike yer unlamented late husband, this doesnae intimidate me."

His hand drifted lower, fingertips a few inches from her breast bone.

"Here, ye are fiercely loyal, unstintingly kind, and so passionate. Ye are beautiful, Brianna. Both inside and out. I know this, and I wouldnae change a bit of it. I cannae imagine a better woman to have at my side."

"At yer side? Truly? Ye would look to me for advice?"

"And gratefully accept it."

Brianna hesitated, torn between the desire to hug him to her and roll her eyes at him with cynicism born of past experience.

Conn scowled. "Ye only marry Gavin because he doesnae challenge ye. All yer life he has done yer bidding. Ye would soon be miserable in such a marriage. Would ye continue to respect the man? Or would ye lose yer regard for him?"

She shot him a startled look. She could not call him a liar, for his words struck a chord in her heart. But she didn't have to like the truth he pointed out. Her lips nudged downward in a thoughtful frown.

He shrugged. "Think on it, dearling. In the meantime, I believe ye have some shopping to do."

To her surprise, he followed amiably as she chose spices for the kitchen, commenting knowledgably when she asked his opinion, and made no complaint as she moved from one tiny shop to another. He carried her basket without comment after she passed it to him in order to inspect a length of lace. Her fingers caressed the web-fine needlework longingly, but she put it away with a sigh. Finances being what they were at Wyndham, she would not purchase what she did not need.

Tam met up with them as they exited the shop, leaving a group of youngsters behind.

"Yer dog has made a number of friends, I see."

Brianna nodded. "He is often with Jamie, and these are his friends. They know him well."

"So, ye willnae train him to herd cattle?"

"He does that instinctively. The master herdsman is pleased with him. But Jamie needs him more."

She paused to speak to a pair of old crones seated on a wooden bench. Conn waited patiently, tossing a stick for the dog, who retrieved it over and over. Brianna's lips curved upward in amusement.

As they made their way back to Wyndham Hall, Conn spoke. "I meant what I said yesterday. I dinnae believe ye should marry Gavin."

She quirked a brow at him. "I suppose ye think I should marry ye?"

He nodded his head emphatically. "Aye."

"But, why?" She halted in the middle of the trail and turned to him, a troubled frown on her face.

"Brianna, the stories ye heard of me werenae much exaggerated. I took few of the lasses to bed, but the rest is fairly accurate. Everything always came easily to me. But the one thing that mattered most, I drove away with my thoughtlessness.

"Ye were right to tell me 'nae'. I dinnae understand what it meant to need someone like ye in my life. And I arrogantly treated ye with less respect than my horse, expecting ye to comply with my plans with no fuss. I ask yer forgiveness and promise ye I will never take ye for granted."

A faint smile quivered on her lips. "A pretty speech. How much of it is sincere?"

"Och, that stings. Though learning to speak with ye on all matters will take some practice, I mean to do it, and ye have my thanks for keeping me to my word should I forget."

Brianna gave him a thoughtful look and turned back to the trail. They walked in silence until they reached the edge of the woods. The hall loomed just across the glen. She glanced sideways at him. "I will be fine from here."

"Brianna."

She stopped.

"Ye dinnae belong to Gavin. Ye belong with me. I will do whatever it takes to convince ye of it. I will wait for ye until ye are ready. I will make whatever promise ye ask of me." He shook his head slowly. "But I willnae stay and watch ye marry Gavin. I willnae be here after tomorrow."

Conn paced the small room accorded him as a guest. It mattered not the size or appointments of the room, only that it allowed him to remain near Brianna. Until tomorrow. He slapped the palm of his hand on the wall next to the narrow window. *She cannae marry him! I must make her understand. But what else can I do?*

He snorted. *I should challenge Gavin, but injuring or killing him willnae help*. He recoiled at the thought of Brianna in Gavin's arms. *Albeit, having a good reason to smash my fist into his face would definitely help me.*

He whirled at a knock at the door. He took the missive from the young lad's hand, placing a small coin in his palm in thanks. The single sheet of parchment was folded and fastened with Wyndham's seal. He ripped it open. A single red rose petal, its edges beginning to dry and curl, dropped from the center. He caught it as he scanned the page. There were only three words.

Forgive me?
Brianna

He frowned at the words. *Forgive ye? For what? Disbelieving me? Lying?* Or for marrying Gavin?

He crushed the paper in his fist, a curse snarling from his lips. He'd already forgiven the first, trying hard for the second, but damned if he would forgive her for marrying Gavin when she knew in that stubborn heart of hers she belonged to him.

Opening his hand, he smoothed the paper as he re-read the words. The delicate tracery, a skill so few possessed, showed strength and determination, very much like her. He folded the paper carefully, placing the rose petal in its center, and tucked the small package into his sporran. He'd won a response from her, but he wasn't certain if it was the one he wanted.

Gavin gulped the hot mulled wine, grateful for its warmth against the early morning chill. A few servants stirred about the hall, poking the fire in the great hearth back to life and setting out platters of bread and cheese for the early risers.

Brianna beckoned to him from the edge of the room, indicating he follow her into the lord's private chamber just off the hall. Startled to see her up so early, he rose and accompanied her to the room. Something about her measured movements sent warning bells off in his head, and he shut the door softly behind him.

"'Tis good to see ye this morning. Are things well with ye?"

She bit her lip and glanced away. He crossed the room, fighting the familiar urge to comfort her. "Ye have something that needs saying, aye?"

For a moment, she did not reply. Squaring her shoulders, she faced him. "I want you to know I cannae marry ye."

Hollowness twisted his stomach, and he sucked in a sharp breath of surprise.

Her eyes darkened and she canted her head to one side, an anxious look of appeal on her face. "Even when I was but a lass, ye were the one person I knew I could trust. Even though I led ye into danger, ye always had a care for me. That has meant more to me than ye could ever know."

Gavin grimaced. *More than a care, lass.* But he couldn't voice the words.

"Yer love and patience meant the world to me these past weeks. It gave me strength to be honest with myself."

Slowly, the band constricting his heart eased and he gave a short nod. "Ye have decided to marry MacLaurey." He could not disguise the harshness of his voice, and a look of pain crossed her face.

"I have."

Her words were simple, honest, yet they sounded bleak to his ears. He gritted his teeth. "Is there any chance..." His voice trailed off. He'd known the depths of her anger at the laird, but he had obviously misjudged her heart. He would have sworn there was no way in hell Conn could win her back.

She stepped forward, closing the gap between them, her hands settling softly on his arms. He reached for her, folding his arms about her.

"I am sorry," she whispered against his chest. "I am so sorry to break my promise to ye."

He released her reluctantly, then tucked a finger beneath her chin. "Ye are happy? This is yer true wish, not just because of the bairn?"

"Aye. It is my wish. He is much like me, and though I doubt we will always agree, we will always be equal partners. This he has promised me, and I now trust him to keep his word." She tilted her head. "And we will have our bairn. Mayhap others, as well."

Gavin touched the back of his fingers to the side of her face and read happiness in her eyes. "Then I release ye from yer promise."

"Ye dinnae hate me? I have wronged ye."

He managed a small smile. "Nae, lass. Never that. Ye have my heart, ye know."

Brianna strode from the lord's chamber and crossed the great hall, her pace increasing with every step as her elation grew. Through the open door, she saw Conn standing next to Embarr on the far edge of the yard, saddled and ready to go. *He leaves this soon?* She gasped and broke into a run, her feet flying down the steps and across the grassy yard, her hair and skirts billowing in the air.

Conn glanced up sharply, dropping Embarr's reins as he spread his arms wide. She flung herself against him, and he scooped her up, swinging her around as laughter and tears caught in her throat. Lowering her to the ground, he crushed her to him, burrowing his face in her hair.

"Will ye marry me now?"

Brianna pulled back, still within the circle of his arms. Her eyes danced. "Nae. I have a few belongings to pack, and ye have a castle to ready for me."

Conn's eyebrows shot upward. "Aye. I do. But I would marry ye here at Wyndham before I go. It shouldnae be too difficult. Ye have had plenty of practice."

Her chin tilted at a haughty angle, but she laughed. "I have only had two weddings. Ye missed the last one."

"I want all of Wyndham to see ye happy. We could wed tomorrow—a priest, food for a feast—what else do we need?"

"I cannae marry ye tomorrow. That was the day..." Her voice trailed off and she glanced over her shoulder, feeling Gavin's absence.

"Then marry me today. I could stay a day or two while ye pack yer things. Corfin is in good enough shape to welcome ye home."

He bent and kissed her until her head fairly spun and she could scarcely catch her breath. At last he released her. "I will speak to the priest. Ye must have things to attend to. The feast, yer wedding dress. I wouldnae mind if ye wore what I found ye in, but since there will be witnesses present, ye best find something to keep their tongues from wagging."

Brianna shrieked in mock outrage and raised a fist, pummeling his chest. "Beast!"

Conn chuckled and dodged her half-hearted blows. Reaching into the bag behind Embarr's saddle, he pulled out a length of lace and ribbon. Brianna gasped in surprised delight.

"'Tis beautiful!"

"I saw ye admiring the lace yesterday and I wanted ye to have it. The ribbon is the color of the gown I saw ye in at Dundonald Castle. It suits yer eyes."

"Thank ye!" she breathed, astounded at his thoughtfulness. Tears pricked her eyes. Accepting his gift, she kissed him. It felt surprisingly good for her to kiss him, rather than the other way around, and she lingered, tasting the warmth of his lips. She wrapped her arms about his neck and leaned into him, astonished at how right it felt to curve into his body.

At last she broke away, breathing heavily, feeling definitely overwarm. "I will see to things here," she murmured. Her hands slid from his shoulders to his waist, her gaze following. "Ye may want to wait a bit before talking to Father Roderick."

Conn's laugh warmed her heart. "Aye, we dinnae want to alarm the priest, aye?" He gently pushed her hair over her shoulder, fingers lingering. "Will ye wear the pendant I gave ye, also?"

Brianna's face fell. She lifted a hand to her throat. "I do not have it."

An eyebrow quirked at her. "What do ye mean?"

I willnae begin my married life with a lie or a half-truth. "When ye dinnae arrive for the wedding, I gave it to Gavin to be sold."

"Why? 'Twas a gift."

"Aye. But I have no need for such, and the coin would buy us much grain this winter."

"But I gave it to you."

"Cold stone and metal willnae fill our bellies."

Conn stood silent for many long moments. "We are both practical. I was willing to lose my home to roust Malcolm, and ye gave up a pretty gift to feed yer people. I cannae blame ye. But it will be my pleasure to see ye adorned with beautiful clothes and jewels and have nae concern that doing so keeps food from any mouth."

"I must admit, when ye gave it to me I had no care to wear it and be marked as yer possession."

Conn laughed. "There is the lass I know and love. Yer honesty warms my bones. Dinnae ever change, aye?"

She slanted her eyes. "The babe will mark me as yers soon enough."

The hall was packed with people. A collective intake of breath mingled with murmurs of approval alerted Conn to Brianna's presence at the head of the stairs. She floated along the gallery that ringed the room, glowing in her wedding splendor. His heart swelled, feeling her presence as intently as his own heartbeat. Seeing her, knowing she would soon be his wife, created an ache deep inside.

He grinned suddenly. She was now his responsibility, not his duty. No longer an outlaw, she was his bride. Perhaps some men preferred docile, acquiescing wives, but he looked forward to the fire and passion she would bring to their marriage.

She hesitated at the top of the landing. Her eyes locked with his and for a moment Conn wondered if she would descend the stairs. He splayed his arms at his side, a silent invitation, a promise of desire and keeping. She smiled and color flooded her cheeks. From the other end of the gallery, an older man appeared at her side, dressed in festive finery. He took her arm and led her down the steps.

She glided slowly across the hall between the rows of Wyndham folk and a few from Morven. Conn's eyes lingered briefly on Brianna's teal blue velvet gown, his ribbon gift twined through her curls. A sparkling band circling her brow held the delicate lace in place over her head. And nestled atop the mound of her breasts winked a splendid sapphire pendant.

At last she halted before Father Roderick, and the priest glanced from Conn to Brianna and back. He cleared his throat.

"Conn MacLaurey?" he asked. Conn nodded. With a nod, the priest placed Brianna's hand in his, and Conn stared into the happy eyes of his bride.

Chapter Twenty-eight

Conn wondered when he could tastefully and unobtrusively remove his new wife from the feast. He smiled at an elderly lady who wished him and his bride good health, and nodded at a man who raised his glass, saluting Conn's good fortune.

Bray stalked to his side as Conn perused the crowded hall. "I am glad ye made it. Ye look well enough for a man who wasted no time on the trail."

"There were a few of us who did not wish to miss your *cérémonie du marriage*. It was well done, laird." Bray motioned toward Brianna. "Ye best claim her before she collapses."

Conn followed his direction and spotted her standing in the midst of a chattering group of young women, a strained look on her face.

With a start, he realized the long day and her pregnancy likely exhausted her, and he jerked away from his indolent stance at the fireplace. Shoving his mug of ale into Bray's hands, he strode toward his wife. He made his way through the crowd, nodding absently to well-wishers. Reaching Brianna's side, he slid an arm around her waist and felt her sag against him.

"Are ye well?" he whispered as he kissed her ear.

She turned bright eyes and a tired smile on him. "Och, I am fine."

Conn gave her a tender look. "Dearling, when ye need something, dinnae deny me the opportunity to provide it." He guided her to the side, away from listening ears. "Wait a wee bit, then excuse yerself. Go up to yer room. I will be there shortly."

"I shouldnae leave the guests—"

Conn stopped her protest with a finger to her lips. "They will be here until the food and wine are gone." His attention wandered to the softness of her lips and he slowly rubbed his finger against their gentle curve. "'Tis time for us to retire."

"Och, then we can retire together. They willnae follow us up. I am no maiden, and I am already with child, though I would prefer to keep that to ourselves a bit longer."

"Ye are right, but I still think I will get Bray to stand guard at the foot of the stairs. Blushing virgin or not, 'tis still a wedding and I would rather avoid any pranks, however well-meant."

"A fine idea. I shall go now." She wound through the room, pausing to greet guests along her way. Conn watched the swing of her hips for a moment, then strode to Bray to ask his favor.

"*Oui*, I will keep the marauding horde from your doorway," he vowed, hand over his heart in jesting promise. With a nod of thanks, Conn took his leave. Ahead of him, Brianna paused at the foot of the stairs. Jamie, clearly both exhausted and over-stimulated by the excitement, threw himself at her, wrapping his arms fiercely about her waist.

"Anna!" he howled. "Dinnae leave me, Anna!" He buried his face in her skirts, sobbing into the costly velvet. Brianna pried his hands from the fabric, pushing him slightly away as she hunkered down to his height.

"Wheesht, lad!" she admonished him. "Why do ye *haiver* so?"

"Ye are leaving me again," he sobbed. "Like ye did before. Ye are leaving, and ye are never coming back!"

"Och, ye know that isnae true. Ye can visit me at Morven whenever ye wish once I am settled there."

Jamie drew back, giving his sister an accusing stare. "Ye are, too, leaving me. And I willnae let ye!" His lower lip quivered and Brianna took a deep breath.

"Jamie, Da and Auld Willie will be here. And I will leave Tam here for ye, too. Ye willnae be alone. And Una will tuck ye in at night."

"But she willnae tell me stories." He leaned backward, straining against her grip on his hands.

Conn strode to them, placing a hand on Brianna's shoulder in support. "We will be here a couple more days, lad. Then, if ye are agreeable, ye can ride with us to Morven and see where yer sister will be living. Would ye like that?"

Jamie glanced at him and snuffled, dragging the back of his wrist across his nose before he answered. "Can I really go with ye?" he asked, cautious hope on his face. Brianna gave Conn a startled look, but he smiled at Jamie and patted his head.

"I would imagine ye could do a lot of things if ye would refrain from rumpling yer sister's good clothes," he told him in a conspiratorial whisper. "The lasses dinnae like their clothes getting all mussed up."

"Anna doesnae mind." Jamie stoutly defended his sister. "She isnae like other lasses. She even likes *puddies*!"

Conn grinned. "Good. Because there are a lot of frogs at Loch Mor. Now, ye need a good night's sleep so ye can start packing yer things on the morrow." He gave the lad a nod. "Off ye go."

Jamie started to leave, then rushed back to give Brianna a quick hug. "Can she tell me a bedtime story?" he asked Conn.

Conn shook his head. "Nae, lad. Not tonight."

Jamie's lower lip slipped out in a pout. "Why not?"

Conn leaned down and whispered in the lad's ear. "She is telling *me* a story tonight."

Jamie's face registered surprise. "Truth?"

Conn nodded solemnly. Jamie appeared to give it some thought, then looked back at his sister. "Aye, then."

With that, he took himself off to bed. Brianna turned to Conn, a look of bemusement on her face. "What did ye tell the lad?"

"Seems Jamie has a new appreciation for marriage." Conn grinned. "He will learn the truth in a few years."

"And what would that be?"

"That husbands get a bedtime story *every* night."

Brianna had almost finished brushing her hair when she saw the opening of the door reflected in her mirror. Laying her brush carefully on the table, she waited as Conn walked through the door, closing it securely behind him. He crossed the room and stood behind her, filling his hands with the mass of her hair.

He leaned close, his lips teasing the edge of her ear. "I love yer hair, the way it glows like moonlight." He pulled her against him, running his hands up and down her arms. Invisible sparks arced between them where their bodies touched.

"I love the way it spills across my hands, the way it smells." He wrapped his arms around her shoulders, nuzzling the side of her neck. "And I love the way ye feel in my arms."

His hand drifted to the ribbon at her neck. Grasping it, he slowly slid the pendant up her skin, eliciting goose bumps along its trail. "How did ye get this?"

"I had given it to Gavin to be sold, but there is no place in Wyndham's village to sell such a piece and he held it until he would make a trip elsewhere for grain."

"I suppose it should bother me ye gave my gift to another man, and in some small way it does. But I understand the why of it, and I am particularly pleased he saw fit to give it back to ye. I promise ye, Wyndham willnae go hungry this winter."

Brianna slipped the pendant from her neck and laid it on the table before her. She closed her eyes and sighed, tilting her head back against his shoulder, giving in to the sensations of pleasure shooting through her. She looked into the mirror, to his storm-dark eyes, and smiled at him. "I think I may like ye," she murmured, arching an eyebrow.

He laid his lips against her cheek. "Want to find out for sure?" he challenged in a husky whisper that made her knees quiver, and made her glad she was seated.

His warm breath fanned across her skin and sent ripples of delight down her spine. She shuddered as she sucked in her breath.

"Aye."

Conn pulled her from her seat and into his arms. She wound her arms around his neck, melting into his kiss. Scooping her into his arms, he carried her to the bed and laid her on the soft coverlet. Her hands flew to unfasten his leine and he pulled back only for the instant it took him to fling the garment to the floor. He stretched out on the bed, pulling her down beside him, running his hands over the nearly transparent muslin of Brianna's under gown, past the delicate embroidery, to the hem caught beneath her legs.

Brianna wriggled until he tugged it free, leaving it loosened about her, then lay back to catch her breath. Running her hands over his shoulders and across his chest, she thrilled to the feel of his skin pulled across taut muscles. She followed his gaze as his eyes over her body, knowing she was subtly different, aware he noticed the changes. He explored the roundness of her breasts and the slight mound of her stomach with his hands, sending new tremors through her. Splaying a hand across her belly, he caressed it gently.

"Have ye felt the bairn move yet?"

Brianna shook her head. "I thought I did once, but I am certain it is still too early."

He kissed where his hand had lain, and Brianna laughed as his chin tickled her through the sheer fabric. He grinned at her. "My loving ye is funny?"

"Yer whiskers!" she replied, squealing as he rubbed his cheek vigorously across her belly. But her laughter changed with a sudden intake of breath as he ceased his play and trailed his kisses lower and lower as she arched against his touch. She reached for him to bring him closer, but he resisted.

"I am afraid of hurting the bairn. Not for all the pleasure in the world would I risk harming him."

"Ye cannae hurt the bairn," she assured him, stroking his arm. "Dinnae stop."

Conn chuckled. "Then I willnae let ye hold back, either. I promise ye will have yer pleasure. I am not so muddle-headed this time."

"Show me what I have been missing, Conn. I would be yer wife in full."

His gaze locked with hers. "Ye shall be."

He knelt beside her and gathered her hands in his. He kissed each finger, opening her hands slowly to kiss her palms. She shuddered as the tip of his tongue slid across her skin, and he looked up, a wicked smile on his face.

Sliding off the bed, he unwound his plaide, leaving his clothing in a heap on the floor. Brianna couldn't help the lift of her brow as she beheld his form.

"Ye dinnae appear so in the moonlight."

"'Twas over much too soon, dearling. This night, we have as much time as we wish."

Her insides tightened at his bold promise and she pushed to a sitting position, motioning for him to turn. She lost sight of his cocky smile as he faced away, but she was content to admire the strong line of his back and buttocks. For a moment.

With a laugh, Conn faced her again, arms folded across his chest, feet planted a foot or so apart. "Yer turn."

Nerves fluttered down her arms as Brianna accepted his challenge. Running her fingertips across the tops of her breasts, she fingered the tie at her neck for a moment before grasping the loose end. She pulled it slowly downward, exposing her breasts inch by tantalizing inch. His eyes flashed and Brianna reached for the hem of her shift, pooled about her on the bed.

With a twist, she yanked the fabric over her head and it floated to floor without so much as a whisper of sound. Her skin prickled and she shivered.

"Cold?" His voice rasped.

"Titillated." She smiled.

Conn groaned. "I have married an educated woman."

"Ye know I am not a simpering virgin."

He sank onto the bed beside her, running his eyes hungrily over her before meeting her gaze. "Ye are a bold young woman who is not afraid to state her mind, and who is used to giving orders." One side of his mouth quirked upward. "I will do whatever ye bid me this night."

"I dinnae have enough experience to command yer performance."

His grin widened. "By the end of the night, ye will."

Brianna felt Conn's breath stir the hair at her neck. "Wake up, dearling," he whispered in her ear. She sighed and snuggled her backside closer against him, feeling her heart rate jolt at the memory of her pleasure at his hands. She moaned softly. He jostled her and she opened her eyes. Pale light streaked through the window, and the manor house was silent.

"Shh. Dinnae move."

"I dinnae think I can." She pulled a leg free from beneath his and stretched slowly, feeling her muscles' light protest.

Conn chuckled in her ear. "We have company, my love."

Startled, she glanced quickly about the room and spied a small bundle in the chair beside the fireplace across from their bed. She started to sit up, but Conn's hand stopped her even as she remembered she was naked beneath the bedding.

"'Tis Jamie, and he is asleep," he murmured. "Tam is curled beneath the chair."

"How long do ye think he has been there?" she whispered back, a bit shocked to think Jamie had wandered in sometime during the night. Her cheeks warmed.

Conn's soft laugh rumbled in his chest. "Not long, I dinnae think. He wasnae there when I got up an hour or so ago, and ye have been sleeping since." He pulled the edge of the bed clothes closer around her neck. He slipped from far side of the bed and wrapped his kilt about his waist. Crossing to the chair, he hunkered down beside it.

"Jamie?"

Tam crept from beneath the chair and licked Conn's arm. He ruffled the dog's ears.

The lad stirred and rubbed his eyes sleepily. "Conn?"

"Wheesht, lad, dinnae wake yer sister."

Jamie nodded solemnly.

"What are ye doing in here?"

Jamie glanced over the arm of the chair, and Brianna saw the bundle lying on the floor. "I packed so I can go with ye and Anna."

Conn smiled. "That is a good idea. When it is morning, I bet she will make sure ye have everything ye need. Right now, ye need to hie yerself back to yer own bed and get all the sleep ye can. Ye need to be ready for our trip in a couple of days. Can ye do that?"

Jamie's brow furrowed. "Are ye sure I have to go back to bed?"

Conn merely tilted his head at Jamie. Brianna smothered a laugh. She knew Jamie needed to be reassured, but the sooner Jamie learned to trust Conn, the quicker they would become friends, and a dose of authority now would certainly help, too.

"Ye willnae leave me, will ye?" Jamie asked.

"Nae, lad. I dinnae lie to ye. Ye are welcome to come with us for a visit in a couple of days."

Jamie sighed his reluctant acceptance and wriggled out of the chair, stopping to pick up his bag. With a heavy yawn, he wandered from the room, dragging his belongings behind him as Tam dogged his heels.

"Thank ye," Brianna whispered.

"Hmm?" Conn rose and shut the door firmly, testing the latch.

"He is so happy to be going with me. I know he can be a handful."

Conn returned to the bed. "We will let Gillis take care of him from time to time. Dinnae *fash* yerself."

"Still, I wanted to let ye know how much I appreciate ye letting him come with us for a bit."

The kilt slipped to the floor around Conn's feet. "How much?" He grinned.

Heat skittered through her as she whisked the bedding back in invitation. "Let me show ye."

Chapter Twenty-nine

The hall, lit only by candles and a fire in the hearth, was a cozy haven against the rain dimming the late afternoon sky. Brianna and Conn lingered over a late meal amid a handful of guests who had apparently imbibed more than they should have the night before.

"I imagine the rain drumming on the roof is giving that one a pounding headache," Brianna murmured with a brief nod to a man several seats away, head in his hands.

"Aye. But that willnae stop him from licking the bottom of his glass the next time."

Brianna stroked the back of Conn's hand. "Do ye think we should leave tomorrow or the day after?"

He covered her hand with his. "It may take longer to pack than ye think."

"Why?"

Rising to his feet, he pulled her against him, and her heart quickened to feel his response to her. "Because I believe I am about to hinder the process."

Passion flooded her, and she cast a quick glance around the room from the corner of her eyes. "Indeed? Mayhap we could discuss this a bit more privately?"

Keeping one hand laced with hers, he led her up the stairs. Inside the bed-chamber, Brianna backed him against the door, smothering his laughter with a heated kiss, her hands tugging his leine from his belt.

She ran her palms up the length of his torso, fingers sliding through the hair on his chest and flicking across his tight nipples. With a sound that was half-groan, half-snarl, he snatched at her skirts, pulling them around her waist. Twisting about, he lifted her in his arms and pinned her against the wall. He quickly rucked his kilt upward and pressed against her.

"Shall I ask yer advice on this?" he teased. "I believe I like my opinionated wife."

Brianna grabbed his ears and gave them a mock twist. "Shut up, Conn." She wrapped her legs about his waist and pulled him to her with a quick jerk. He pounded into her, passion surging beyond her control. Within moments, she gasped, her head hard against the wall as she arched against him. Conn buried his head between her breasts, his breath coming hard and fast. Waves of pleasure spiraled through her, and Conn leaned gently into her, pinning her in place.

She ran a languid hand through his hair. "Ye can put me down now."

Conn laughed. "Aye, but I like this too much to move." With a groan, he let her slide to the floor, then rested against her once again. "Shall we move to the bed, milady, for a wee snooze? Ye drained me of all my manly intentions before we scarce crossed the threshold."

"A nap sounds good, as long as I am with ye."

Conn glanced down. "It seems we are still in disarray."

For the first time, the cool air against her bare legs, tangled with his, registered, and heat stole up her neck, shocked at what he provoked in her.

A frantic pounding at the door interrupted them, and she hastily shoved her skirts down.

"Who could possibly think to intrude?" Conn muttered as he straightened his kilt. With a quick glance at her, he opened the door. Una burst in, her hands fluttering high in the air.

"Brianna, come quickly!"

"What is wrong, Una?"

The woman gave her an agonized look. "'Tis Jamie. He has—"

Flinging a brief glance of apology at Conn, Brianna spun the other woman around, shoving her out the door. They flew down the hallway to Jamie's room, and Brianna came to a startled halt just inside his door. Cook's daughter knelt beside the lad, who was almost completely covered in mud. His teeth chattered and he twitched violently as the lass wiped the mud off him with a piece of rough cloth.

"Get him into a warm bath, Kirsten." Brianna stepped quickly to Jamie's side, grabbed a towel, and used it to rub some warmth into his thin arms.

"I am waiting for hot water, milady." Kirsten pulled Jamie's breeches off and helped wrap him in a blanket warm from the hearth.

Brianna cast a worried look at Una. "See where the water is."

With a nod, Una hurried from the room. Brianna turned back to Jamie, who snuffled and rubbed his eyes. "How did ye get so muddy, hmm?" She pulled the corner of the blanket over the top of his head for added warmth.

"I had to say good-bye to my friends," Jamie sobbed, clearly upset.

"What happened, dearling?"

Jamie kicked at the pile of clothing at his feet. "It wasnae raining when I left. And when I ran home—like the wind," he assured her, "I took the short cut and tripped and fell down the bank to the burn and landed in the marsh." His voice ended on a mournful note.

With gritted teeth, Brianna decided to address his adventure alone—to the burn, nonetheless—at another time. "How long were ye outside?"

Jamie snuffled and dragged a filthy hand across his face. Kirstin glanced up.

"He took the dog and left just after the morning meal. The dog came back all in a fit, covered in mud himself." Kirsten nodded toward the corner of the room. "He must have pulled Jamie out, then raced to the hall for help getting him home, poor lad."

Wrapped in a tight ball, mud caked in his long coat, Tam shivered against the hearth. Brianna's heart plummeted to think of Jamie's fate had the dog not been with him.

Una bustled through the door, carrying a bucket of hot water. Two servants followed, each carrying two buckets, which they poured into the tub already wrestled into the center of the room. Brianna tested the water and nodded approvingly. She stripped the blanket from Jamie's shaking body and reached to lift him into the wooden tub. Conn's hands took the burden from her and she gave him a grateful nod. She rose and gathered Tam in her arms and dumped him into the tub as well.

Jamie gasped in surprise then giggled as Tam floundered in the water. Apparently deciding he appreciated the warmth, the dog found his footing and stood patiently as Brianna and Kirsten rinsed the mud away.

Soon, the pair was scrubbed clean, and Jamie's shrieks of delight as Tam pranced about in the water filled the air. Fresh water replaced the muddy, and both Jamie and Tam were given a final rinse. Tam was sent to his blanket by the hearth, Jamie directly to his bed.

"I dinnae want to go to bed," he wailed tiredly. His protest ended in a hiccup as he grudgingly followed Brianna. Conn tossed him onto the bed and Brianna piled the blankets atop his small body. Sitting beside him, she ran her fingers through his red-gold hair.

"Tell me a story," Jamie whispered, his eyes drooping.

"Do ye remember the story about the selkies who danced in the moonlight?"

"Uh huh," Jamie replied, the sound scarcely louder than a sigh.

Brianna smiled fondly, blinking back tears as she tried not to think of how easily he could become ill. "Well," she said, her voice calm and soothing, "the selkies came out of the sea and shed their seal skins, dancing on the land in the moonlight…"

Before she finished the tale, Jamie was asleep. Conn pulled her from the bed where she huddled, spoon-like, with Jamie tucked close against her.

"Let Una stay with him while he sleeps." He wrapped his arms around her, cradling her head against his shoulder.

"He gets ill so easily." She fought back tears. "We should know how bad this is by morning."

Jamie fretted at being restricted to his bed, though Brianna found no signs of fever. He ate a few bites mid-morning, but refused more, demanding to be let out. She finally let him go, wringing a firm promise from him to stay at the hall unless he was with Rabbie or Duncan.

"Do ye think he will be strong enough to travel tomorrow?" Conn asked her as they strolled across the grounds.

Brianna leaned against a tree with a shrug. "I believe another day or two will see him completely recovered. He will do better to get a bit of rest before all the excitement of travel and a new place." She gave Conn a wry smile. "Ye know we dinnae dare leave him here."

Conn laughed. "The lad would follow us on foot. I believe stubbornness runs in this family."

Brianna pushed away from the tree, pinching back an answering grin. "Do ye say I am stubborn?"

"Dearling, ye are willful, confident, determined," he avowed. "I am astounded every day by yer resolve."

She tossed her head. "Would ye like me if I were weak-minded?"

"Are ye fishing for compliments?" His eyebrows lifted in query.

"Do I have to?" she challenged.

"Mayhap we should continue this discussion of yer boldness inside. Behind a closed door would be my choice."

Brianna draped her arms across his shoulders and leaned forward to nibble an ear. "Bold? I thought ye said I was stubborn."

Conn shivered. "Ye are both today." He slid his hands around her to cup her bottom, pulling her hard against him. "I like it."

"Then we best discuss yer likes and dislikes further, aye?" With a tug on his arm, she pulled him toward the hall and up the stairs. Una's appearance at the head of the steps struck like a splash of frigid water as Brianna noted the concern in the woman's eyes.

"How is Jamie?"

"He has started coughing. I put him to bed. He is calling for ye."

Brianna bolted for Jamie's chamber, Conn and Una on her heels. Kirsten sat on the edge of the bed, wiping Jamie's forehead with a damp rag as she spoke soothingly to him. She stood, allowing Brianna in her place. Laying a hand on Jamie's forehead, Brianna slid her palm down his cheeks, feeling the heat burn against her skin.

"He needs medicine."

"Ye have more knowledge of the herbs than I." Una handed Brianna a key from the bundle at her belt.

Clutching the slender piece of metal in her fist, Brianna hurried to the small room beyond the kitchen where the herbs and spices were stored. She inhaled the familiar fragrance in the cool, dry air, recounting the hours spent reciting the herb lore with her mother.

I thank ye, Ma, for yer patience with me. May it help cure wee Jamie. Working quickly from the depths of her memory, she measured and blended, adding the precious honey to treat his fever and cough and soothe his irritated throat. She poured the mixture into a mug and hurried back upstairs.

Jamie pushed Una's hands away restlessly. Conn sat on Jamie's bed, his back against the headboard, cradling the lad in his arms as Una wiped his feverish body.

Brianna gave Conn a look of gratitude, warmed to her toes to see him caring for her brother. Handing the mug to Una, she sat beside Conn and stroked Jamie's pale face.

"Jamie, I want ye to take this for me. It has plenty of honey in it, and I promise ye will like it."

Jamie tossed his head, but Conn gently held him as Brianna took the mug and dribbled some of the liquid between Jamie's lips. He whimpered and frowned and tried to slide from Conn's grip, but Conn held him until Brianna coaxed the last of the herbal mixture down his throat. Laying the lad back on the bed, he tucked the blankets around him.

"Will he sleep now?"

Brianna shook her head. "The draught was for his cough and fever. His tiredness will make him sleep. I need to be with him. I cannae leave him now."

Conn stroked her cheek. "I understand. Yer kind heart is one of the reasons I love ye." He took her hand and led her to the large chair next to the bed. Sitting, he pulled her into his lap, covering her with a light blanket tossed over the chair's arm. He wrapped his arms about her.

Brianna snuggled against him, trailing a finger down his arm. "Ye love me?"

"Aye. But dinnae let it go to yer head. It comes as easy to me as breathing."

A soft laugh escaped her. "I am never quite sure what ye will say next."

"How about, do ye love me?"

"It is rather astonishing, but, aye, I love ye."

"I thought liking me was a bit of a stretch," he reminded her.

"Loving ye will last longer."

He placed a kiss on her neck. "Can ye see Jamie from here?"

Brianna nodded.

"Good. Then we will watch him together."

Brianna collected the remains of Jamie's breakfast and handed them to Kirsten. Jamie's laughter, while not as robust as normal, relieved her as she watched him and Conn toss a rag ball for Tam to chase. She would gladly forgive the chaos in the room to see the lad return to health.

"I know ye need to get back to Morven," she said to Conn as he flipped the ball to Jamie and joined her on the bench under the window. "'Tis three days past time ye thought to leave and 'twill be a few days more before Jamie is able to travel. Besides, I need a day or two to see to my own packing."

"Are ye trying to get rid of me?" he teased, pulling her to him as he dropped a kiss on her ear. She turned her face to him, landing the next kiss on her lips.

"Never. But ye have been here far longer than ye planned, and I know there is much to do at Morven."

Leaving Jamie in Kirsten's care, she linked an arm through Conn's. They strolled downstairs and out into the misty sunlight. Fog rolled across the glen, sparkling like diamonds among the autumn leaves. "Morven needs ye. I can follow with Jamie in a few days."

Conn considered her words, his lips pulled to one side. "I dinnae like leaving ye here."

"I will miss ye terribly, but 'twill only be a couple of days."

"I will send an escort for ye from Morven."

"Och, I believe Auld Willie can handle that. Since we are now free of Malcolm and his ilk, only a small escort is needed. 'Tis not so far to Morven."

"We never discovered who betrayed ye to the sheriff." Conn frowned.

"But nothing has happened since Malcolm died," Brianna pointed out. "Mayhap 'twas Malcolm all along."

His eyes clouded, still troubled, but he gave her a hug. "Aye. Ye are likely right. He was a very ambitious man. Mayhap he desired this beautiful gem of land as well as Morven."

"I know this is my home, and I am partial, but it is a verra beautiful place."

Conn placed his hands on her shoulders and gently turned her to face him. "And this," he said, nodding emphatically to her, "is the most beautiful thing in it. Ye are precious to me."

A shiver danced up Brianna's spine. "We will be fine, Conn. I promise."

Chapter Thirty

Brianna waved goodbye to Conn as he mounted his stallion. Auld Willie stood at her side, hands clasped behind his back.

"'Pon my soul," he vowed. "I will take good care of them."

Conn favored him an intent look. "I hold ye to yer word." Accepting another kiss from Brianna, he reined Embarr down the trail at a hard gallop.

"Thank ye, Auld Willie. I have much to do. I will leave the matter of an escort to ye."

She picked up her skirts and hurried inside, her mind churning with a list of items to pack. Una met her in the hallway, directing two lads with wooden chests hoisted on their shoulders.

"Thank ye, Una. I will need help if I am to be packed to leave in two days."

"Leave the heavy work to the lads. Ye dinnae need to be lifting these chests in yer condition."

Startled, Brianna glanced about, but none seemed to have overheard Una's words. Taking the older woman by the arm, she pulled her aside. "What do ye mean?"

Una pursed her lips. "Dinnae forget I am the one who measured ye for yer wedding gown. And the one who noticed ye havenae had yer courses in more than three months."

Brianna felt heat flood her cheeks. "Ye dinnae say anything."

"Nae, lass. What is there to say? Only that ye need to start taking care of yerself." She shooed Brianna toward the steps. "First, ye must eat properly, and then a nap is in order. Ye need yer strength, and ye have missed too many meals of late."

Brianna gave Una a quick hug. "Thank ye for taking such good care of me and Jamie all these years."

Una patted Brianna's cheek fondly. "Ye are a credit to yer ma, lass. Dinnae let anyone tell ye different."

"Wheesht, Jamie!" Brianna muttered crossly. "Ye arenae coming to live at Morven, only visit a few days. Ye cannae take all of this with ye."

She pointed to the toys Jamie dumped beside the wooden chest. Carved animals, wooden swords, and even a hoop from a barrel lay scattered around. "Ye may take two."

Jamie hunched his shoulders in stubborn protest. Brianna gave an exasperated sigh.

"What if ye left something behind at Morven? Or if something was broken during the travel?"

Jamie's hand clenched around the fragile, carved windmill, and his glance lingered on the wooden hobby horse. "Can I take my horse and a ball?"

Relieved, Brianna nodded permission and Jamie gathered the rest, making several trips to tote them all back to his room.

"I dinnae know the lad had so many toys," she groused to Una. "He is entirely too spoiled." She ran her fingers through the contents of the chest. "Put a couple of his shirts in here and an extra pair of trews. Then have a lad carry all this to the cart. I would like them to leave soon so they dinnae have to finish their journey in the dark."

"Ye will leave in the morning?"

"Aye. Ewan will drive the cart with my things to Morven and let Conn know Jamie and I will be there tomorrow."

Una touched Brianna's arm. "Be careful, lass. Ye will take care of yerself and send word about the bairn, aye?"

Brianna felt tears prick her eyes. "I will. I want ye with me when the time comes. Will ye help birth the bairn?"

"Of course I will. Let me know when yer time draws close."

Jamie galloped into the room, astride the pole of his hobby horse, shouting the Douglas war cry. Tam skittered behind him, adding his barking to the din. Brianna covered her ears as Jamie circled the room once, then darted out the door, Tam's toenails sliding on the wood floor as he made the turn in Jamie's wake.

"He certainly is better! But it will take ye, Da, Gavin and Auld Willie to manage him." She grabbed the box at her feet. "Una, latch this chest while I push down on the lid. If we leave it open, he will try to stuff something else into it."

Two lads lifted the chest and carried it to the waiting conveyance. It was already loaded with two similar boxes, and Brianna surveyed the lot, mentally tallying their contents to be sure she left nothing behind.

Ewan stepped onto the cart. "We will get this to Morven and let the laird know ye will be there tomorrow. Ye have an escort, aye?"

"Auld Willie is handling the details." She waved off Ewan's concern. "'Tis only a few hours' travel. My uncle's advice served us well when we fought against the reivers, and his knowledge of the land is unquestionable. I trust him to get us there safely."

Jamie bounded down the steps and flung himself against the loaded wagon.

"I want to ride with Ewan!" He struggled to find a hold on the wheel. Tam bounded over, placing his front feet on the wheel as he peered into the cart.

"Jamie, ye will ride with me tomorrow," Brianna reminded him, grasping Tam's collar and dragging him back.

"Nae! I want to go with Ewan!" His feet found purchase and he hoisted himself onto the seat.

Ewan gave the lad a ferocious scowl and grabbed the collar of his shirt. "Ye will do as yer sister says and be quick about it," he growled. He nudged him onto the ground. Jamie whirled, meeting Ewan's scowl with one of his own. The two locked stares, and after a moment, Jamie dropped his gaze. Ewan grunted.

"Now apologize, lad."

Jamie hung his head. "I am sorry."

"For?" Ewan prompted him.

"For not doing what ye told me." He sighed and turned pleading eyes on Brianna. She nodded, biting her lip to keep back a smile at his obvious discomfort. Ewan gave her a quick grin.

"I would watch the lad if I were ye. I heard the brownies in the woods were looking for troublesome lads this night."

Brianna managed another nod. She didn't like the idea of threatening the lad with tales of faeries and such, but Ewan evidently struck a chord, for Jamie took a step backward and grabbed her hand, his manner contrite. Tam plopped his furry rump on the ground beside him and licked his free hand.

They waved as Ewan and Duncan left, wooden wheels creaking softly down the road. As they turned toward Morven, Jamie tugged at Brianna.

"Can I sleep with ye tonight?"

Brianna regarded him askance. He shifted from one foot to another.

"Mayhap. But only if ye stay out of trouble."

Jamie nodded vigorously and darted inside the hall.

"How much longer 'til we get there? Why are we going so slow? I know my pony can go faster than this. When can I have a big horse like ye?"

Brianna's head whirled with Jamie's questions as he rapid-fired them at her in his boisterous way. Not sure which question to answer first, she merely listened as he rattled on, not pausing long enough for her to say a word.

Behind her, Auld Willie and Rabbie sat their horses, lagging behind, she suspicioned, to keep from being part of Jamie's constant comments, questions and complaints.

She still struggled with Auld Willie's decision to travel with only himself and Rabbie for an escort. *There is no problem between Morven and Wyndham now Malcolm is gone*, he'd told her as they prepared to leave. *The men are busy preparing stabling for the cattle against reivers, and winter will be here soon.* In fact, the cold air sported snowflakes to support his claim. It would have been little effort to call up a few more riders, but Auld Willie had scowled as she started to question his logic, and she wavered between loyalty to her uncle and his seeming lack of concern for their safety.

She glanced at the trees, their partly denuded branches thick overhead. *I dinnae like this. We have passed no others on the road, and I am jumpy. 'Twould be better had I insisted on a larger escort.* With a mental shrug, she urged her horse to a faster pace. *We are more than halfway to Morven. Mayhap I worry for naught.*

Auld Willie rode up beside her. "'Tis time for a break," he announced.

"I need to piss!" Jamie declared.

Brianna reined Maude to a stop and dismounted. Tying her reins loosely so Maude could graze, she watched Rabbie help Jamie with his pony as she stretched the soreness from her back. Auld Willie offered Jamie a sip of water from his leather flask.

He took a long pull and handed it to Brianna. "I want to eat, now."

"Wheesht, lad. We will be in Morven in a couple of hours." Auld Willie tossed him an oatcake. "This will get ye by 'til then."

Brianna glanced about nervously. A prickly sensation traveled up and down her spine. "Come. Let us be away."

"I wanted to bring Tam," Jamie groused as Rabbie shoved him onto his pony.

Brianna mounted her horse. "The herdsman wanted time with him. I know ye like him, but he was bred to work cattle. He will be there when ye get home."

"Conn would have let him come with me."

"Conn is Laird MacLaurey to ye, lad. And he understands dogs need guidance sometimes just as much as wee lads."

"Do ye think Conn will let me have a new horse?" Jamie kicked his pony faster to keep up with Maude's longer stride.

Brianna sighed. "Ye need to ask Da about a new horse, not Conn. Ye arenae Conn's responsibility."

"But he likes me. Mayhap he will let me have a new horse."

Brianna's eyes met Rabbie's over Jamie's head. Jamie launched into a list of virtues for his new horse.

"He will be fast and outrun yer horses, and tall as the trees—as tall as the sky! And I want him to be white as the snow with a black mane and tail."

"He does pass the time, aye?" Rabbie chuckled as Jamie's voice droned on.

"Rabbie!" Auld Willie's voice rapped over Jamie's babble. "I left one of the bags along the trail where we stopped. Ride back and fetch it for me."

Rabbie shrugged and reined his horse back down the trail. He quickly disappeared around a bend, his jaunty whistle fading on the breeze. Brianna pulled her arisaid closer against the light swirl of snowflakes and urged Maude to a faster pace.

Jamie bounced beside her, his stout pony trotting to keep up. "Slow down, Anna!"

A sharp, muttered expletive from Auld Willie caused Brianna

to swivel in her saddle. Auld Willie gave her a sheepish look.

"I dinnae mean to say that out loud. I need a short privacy stop. I feel my years these days—cannae go long between privies." He motioned them on. "I will only be a moment or two."

Brianna's unease grew by the minute. Leaving the protection of the two men sent warning bells ringing in her head.

"I want to go back, Anna," Jamie whined, pulling his pony to a halt.

The need for protection warred with her ability to deal with Jamie's increasing tiredness. Her own curse stifled beneath her breath, she gave Jamie a bright smile.

"Let us race to the big rock and give Auld Willie a moment to himself."

With a whooping cry, Jamie leaned low over his pony's neck and shook his reins. Grabbing the bit, the pony darted forward, ears flat against his skull. Jumping to the pony's challenge, Maude joined the race. Brianna quickly adjusted her seat and steadied the mare, making sure Jamie won by a short nose.

Jamie plumped back into the saddle, shouting in triumph as he waved his hands in the air. His pony gave a quick buck, and Jamie slipped to the side, landing in the dust of the trail.

"Oh!" he exclaimed in surprise. Brianna slid from Maude's back and hurried to his side. She laughed at the disgusted look on his face, assured only his pride was injured. She helped him to his feet, brushing away the dirt and leaves clinging to his clothing.

"My pony!" he shouted, pointing after the animal rapidly disappearing down the trail.

"Stay here!" Brianna scrambled after the fat pony. He dodged this way and that, and it took her several moments to finally outsmart the four-legged menace. Not sure whether to laugh or insist on roasting the troublesome pony over a fire, she led him back to the large rock where she'd left Jamie. She glanced around in bewilderment. He was nowhere to be seen.

"Jamie?" she called, turning in a full circle, trying to catch a glimpse of his red-gold hair. "Jamie, if ye think this is a game, I assure ye 'tis not!"

Exasperated, she propped her fists at her waist. "Jamie Douglas. Auld Willie will be here in a moment and we need to get going again." Fear slid cold fingers down her spine. "Jamie? Where are ye?"

Chapter Thirty-one

Brianna searched the shadows and hidden areas among the trees. A ray of sunlight split the gloom, glinting off red-gold hair. She started forward, the rebuke dying on her lips as she saw the lad's wide eyes and the strong arm lying firmly across his neck. Jamie and his captor took one step forward from the shadows.

"Auld Willie?" A wave of dizziness swept over her, and a cold sweat broke out over her body.

"Wheesht, lass. Dinnae fash yerself. It happens so fast. Ye will scarce be aware." He sighed tiredly. "'Tis the waiting that is the worst."

"What are ye doing?"

"It has been harder than I thought to make things right."

"What things, Uncle? What isnae right?"

"'Twas not yer da's fault he was born first. But Wyndham should have been mine." He stepped closer and Brianna noted the strained look of his face, the way his eyes darted from one place to another, unable to rest, unable to find peace. Madness.

"Wyndham has always been yer home," she protested gently, shoving the rising panic deep inside her.

"The running of it should have been mine! Yer da was never the leader I would have been." He waved a hand about wildly in agitation. "For the past five years he has done naught but sit and stare at the fire in a drunken stupor, seeing naught but a dead wife!"

"He was a good leader. He will be again."

"Nae, lass. His time is over. With ye and Jamie out of the way, Wyndham will come to me as it should."

"And then what, Uncle?" Brianna demanded, anger overtaking her fear. "Who will it fall to after ye are gone?"

Auld Willie looked around the glen, bewilderment on his face. "Geordie…"

"Geordie is dead, Uncle." Brianna took a cautious step toward the old man. "He is dead and ye never even acknowledged him as yer son."

She pushed him, nudged him one step closer to madness. *Unleash yer anger on me, auld man. Let Jamie go.*

Auld Willie's face darkened. "Ye dinnae know what ye say, lass," he snarled. "His mother tried to play me false, but I dinnae fall for it."

"So, he wasnae yer son? He was no blood kin of yers?"

His mood changed abruptly. "Aye. He was my son." His voice fell softly, finally admitting aloud what he had lost. He let Jamie slip from his grasp and turned away. Brianna motioned wildly for Jamie to run, but he stared at her in shock, rooted to the ground.

Please run, Jamie! She took a step forward, shooing Jamie into the woods with her hands, and he leapt as though sprung from a trap and darted behind a tree, out of harm's way.

Breathing a sigh of relief, she faced her uncle.

"Auld Willie?"

He turned his sorrowing gaze to her. "Ye were supposed to be easy to get rid of. I dinnae want to do it myself. Ye have always been special to me. But we couldnae let Wyndham go as yer dowry."

"Wyndham is Jamie's, Uncle."

"Yer brother is sickly. Ye would have inherited Wyndham. We couldnae risk it."

"Who is *we*?"

"I only wanted Wyndham. Malcolm wanted Morven. But Conn came home, and the two of ye were to wed. We couldnae let that happen. With ye both gone, we would have had what we wanted."

"Wyndham is Jamie's inheritance!"

"Not if he is dead!"

The vehemence in Auld Willie's voice stunned Brianna, and she reeled from the hatred spewing forth. He advanced on her, words pouring from his lips amid the spittle of rage. "Because of Jamie, I had nothing to offer my own son!"

He lunged at her, and her feet failed her. She scarcely cleared one step before he grabbed her, knocking her to the ground. She rolled awkwardly, fighting him as they locked together, her strength no match for his. He rolled atop her, her arms beneath his knees as he pinned her to the ground. His breath wheezed in his chest, his weight numbing her arms.

"Ye were always a stubborn lass." He pulled a dagger from its sheath at his waist and held it at her throat. "'Tis time to end this."

A ferocious growl rolled like thunder across the small glen. Leaves rustled in a tempest as Tam launched himself at Auld Willie, a length of broken tether dangling from his collar. Brianna twisted to the side as the force of the dog's attack struck Auld Willie on the side. He cried out, grabbing at her for balance, and the blade of the dagger bit into her shoulder. He fell heavily to the ground beside her and she rolled away, blotting out the searing pain as the dagger jolted from the wound, blood trailing hot down her arm. She scrambled to her feet amid a swirl of skirts and an angry dog who danced between her and Auld Willie, barking furiously.

Auld Willie ignored Tam and reached for her, tearing at her gown as he dragged her back to him. Her feet slipped on the slick, damp leaves and she landed hard. Rolling to her back, she clawed at her uncle's face. Tam landed with a roar on Auld Willie's back, and he gave a shout, reaching behind him to ward off the dog's attack. Brianna shoved him aside, hands fumbling in the leaves for the fallen dagger.

Conn drew his horse to a halt. Beside him, Gillis gasped.

"*Mon Dieu!*" Bray exclaimed.

Jamie appeared in the path before them, struggling for breath. He fell to his knees, his hands clasping his stomach as he sobbed incoherently.

Conn leapt to the ground, covering the distance between them in three long strides. He grabbed Jamie and shook him.

"Where is yer sister, Jamie?" Images of every imaginable horror snaked through his mind and his voice rasped harsh with worry.

Jamie hiccupped and wriggled in Conn's grip, pointing down the trail. "She is back there. I was supposed to hide, but I ran away."

Realizing he frightened the lad, Conn loosened his grasp. "Ye are a brave lad, Jamie. Is she hurt?"

"Auld Willie has her!"

"What do ye mean?"

"He wants to give Wyndham to Geordie—but Geordie is dead!"

Conn glanced over his shoulder to Bray, who had dismounted and stood behind him, listening to Jamie's tale. "Does this mean anything to ye?"

Bray frowned. "There is a rumor Geordie was his *fils illégitime*. It is possible he is the one who gave Brianna over to the sheriff. His son's death could have pushed him into madness."

Conn turned back to Jamie. "Stay with Gillis." He rose quickly and mounted his horse. Embarr tossed his head and launched himself down the trail, Bray following close behind.

They reined their horses to a sliding halt next to Maude, Conn's feet on the ground before Embarr stopped moving. He hurried forward a few steps, searching the road and immediate area for signs of Brianna or Auld Willie. Furious barking sent him racing toward the sound, and he slid down a small embankment, hands flung to the side for balance.

He stumbled to a halt. Auld Willie stood over Brianna, his hands covered in blood. Tam fought frantically against his tether caught in the fork of a slender sapling. The long blade of a sword blinked in Auld Willie's hands, the tip poised over Brianna's chest. She twisted to avoid the blow as the blade plunged downward. A spark of light flashed in her hands and Auld Willie stiffened, his arms losing their purpose as his hands loosened, releasing the sword.

He fell to the ground, staring up at the brown and gold canopied sky as snowflakes settled onto his sightless eyes. Brianna lay in the leaves beside him, her breathing harsh. Conn knelt beside her, pulling her into his arms. She cried out and he saw tears spring from her eyes.

"Are ye wounded?" He released her enough to run his palms over her, drawing a quick breath at the large blood-stain over her chest. Laying her carefully back onto the ground, he slipped his plaide from his shoulders, covering her for warmth.

"She has been hurt," Conn murmured to Bray as he slid through the leaves to his side. "Check the auld man. I believe she pierced his black heart, but make sure, aye?"

He stripped off his shirt and ripped it into strips, ignoring the icy sting as snowflakes lit on his skin. Pressing a pad of folded cloth to the wound in Brianna's shoulder, he wrapped a long piece around her chest and arm, holding it in place. Satisfied with the bandage, he lifted her into his arms.

"She has fainted?" Bray asked. Tam, released from his tether, nuzzled Brianna anxiously.

"Not..." Her voice was a soft sigh against Conn's chest.

"She has lost blood," Conn replied, his words clipped, tight with fear. "I must get her to Morven!"

Bray helped him to the top of the embankment, and Conn handed Brianna to him only long enough to mount Embarr. He settled her tight against him and spurred the horse to top speed, leaving the others to follow, praying as Brianna's body went slack in his arms.

Brianna opened her eyes, blinking against the flickering light, and bit her lip against the pain of consciousness. The warm caress of a hand on her cheek soothed her, and she leaned into the comfort.

"Easy, dearling."

She turned her focus to the face hovering above hers, storm-dark eyes the only detail she could determine in her hazy vision. Sighing as she recognized Conn's visage, she closed her eyes again.

"Brianna?"

She responded by lifting her eyebrows, but other movement was beyond her, the ache in her body dragging her into relentless darkness. The reprieve of painless sleep coaxed her into its grasp.

The next time she woke, both her vision and memory returned with agonizing clarity. *I left Wyndham...* With a moan, she tried to force the rest of the memory away.

"Brianna? Are ye in pain?"

Tears flowed from the corners of her eyes as she shook her head. "Nae. Not so much."

"Can ye tell me what happened?"

"I dinnae want to remember." *But I do. The man who plotted with us to get our cattle back, the uncle I trusted with my life, betrayed me to the sheriff. Auld Willie tried to kill me and Jamie.*

She clenched a fist, the memory of the dagger's jeweled hilt burning the palm of her hand. She'd found it beneath a layer of leaves and known instantly what it was. And knew just as certainly Auld Willie was dead.

Her head pounded, and she could no longer hold her grief inside. Conn's arms came about her and she sobbed against his chest. Finally, drained, she took a deep, shuddering breath. He smoothed a strand of hair from her cheek.

"How do ye feel?"

"I hurt."

"Yer shoulder was a wee bit of a mess, but it is healing. Ye came down with a fever and have been sick for nearly a sennight. But ye have been fever-free for a couple of days now. I am glad to see ye awake."

"What are ye not telling me?"

"Ye are fine. Ye just need rest."

She stiffened. "Where is Jamie?"

Conn's low chuckle partially reassured her. "He is running about with Gillis and that braw dog of yers, driving the lad to distraction with a hundred questions a day. Dinnae worry about him."

"Rabbie?"

"Bray found him addled from a clout to the head. He needed a few stitches and a bit of rest, but he will be fine."

"What else?" She felt herself tiring.

"Nothing to *fash* yerself over. Get some rest."

Her throat went dry. "The bairn?"

Conn shook his head. "I dinnae know, dearling. Ye have been bleeding, but ye havenae lost the bairn—yet."

Her breath came in hiccups. Conn tightened his arms about her. "Ye will stay in bed until ye and the bairn are healthy again," he told her. "Ye have no idea what happened to my heart when I found Jamie in the middle of the road, too winded to speak. He gave me a garbled story about Auld Willie, and when I found ye, I felt my life was about to be over."

He gently stroked her back as her shudders eased. "Ye had lost so much blood, but ye saved yerself. I have never been so helpless in my life."

"Hold me."

Conn stretched out beside her on the bed and held her against his heart. "*Coorie doon*, dearling. Snuggle down and rest. Ye are safe with me."

Epilogue

April 1387, Corfin Castle, Morven

The cry of a newborn echoed loudly in the silence of the great hall. Conn bolted from his chair and took the stairs two at a time, his nerves stretched to the breaking point. Behind him, murmurs sifted from the lips of those who'd shared his long wait. Brianna had been in labor for more than a day, and he grew frantic with worry.

Bursting through the doorway of the laird's bedchamber, ignoring Una's glare, he strode to the edge of the bed. His eyes searched Brianna's face before allowing his gaze to settle on the bundle in her arms.

"'Tis a lad," she told him drowsily, the weariness in her voice tearing at his heart. "I thought we should name him Ian, after yer da."

A huge grin split his face as he settled beside her on the bed, peering over the tiny bundle who'd caused such an uproar in their lives. Young Ian was, at this moment, asleep, content in his ma's arms.

"Ye dinnae want to name him after yer father?" Conn asked, touching the tip of a finger to the babe's satin cheek.

"He is a MacLaurey. I like Ian."

He leaned over and kissed her softly. "Thank ye for giving me a chance to know my son." He lifted the bundle from her arms and cuddled the babe against his shoulder. "*Coorie doon*, my wee lad. Ye are safe with me, my wee laddie."

Tam entered the room behind him and leapt upon the bed,

snuggling close to Brianna, and propped his chin on his paws, a watchful look on his face as the bairn gave a small cry and waved a tiny fist. Jamie hesitated in the doorway, the anxious look on his face breaking into a grin as Conn bid him enter.

"Yer wee cousin bids ye welcome, Jamie, lad. Do ye think ye can give him pointers as he grows up?"

Jamie nodded his head vigorously. "Aye! I will teach him to run and swim and tickle trout in the stream." He beamed at Conn. "Da showed me how the other day. I havenae caught one, yet, but he did!"

Brianna chuckled tiredly and Conn rose, shooing Jamie and the dog out the door as he placed wee Ian in his cradle. Jamie bounded across the floor, arms windmilling in excitement.

"And I will let him ride my horse when he is bigger. 'Twill be black as night and fire will come from its nose! And 'twill be as tall as the sky—bigger!"

He turned in the doorway, a finger to his lips as he glanced at his sister. "Conn? Dinnae tell Anna, but I am glad wee Ian isnae a girl. Would ye have minded?"

Conn traced the curve of wee Ian's cheek with his fingertips, a fullness blossoming in his chest he had never felt before. "Nae, Jamie. I wouldnae have minded at all. Ye see, she would have been just like her ma."

A Note to my Readers

Thank you so much for sharing the journey with me. This is the fourth book in the Highlander's Bride series. Of all the books, this one connects most with the one before it, though it is not necessary to read them in order—just more fun ☺

The Highlander's Outlaw Bride is actually the first Highlander book I ever wrote. It was written as a challenge by author-friend, Katherine Bone, after I took a year's sabbatical from writing and wanted to try something fresh. Katherine suggested I write an historical romance, her own genre, then, a mere three months later, recommended I enter it in the Golden Claddagh Contest, hosted by Celtic Hearts Romance Writers. I can remember telling her, "Gee, Katherine, I just started it. I don't know…" It did not faze her in the least I had only two months to complete the novel.

I did, and it won its category, proving her to be a very astute and helpful friend, and The Highlander's Outlaw Bride now takes its place in the series. I sincerely hope you enjoyed it.

For those of you who follow my Wonderful Wednesday blog and have met Freki, yes, Tam is modeled on her antics as a puppy. Tam is also a fond compilation of memories growing up amid a pack of Collies. In Medieval Scotland, the colley would have more closely resembled the Border Collie than the modern-day Collie, hence the portrait on the book's cover.

I love to hear from readers! Look for news and fun on my blogs.

Bits 'n Bobs showcases writings from many authors as well as my own books, and writing related interest features.

Wonderful Wednesdays is a personal blog, typically dedicated to the dogs, gardening, and whatever else takes my fancy.

You can find both at www.cathymacraeauthor.com

Other books by Cathy MacRae

The Highlander's Bride series:

The Highlander's Accidental Bride (book 1)

The Highlander's Reluctant Bride (book 2)

The Highlander's Tempestuous Bride (book 3)

The Highlander's Outlaw Bride (book 4)

Highland Escape (with DD MacRae)

Enjoy an excerpt from

Kinnon's Story
(working title)

Cathy MacRae

Chapter One

1380, Châteauneuf-de-Randon, France

Kinnon Macrory stared into the face of death.

'Tis nae fair. After all the battles I have survived, to arrive at this. He would have sighed at the injustice of it, but he was, quite frankly, afraid to make an unnecessary move.

The black mask surrounded dark topaz eyes, burnished fur, and a fine set of strong, white teeth revealed from beneath snarling black jowls. The Alaunt's ears pressed flat against his skull in warning, and his hair stood up along his neck and shoulders. As did Kinnon's.

Shite.

He lifted his gaze carefully from the reddened hand laid across the dog's neck. The slender fingers could have belonged to a nobleman's daughter, but the nails were short and the skin rough. Amazing what the mind registers when death is imminent. The owner of the hand wore a serviceable gown, patched areas meticulously sewn, sleeve cuff turned back on itself, almost hiding the raveled edges. A smudged apron covered the gown, the bucket of milk at her feet attesting her job before he walked up. And came face-to-face with death.

"Do ye mind calling off yer beast?" He offered a winsome smile, splaying his hands at his side, a small bag of coins in his left palm. The young woman stared at him, hardly giving the bag a look.

He tried again. "*Chien?*"

The young woman's gaze did not waver—clear, cold blue eyes

bore into his. Wisps of black hair curled damply against her temple, attesting to her work ethic. Her thin nose sat atop full, red lips that neither smiled nor frowned at him.

The dog growled, a deep menacing sound originating from his enormous chest that warned Kinnon from making a further move—if he wanted to keep his throat intact.

Kinnon did.

His heartbeat kicked up. The impressive muscles in the dog's forelegs rippled, his claws gripped the ground, his hindquarters bunched. Endless moments passed as Kinnon roundly cursed the man who sent him to this farm on an errand better suited to one of the camp lackeys.

"*Se calmer*, Jean-Baptiste," she murmured as the dog leaned forward.

"Jean-Baptiste?" Kinnon couldn't help himself. "Ye call this beast John the Baptizer?"

The woman gave him in inscrutable look, but the edge of her lips quivered, threatened to smile. "He has changed the religion of more than one man, *monsieur*."

Kinnon's eyebrows shot upward. "Aye. I can see that happening." He eyed the enormous beast, his shoulder almost even with the woman's waist, his possessiveness clear. With his mistress's soft command, the dog settled, but his eyes did not waver, his threat remained unmistakable.

"I was sent here to ask ye for what supplies I could buy." Kinnon gently flipped the small bag in his hand. The movement and clink of coin drew the woman's attention.

"You brought coin?" She snorted and hefted the milk bucket in one slender hand. Kinnon moved instinctively to take the burden from her but froze at the snarling response from Jean-Baptiste. Cool blue eyes met his, and this time, the young woman smiled.

"*Merci*, but I can manage. If you would like to keep yourself intact, please take a step back. Jean-Baptiste and I do not like to be crowded."

Kinnon let out his breath and took the required step backward. "Aye. And I thank ye."

She raised her eyebrows. "For what?"

"For not letting yon beast change my religion."

The young woman jerked her chin, indicating him to follow. Keeping a respectful distance, Kinnon trailed her.

"What is it you wish to purchase?" Her voice hitched as she swung the bucket onto the back of the small cart against the edge of the stone stable. Moss grew over the crumbling edges, softening the once-pristine façade. Hay spilled out into the yard, fresh and clean, its odor mingling with the sharp tang of manure.

"My commander sent me for chickens, eggs, beef—whatever ye can spare." He gave her a sideways glance. "The coin would purchase material for a pretty gown for ye, or mayhap a bit of ribbon."

The woman gave him a stern look. "I have no use for such fripperies. The soldiers usually simply take what they want, and our cupboards bear the brunt of their greed."

"Bertran wouldnae condone such behavior."

"His isnae the only army in these parts, *monsieur*. The English have garrisoned here many years."

"That would explain ye speaking English, though yer accent is quite lovely." Kinnon gifted her a winsome grin.

"Your *accentuer* is strange. Neither *Anglais* nor *Français*. It is not one I recognize."

"Nae English. Scots."

She lifted fine eyebrows. "You are Scottish? Fighting here, on French soil?"

Kinnon's grin broadened.

"Och, aye. As part of the Auld Alliance, we Scots are grateful for any chance to fight the bluidy English."

Wiping her hands in her apron, the young woman nodded. "Do you have a wagon?"

"Aye. 'Tis in that copse of trees. Bluidy rocks around here make driving it a bit of a nuisance."

"We will pick out what you need and load the cart. Jean-Baptiste can pull it to your wagon." She led him into the stable.

Kinnon eyed the beast's beefy shoulders. "A good use for his muscles."

"He can take down an angry bull with a mere tug of his head. His ancestors were bred in the mountains and came with the Romans as fighting dogs. He fears nothing, yet cares for us with gentleness."

"Us?"

She nodded. "My sister lives here as well. She is gathering eggs."

Kinnon paused. "Mademoiselle, I have been too long at war, but even so, my ma would say my manners need polish. If we are to do business, I should introduce myself. My name is Kinnon Macrory." He held out his hand.

"My name is Melisende. Let me see the color of your coin."

About The Author

Cathy MacRae enjoys combining her loves of Scotland and happy-ever-afters. When not writing, she finds herself in the garden, playing with the dogs, or cooking.

She also enjoys hearing from readers. You can read more about Cathy and her writing on at http://www.cathymacraeauthor.com and email her at cathymacrae@cathymacraeauthor.com.

Information on upcoming books and projects are listed under 'News', and you will find lots of writing-related blogs under the 'Bits 'n Bobs' tab, including author interviews and book releases for fellow authors, as well as some fun posts on Scotland.

Look under 'Wonderful Wednesdays' for bits on gardening, corgis, and the newest member of the family, Freki. See how she came up with the name and watch Freki grow up amid two very short-legged dogs.

Made in United States
Orlando, FL
21 April 2022